KEVIN

BLUE TEAM BOOK 4

RILEY EDWARDS

KEVIN
BLUE TEAM BOOK 4

RILEY EDWARDS

Copyright © 2022 by Riley Edwards

Cover design: Lori Jackson Designs

Written by: Riley Edwards

Published by: Riley Edwards/Rebels Romance

Edited by: Rebecca Hodgkins

Proofreader: Julie Deaton, Rebecca Kendall, Jo West

Kevin

PRINT ISBN: 978-1-951567-23-1

First edition: January 25, 2022

Copyright © 2022 Riley Edwards

To my family - my team – my tribe.
This is for you.

1

GODDAMN IDIOT!

I watched Bronson Williams get back into his rental then looked back at the pile of rocks he'd left on Max Brown's brand-new Cherokee.

A former Navy SEAL sniper was not the type of man you wanted to screw with. Yet, there Bronson was, poking the beast.

Revenge tended to make people stupid, but in Bronson's case, it was more than that. He had no idea who he was up against. How could he? The guy was an average Joe, living an average life far removed from the circles Max Brown ran in. All Bronson knew was that Max worked for the man he thought was responsible for his brother's death.

Stupid, stupid idiot.

The four rocks Bronson had left would piss Max off. But they'd send Zane Lewis, Max's boss, straight to the red zone. I didn't need Zane going nuclear. A gonzo Zane could mean anything. None of those things would be good nor would they persuade him to help me.

And I needed Zane's help. Without him, my missing

teammate would die or I'd have to scrap a ten-year mission and pull the rest of my team from the field.

I had no other options.

My problem was Zane was my only hope and the man's hatred for the CIA was carved in granite—and I had ties to the CIA. I didn't need Bronson Williams and his misguided bullshit getting in my way.

I had one shot at saving Theo.

I was out of favors. I used my last one when I contacted Lucas Grant and called in my marker. He'd come through big time, arranging a meeting with President Graham. To say the POTUS was unhappy there was a covert operation running that he hadn't known about would be a grave understatement of the president's anger. The man was rightly pissed and being such, it was *his* suggestion to call in Z Corps. I felt no remorse for playing the President of the United States. I needed Zane and one of his teams.

But first things first; Bronson had to be neutralized.

I pulled out of my parking spot and pulled right behind Bronson's rental. I didn't waste time with normal tactics. I didn't need to; the guy had no idea I'd been following him for days.

Today would be the day he learned he should've paid more attention.

There was no thrill in this particular chase. There was no adrenaline rush as I neared my target. My chest ached and an ugly ball of regret knotted in my belly.

How had everything gone so wrong?

I COULD SPOT a liar from a mile away.

A well-trained government liar? They were even easier.

And the woman sitting across from me in the White House briefing room was a well-trained government liar.

A drop-dead-smokin' hot liar with arresting eyes and pouty lips.

I could spot 'em but my boss could sniff 'em out, which was something Zane did the moment we walked into the room and he caught a whiff of her expensive perfume.

President Graham was at the head of the table, Zane at the other end. Owen, Gabe, Myles, Cooper, and I filled in the seats between them.

And Layla—the professional liar—was sitting directly across from me.

"Thank you for joining us," President Graham started.

"With all due respect, Mr. President, I don't work with the CIA," Zane said.

Layla didn't blink. She didn't flinch, her nose didn't even twitch.

"I don't understand, we're not dealing with the CIA on this op."

"I thought Tom briefed you before he left office," Zane went on.

"Indeed he did."

Still no signs of discomfort.

"Then I'm positive he told you I'm out of the spy game. Moving on from that, I'm sure he told you I don't like to be lied to and most of all I don't like my time wasted."

The woman wore an almost bored expression as she listened.

"And I'm quite sure I haven't lied to you, and moving on from *that*, I don't appreciate the insinuation that I have."

"Then what's she doing here?"

Layla's eyes went hard and they sliced to Zane.

"Layla Cunnings is a DoD civilian contractor. She works in intelligence."

"What region?" Zane asked.

"Southwest Asia," Layla answered.

"Turkey, Armenia, Georgia, and Azerbaijan," Zane quickly rattled off the countries.

"Impressive, Mr. Lewis, you know your combatant commands."

She was a spunky liar.

"What's more impressive is you managed to get Graham's ear and arrange this meeting."

"I have connections and—"

"I bet you do," Zane cut her off. "I don't work with the CIA."

Layla's cheek jumped—the first sign she was getting flustered. She got a pass on the hardening and narrowing of her eyes. I was chalking that up to Zane being Zane, which translated to rude. But he had not lied; he hated his time being wasted, and after his last run-in with the CIA he vowed never to work an op with them again.

"I'm not with the CIA," Layla spat.

"Right, you're a civilian contractor for the DoD. And when I worked for the CIA I was an escalator repairman. You cannot imagine the access you get to buildings using that cover. I was also a limo driver, a great one, too. It's amazing the shit people say when they think that partition is soundproof. I had lots of different *jobs* when I worked with the CIA. Yet I only had one—to gather intel by any means necessary. I'm clear of that and my men are clear of it."

"Theo Jackson," Layla said.

I didn't need to be looking at Zane to know she'd dropped a bomb.

"You know that name, yet you expect me to believe you don't work for the CIA."

"He's the reason I left. I disagreed with the way the agency wanted to handle him."

"Handle him?" Zane's voice turned abrasive and menacing.

Handle him was CIA lingo for a kill order.

At the sound of his tone, I went on high-alert. I shifted my gaze to my teammates and they, too, were alert and ready.

Layla had no reaction to Zane's clipped question.

I took in her crisp white button-down shirt, the diamond studs in her ears, the Tag Heuer watch on her wrist and figured her jewelry alone would cost a whack. Couple that with the designer outfit, heels, perfectly styled hair, and makeup, the woman screamed high maintenance.

Her demeanor remained professional and detached when she addressed Zane.

"After he left you and your platoon in Egypt he followed the intel you helped him find and went to Spain. He found his target. The problem was Langley doesn't like egg on its face and the HVT ended up being an asset that had been on the CIA's payroll for years. Theo was told to bury the intel and was given a new assignment. Theo didn't feel like burying the fact that the CIA had been paying a top Al-Qaeda leader for false intel and the money he'd been paid aided a terrorist organization's quest to kill U.S. service members. Theo wanted an investigation. Langley disagreed. Theo wouldn't back down and was fired. I didn't agree with my boss's assessment of the situation. I thought an investigation was in order, for no other reason than to ensure something like that never occurred again. A few weeks later I was called to the seventh floor and handed my walking papers. Of course, it was a carefully worded resignation I didn't write but was told to sign. Then I was reminded of the oath I took and the NDAs I signed and how both were in effect in perpetuity and was asked to leave."

For some unexplainable reason, I wanted Layla rattled. I wanted the professional façade dropped. I wanted the perfection that was sitting across from me mussed up and the real woman she kept hidden to come out. I wanted to see the fire she kept at bay burn.

It was all there simmering under the surface. The question was, how far would I have to push before it sparked to life?

"Seems to me you need another reminder," I started, and she turned her attention to me. "Unless, of course, we're at the end of days and that NDA is about to expire."

"Are you going to turn me in?"

I couldn't help but smile at her quick comeback.

"It's possible." I shrugged. "Though you just broke your

oath in front of the president so I'm thinking I don't have to call the CIA hotline and report a security breach."

Layla calmly placed her palms on the table and leaned forward.

"The oath I took was the same one you took, Special Operator Monroe. *I will bear true faith and allegiance.* My allegiance has never wavered—not from my country or my brothers and sisters in the field. I've been assured your team can be trusted with—"

Seems she'd done her homework and looked us up. My service in the Navy was easily accessible and my time spent on the Teams wouldn't be hard to find.

"Can you be trusted?" I cut her off.

Her eyes narrowed and I noticed they weren't the hazel I'd originally thought they were. They were green, and the fire was beginning to flash.

"Tell me about Theo," Zane demanded.

"According to public record, he died in a plane crash ten years ago."

Bronson Williams's half-brother died in a plane crash ten years ago minutes after it took off from Cyprus. Everyone aboard that flight was reported deceased.

Bronson Williams was throwing stones—or more accurately pebbles—and making veiled threats against Zane.

The room went deadly silent.

The air grew heavy.

The fuse had been lit.

"Aaron Cardon," Zane growled.

"Theo Jackson's real name," Layla confirmed.

There it was—the connection we couldn't find.

"We need your help locating him," Graham interjected.

Zane's angry stare transferred to the president.

"I don't work with the CIA."

Layla's control finally snapped and her fist slammed down on the table.

"For the last time, I don't work for the goddamn CIA," she seethed. "Theo trusts me. Lucas Grant told me I could trust *you*. The last time I heard from Theo he was following a lead in Armenia. He's been dark for over two months. Our deal was sixty days, no more, between contact. Ten years without fail, every sixty days he's made contact. Now it's been seventy days and no check-in. Lucas said your teams are the best. That you're the only man I can trust with this information."

Lucas Grant was a former SEAL. He was now serving as the president's personal bodyguard. Another piece of the puzzle clicked into place; that was how she got a meeting with Graham.

"Myles?" Zane called. "It's your team. Your call."

"She's got twenty-four hours to convince Kevin why we should get involved," Myles replied.

"A man's life is in danger," Layla hissed. "And you want me to convince you to help me?"

"Not me, Miss Cunnings, Kevin," Myles returned. "You're worried about one life, and I'm worried about four-teen men and their families and how us getting involved is going to put us further in danger. Theo's brother, Bronson, seems to have a personal grudge against Zane, and while right now he's a nuisance, that can escalate in the blink of an eye. So before I send my team to Armenia to search for Theo you need to convince Kevin it's worth the risk."

Layla looked beyond pissed.

The professionalism had slipped and the fire was ablaze.

Her gaze skated around the table, then it landed on me and our eyes locked.

Determined, intelligent, shrewd eyes that edged on the side of battle-hardened. And suddenly I wanted to know where she'd been and what she'd done to make her pretty green eyes so wary. How had she come about her strength—was it learned or was she born with steel in her veins? I wanted to know if there was more fire in her and how much more it would take before she combusted.

It felt like an eternity before she finally said, "Let's go."

Layla stood and motioned for me to do the same.

"Hurry up," she bossed. "We've got ten years' worth of intel to go over."

Damn, the woman was bossy *and* spunky—a deadly combination.

I hoped like fuck she could convince me to take the risk.

3

IT HAD BEEN HOURS, and the longer Kevin Monroe silently stared at the computer screen reading reports the more anxious I became.

No, that wasn't right. It wasn't anxiety I was feeling. It was fear. Good old-fashioned fear. Something I rarely, as in never, felt. Over the years, I had often asked myself if the CIA had coached the fear out of me or if I simply lacked the motor function. Therefore, I took risks without much consideration for personal safety. Or maybe it was because I had nothing to lose—there was no one to care if I was injured or killed. Maybe Aaron Cardon, AKA Theo Jackson, would care, but he wouldn't mourn the loss of me like a real friend would.

But this wasn't about me or my safety. It was about Theo Jackson. I needed Zane Lewis's help, and the only way I was going to get it was if I convinced Kevin helping me rescue Theo was in Zane's best interest.

The problem was, Kevin had been scouring through years' worth of intel, and the man's face had been perfectly blank. He was giving me nothing, and that was saying something seeing as I was an expert at reading people. It was a skill that every CIA officer was taught. It was drilled into us until it became second nature. In the field, you either read situations and people, or you died. I was a master of observation; I could pick up on the slightest deviations. Kevin had no such inconsistencies—no tics, no tells. His eyes hadn't flared or narrowed while he'd read. That was irritating. And that irritation had turned into fear because if Kevin didn't believe me, I was screwed.

I needed Zane and his team; I had no other options. Period, the end, underlined, and bolded. No other options. No one else had the expertise or the audacity to go up against the U.S. government. Zane's reputation was such that it preceded him. He was known throughout the intelligence community as being uncontrollable—a loose cannon. The CIA didn't like uncontrollable loose cannons. They liked rule-followers who didn't break the chain of command and I wasn't sure the word "rule" was in Zane's vocabulary. Contrary to that, he was a legend in the SOC/SAC community. A highly respected former SEAL who back in the day had provided security for CIA officers in the field. One of those officers was Theo Jackson. I was banking on Zane's fabled loyalty.

It was a thin thread, but I was desperate.

I did have an ace—a piece of intel that would bind Zane to the cause. Unfortunately, Theo had sworn me to secrecy. Before he went undercover, I promised him I'd never tell Zane or Garrett Davis the truth. I promised to protect them both if the worst-case scenario happened. But now that it had happened, I wished I'd never made that promise. The truth would save Theo, but it would dredge up the past that Garrett wanted to stay buried.

A promise was a promise. I had no choice but to keep it.

Keep it and pray that Zane and Garrett don't put the puzzle together. Which was highly unlikely, but I had to take the risk to save Theo.

"You said last contact was sixty-five days ago?" Kevin finally asked.

His monotone voice grated on my nerves more than it should've. Now that we were alone Kevin's demeanor was far different than the antagonistic—no, not antagonizing; he hadn't been hostile or aggressive as the word suggested. He'd been almost playful back at the White House. Teasing in a way that had been borderline rude, but not mean. As if he was trying his best to goad me into an argument. I liked that much better than the flat, tedium tone he now had.

"Seventy," I corrected.

"Last known location was Argentina?"

Now I was getting irritated.

"Is there a reason you're wasting time testing me with the smallest of details? You cannot actually think if I were going to lie, I'd forget the particulars."

"What I think is you're a professional liar. But even the best slip up, and when they do, it's with the minutia."

Damn, that hurt.

I didn't want to feel the knife Kevin plunged into my heart, but he was right. I was a well-trained, practiced liar. In fact, I was so good I even believed my own lies. The ones I told myself daily to forget who I really was. When I joined the CIA, it was my chance to leave behind the old Layla and invent a whole new persona. In my later years with the agency, I struck gold and was given a sophisticated cover complete with an artificial life. In the agency, it's called a legend, and it was meant to pass the heavy scrutiny of counterintelligence agencies. When my assignment was over, I kept my legend. I became the Layla Cunnings the CIA had invented.

I liked her much better than Layla Brower.

What I did not do was screw up the minutia. Further from that, I didn't slip up on any of the details while I was working a case.

However, I was telling the truth, making Kevin's questioning moot.

"Theo's LKW was in Armenia. More specifically, in Kapan, a village near the Azerbaijan border."

My gaze went from Kevin's brandy-colored eyes to the computer screen. The transition took only a second but was long enough for me to mentally chastise myself for studying the color of the man's eyes. The brown mixed with an orangish hue was so unique I'd momentarily lost focus. Something that absolutely couldn't happen. Theo's life was at stake. My teammate. A man who had given up his identity, faked his own death, and given up years of his life in the pursuit of truth and justice.

On the screen was the photographic proof a CIA officer had met with a Pakistani Inter-Service Intelligence officer and a Saudi prince days before he attempted a coup. The meeting took place on Saudi soil. Of course, the U.S. government condemned the attempt and denied any prior knowledge of the failed takeover. However, the crates of guns and stacks of U.S. currency contradicted that claim. The denial was par for the course. The issue was that five days later the ISI was found responsible for funding an attack on a CIA camp on the Afghanistan-Pakistan border. That attack killed seven Americans.

"How did Theo know about the meeting?" Kevin asked.

"I gave him the coordinates."

"How did you know about the meeting?"

I knew about a lot of clandestine meetings. Meetings that were meant to be off the books, conducted in the shadows in the interest of keeping America and her allies safe.

"I bought the information from the CIA," I answered.

"Bought it?" he spat.

I noted the irritation in Kevin's voice and cataloged the tone. Finally, he was giving me something to work with.

"For the purpose of this mission, all you need to know is, Theo sends me intel from the field. No more than sixty days pass between check-ins. And he missed his check-in."

A few beats of silence passed, and when it stretched, I turned to look at Kevin.

His strong, stubbled jaw was clenched, and his brandy eyes were narrowed. He didn't like me very much and he wasn't hiding it. Why did that make me want to smile? It had been a long time since someone had shown me their true feelings instead of hiding them under layers of deceit. Honesty was a novel concept in the spy game.

"Why you?" he inquired.

Under normal circumstances, I would've lied or deflected the question entirely. But I needed Kevin to tell his boss to help me. I had to win him over, and I sensed the only way to do that was with the truth. Or as much of the truth as I was willing to tell him.

"Because I'm his handler."

"So, you're still with the CIA." His scathing accusation echoed in the empty room.

A cold hard slap of reality—Kevin Monroe wasn't on my side. He didn't now—and would likely never—believe a word I said, even the ones that were the truth. I'd always be a CIA liar to him.

"I haven't been employed by the CIA for ten years," I

reminded him. "Like I told you back at the White House, I was fired when I supported Theo and the investigation."

"The investigation into the payouts to known terrorists?" Kevin inquired but didn't let me answer before he went on. "I don't get it. The CIA's been doing that since Bin Laden hit the radar in the nineties *before* there was an Al-Qaeda to pay. This isn't a new game."

"And how well did that work out? The CIA threw money at the Sudanese government demanding OBL be exiled, and he goes to Afghanistan and declares war on America. Fast forward a few years and 9/11 happens."

Kevin's brows pinched together and the muscle in his cheek jumped before he declared, "I'm familiar with the war, Layla. *Intimately* acquainted with Al-Qaeda. But newsflash—OBL's dead, his network dismantled. I'm unclear what Theo's trying to uncover."

Shit. We were getting off track. I didn't want to debate the CIA's tactics or the outcome of their operations. I needed to stay focused on the mission at hand—Theo.

I knew my attempt to keep my composure failed when I felt my nails bite into my palms as I told Kevin, "There's a traitor."

My honesty was met with a critical, incredulous stare.

"At the CIA?"

"Yes."

"Who do you work for?"

"I'm a civilian contractor—"

"Listen, lady, this can go one of two ways. You keep feeding me your bullshit and I walk away leaving you right where you are now—up shit's creek. Or you cut the spy game, the classified subterfuge, and tell it straight. The choice is yours, but you should know, I'm not playing your game. You're wasting my time and yours."

That was not how this was supposed to go. There was a certain order in which the flow of information was exchanged. I would give the bare minimum, he'd play along and push for more, I'd—insert air quotes—give in and offer more information in exchange for something I wanted. The game as a whole was long and drawn out. In other words —exhausting.

God, aren't I tired enough of the lies and bullshit? Wouldn't it be so much faster and easier if everyone involved would be forthcoming and lay their cards on the table?

"I *am* a civilian contractor."

Kevin shook his head, again not hiding how he truly felt. His disgust was so evident I actually felt his disappointment as his gaze slid back to the computer screen.

Since when had I started caring about someone else's opinion?

I don't.

Yet for some reason, Kevin's revulsion hurt.

I'd never meant to become this person.

Or had I?

Wasn't this version of myself better than the weak, naïve girl I'd been? I'd armed myself with all the tools I needed never to be taken advantage of again. I learned how to be the hunter instead of the hunted.

"My work with the DoD is a cover," I admitted.

Kevin's eyes slowly drifted back to mine, and now that I had his attention, I wasn't sure if I could continue. Hell, I wasn't even sure if he'd believe me if I told him the truth.

But before I could decide what I was going to tell him, a loud explosion blew the windows out.

Is that a sign from God to keep my mouth shut?

"Down!"

I dove to my right, seeking the protection of the kitchen cabinets. Kevin went left and belly-crawled behind the couch. I didn't have the heart to tell him I bought the thing from IKEA and the cheap piece of furniture would offer him no protection.

"We need to move," Kevin called out.

Thanks for the heads up, Captain Obvious.

"Hallway behind you. Are you armed?" I asked as I pulled up my blouse and reached for my compact Glock 43 concealed in a Belly Band holster.

"Yes."

"I'm coming to you."

"Lay—"

I took off running, not bothering to crouch. I was almost across the room when the snap of a bullet breaking the sound barrier hummed by my head.

"Fucking hell, woman!" Kevin snarled and practically tackled me.

I swallowed my yelp of pain when my knees and elbows made contact with the unforgiving wood.

"Get off me," I demanded.

Kevin did not roll off. Instead, with his lips so close they brushed my ear, he growled, "Don't pull that shit again."

My reaction to his snarled demand was unfortunate and ill-timed. I was blaming my shiver on adrenaline and the nipple tingle was most definitely from the danger and not from a handsome man with two-hundred-plus pounds of sinewy muscle pinning me to the floor.

When I didn't answer him, his arm around my stomach tightened.

"Promise me, Layla."

I would make no such promise. I might've been a liar

but even I had my limits and breaking a promise was something I didn't do.

"Don't ever tackle me again while I'm armed. I could've shot you."

My retort was weak; I had better control of my weapon than that. But I needed to say something.

Two more bullets flew through the room and more drywall crumbled.

Kevin didn't loosen his arm when he made a disgruntled groan.

The sound only intensified the nipple tingle and sent another shiver through me.

"Hallway," I muttered.

Kevin rolled to his side, bringing me with him. My gaze caught sight of the large—now glassless—picture window that took up most of the exterior wall. Cheap plastic blinds hung haphazardly on the windowpane and shattered glass littered the wood floor. But that was not what held my attention. From what I could see, all of the lights were on in the apartments across the way, except for two. The third story would give the shooter the best vantage point into my second-floor apartment. The other dark window was on the fifth level. The shooter would be aiming down, and if that was the case, the bullets would be hitting my floor, not the back wall.

"Your laptop."

"It's hashed," I told him. "And I have other backups."

Kevin's arm finally loosened and I scrambled to my knees and crawled into the tiny hallway. To the right was a walk-in closet and to the left, the bathroom. Once I was out of the line of sight of the living room window I stood and kicked off my heels.

I transferred my Glock to my left hand. Then I reached

up and yanked on a length of rope hanging from the ceiling and the attic access door opened.

"Ready?" I asked and pulled down the folding ladder.

"Where's that lead to?"

"The roof."

Kevin dropped his gaze from the opening in the ceiling to me.

He didn't believe me. Or maybe it was that he didn't trust me and thought I had a team of government assassins hidden in the attic.

I tamped down the hurt I had no right to feel and moved to the ladder.

Kevin lifted his hand and grabbed my bicep.

"I go first."

I shoved that hurt aside, too.

"Suit yourself."

Kevin started to climb, pausing for a moment before his head popped up—as did his firearm. He turned, scanning the dark space. I wasn't sure what he thought he was going to see. The first thing I did after I bought the building was have the attic refitted, and the cracked mortar repaired. It was utterly pitch black and sealed tight.

"Reach to your left. There's a light switch on the floor."

Kevin did as I instructed and the space lit with a soft glow.

"Jesus."

I smiled and started up the pull-down stairs behind him. His perfect ass was nearly eye level when he finished his ascent and stepped into the attic, then disappeared from sight.

"You didn't think I was one of those women who went to a party unprepared, did you?"

Another shot rang out and Kevin reached down and plucked me straight up and through the opening.

I was back on my feet trying to get my bearings while simultaneously ignoring the amount of upper-body strength it had taken to lift me when Kevin picked me up again and lifted me over a metal air duct.

I wasn't going to think about how that was a nice thing for Kevin to do. I could've negotiated stepping over it, though I would've had to pull my pencil skirt up, likely exposing my panties in the process. My mind whirled back to that morning and tried to remember what pair I'd put on. White with red hearts and cherubs. Dear Lord baby Jesus, that would've been mortifying.

"Layla?"

"Huh?"

I seriously needed to do laundry more than once a month. Or buy more undies. I etched a shopping trip into my mental to-do list knowing that I wouldn't ever find the desire to do laundry more than I already did.

"What are you thinking about?"

"Nothing."

"Liar."

I needed to get Kevin to tell Zane to help me and I needed to do that quickly. I wished I was a better person and the speed in which I wanted Kevin to leave and go back to Annapolis to tell his boss to gear up a team and roll out solely had to do with helping Theo.

But I wasn't a good person.

I was a lying, manipulating, scheming bitch and I needed to remember that.

I also needed to find another layer of emotional armor because hearing Kevin call me a liar hurt like a son of a bitch.

4

LAYLA'S perfectly bland façade cracked, and she flinched like I'd slapped her. All thoughts of the pretty blush that crept over her cheeks after I'd lifted her over the air duct fled and now, I wanted to know what had put a dent in that fake-ass mask she was hiding behind.

"There's a padlock—"

"Layla—"

"Inside of the Pelican case closest to you."

There were four Pelican cases near me. There was also a small gun safe bolted into the brick wall. She had a safe space above her safe house. I would've been impressed if the boxes that undoubtedly held gear weren't a reminder of who she was.

"Layla—"

She shook her head and talked over me, "You need to close that door and get it locked before someone comes in and finds us up here."

Her disguise was back firmly in place, fortified, and reinforced.

I didn't give one fuck that Layla was right. If someone came in and found us up here, we'd be as good as dead.

"Why'd you flinch?" I asked.

"Close the door," she gritted out through clenched teeth.

"Tell me why you went from blushing to looking like I punched you and I'll close it."

Layla's control slipped and her shoulders tensed. The movement was small, nothing more than a slight strain. But I saw it.

"Let's get something straight right now," I started when she remained quiet. "This." I stopped and gestured between the two of us. "Isn't gonna work if you aren't gonna talk to me."

"It isn't gonna work if someone walks in and starts shooting at us through the ceiling either. Now close the goddamn door and lock it, Kevin."

"Like they shot at your *goddamn* head?" I returned with equal disdain.

No reaction to the reminder she'd almost lost her head. The bullet had been so close she only had inches to spare.

"You don't care, do you?" I asked.

"The real question is, why do you?"

Her retort was so off the wall I was actually rendered speechless.

When my ability to string together a coherent sentence returned—which took several seconds, and it must be noted Layla didn't fill that time with an explanation as to why she hadn't and still didn't look the slightest bit frightened that she could've died—I continued to push.

"Why'd you flinch?"

"I didn't."

"Liar."

There it was again. A minuscule movement. A gesture so insignificant that if she wasn't who she was I would've disregarded it. But she was former CIA, and that teeny recoil was akin to a regular person taking a step back in retreat.

Liar.

Both times she flinched after I called her out.

I wasn't sure if that was telling or if I was being played. Whichever it was, it pissed me right the fuck off.

"Maybe I'd trust you if you answered my questions honestly," I told her.

"I haven't lied to you," she lied.

"You have. Twice. The first time was when I asked you what you were thinking about, and you told me nothing. And the second was just now when I asked you why you flinched, and you lied to me and told me you didn't."

"Right," she sneered. "We both know, there's nothing I can do or say that's going to make you trust me. So, let's drop the bullshit and shut the door."

At that juncture, the smart thing to do would've been to drop it and shut the door. There hadn't been any more gunshots, which could mean the shooter was on their way over here or they could've fled. Enough time had passed that the police would be en route and we had to leave before they showed up.

Yet, I wasn't ready to drop the subject or do the right thing.

"No, Layla. *We* don't know shit because you're giving me nothing."

The woman's silence was utterly infuriating. I bent down and made quick work of pulling up the door, the stairs easily folding into themselves.

"Which case?"

"The one on the left."

I unlatched the box. I wasn't sure what I thought I'd find in the case, but I was staring at a Kevlar vest with a padlock resting on top. Another reminder of who Layla was. A reminder that felt like a sock to the sternum. I ignored the ache and picked up the lock, then went back to the door, found the latch, and locked us in.

"Pull the knot and the rope will pull through the hole."

Smart.

I did as Layla instructed and tied the rope off so it wouldn't slide back down. I returned to the Pelican case and nabbed the vest.

"Do you need anything else out of here?"

"No," she clipped.

When I heard the snap in her voice, I looked over my shoulder to find Layla staring at me. Totally and utterly shut off. More so than she'd been before I'd closed the door, more than when we were looking over the intel Theo had collected, and way more than back at the White House. Her arms hung loosely at her sides, a Glock in her right hand. Her breathing was steady and she wasn't scowling or glaring.

Nothing.

I held my breath until I turned back to the box, then I slowly let it out.

"I won't—" I started but clamped my mouth shut when I heard the front door below us open.

I stood to my full height and gingerly stepped around so I was facing Layla. She gave me a nod and pointed to the other side of the attic. I shook my head in response to her silent directive to go for the door. One creak of the rafters and whoever was downstairs would hear.

A muffled voice rose from the apartment, and I strained to make out what was being said.

I pointed to my ear then to the floor. Layla's head cocked to the side and her eyes narrowed as she listened. Her hand came up with her index finger extended. As soon as I acknowledged her assessment that there was one person below us most likely on the phone, she again pointed to the door. This time her eyes were imploring me to follow her lead. That was the only excuse I could come up with when I nodded my agreement. I watched her lips tip up into a smile and I realized that smile was more dangerous than us moving around in the attic of an old apartment building while there were unknown, very likely armed combatants below us.

Layla didn't waste time and with careful, measured steps she moved across the plywood boards that had been nailed to the rafters. I took another look around and noted the plywood was strategically placed, making a four-foot-wide walkway from the access panel to a door at the farthest side of the attic. There were also a few sheets laid across the two-by-fours where her gear was situated in cases. The insulation and rafters also looked fairly new. The building was older, meaning someone had refitted the attic in the last couple of years. There were six apartments in the building, three on the ground level, three upstairs. Layla's was in the middle of the three on the second level. Either she was smart and rented the middle space specifically for the access panel in the ceiling or she'd hired someone to cut it in after she rented. It was a smart move however it came about.

"The cops are here," drifted up from below. "Grab the laptop."

The voice pulled me from my perusal. I stepped over the metal HVAC line and paused when it hit me that Layla had blushed after I'd lifted her over the pipe. Was that why her cheeks had pinkened? Had I inadvertently...

"They have to fucking be here!" An angry voice sounded.

Layla looked over her shoulder and smiled. When she added a nod and pointed down, I took that as she recognized the voice. I gave her a chin lift and quietly followed her the rest of the way to the door. Once again, I was enthralled by the way she moved. Methodical, slow movements, shifting her weight from the ball of her foot to her heel before she took another step. Streamlined and steady, making her steps soundless.

She stopped to pick up a black backpack that was stowed to the left of the door. Once she had it over her shoulder, she went to work on the combination lock, and seconds later she was pushing the door open. The celerity and deft manner with which she'd navigated the attic—and before that, her close call with death—underlined her training.

Not that I needed the reminder, but it was there all the same.

"I have a car around the corner," she told me after I closed the door behind me.

Of course she did.

"Do you need to lock this?"

"No." She adjusted her pack and I glanced down at her bare feet on the asphalt roof before I looked up and took in my surroundings.

Thankfully the building was flat-roofed, though it provided no cover from the building across the way. Our only saving grace was that it was a moonless night and there was no rooftop lighting. Unless the shooter had thermal, then we were fucked.

"We'll be off the roof and long gone before he thinks to look in the attic," she continued.

"And who is he?" I asked and held up the vest I'd nabbed from her Pelican case. "Here, put this on."

"Seriously. We're—"

"Layla. Put. It. On." I carefully enunciated each word.

And that did it, she shrugged off her pack and held out her Glock.

"Would you mind?"

Damn, she was snippy.

"Sure." I took the gun and passed her the vest.

Once she had it strapped on, I handed her back her weapon and picked up her bag.

"You're in the lead."

It was dark, not pitch black, but hard to see. Even so, I didn't miss the surprise in her expression.

"I'll watch your—"

"I know you will," she cut me off.

Layla said no more. And before I could question her look, she turned and I was staring at her long brown hair brushing the back of a tactical vest. A curl of apprehension started in my gut and traveled its way up my throat until I had to swallow the unease down.

What the hell is that about?

This time when she moved, there was no attempt to be quiet, no worry that someone would hear—thus she ran. We needed off the roof, but I couldn't stop myself from wondering who she was trying to escape from—me or the bad guys?

And then I wondered why the hell it had bothered me so much to see her eyes vacant. What the hell did I care if she was standoffish and devoid of emotion?

Seriously, why the hell did I care?

Because she wasn't devoid of emotion, she was full of...*something*. I just couldn't figure out what that something was. Pain? Loneliness? Grief? Whatever it was, it lingered just below the surface.

And I had a profound need to understand Layla Cunnings.

5

"A LEXUS?" Kevin chuckled.

Well, it wasn't so much a chuckle as it was a throaty snicker but for my sanity's sake, I was ignoring the sound altogether and instead concentrating on the road.

I wasn't driving, he was. But I kept my gaze studiously on the side mirror watching for a tail and bit the inside of my cheek to stop myself from telling him to speed up. We'd passed six cop cars, yes six, so I knew Kevin was driving cautious as not to draw attention to us, but he didn't need to go five miles an hour under the speed limit.

"We're in Prince George's County," I mumbled.

"And what, does PG County have an ordinance in place that requires all getaway cars to be luxury sedans?"

He was teasing me again. I couldn't remember the last time someone other than Kevin teased me. My co-workers at the Pentagon weren't a jovial bunch. When I met with directors and State Department officials, they tended to be staid. And before that, working at the CIA had not been a barrel of laughs. In other words, my life was dull. No, it was worse than dull. It was mind-numbingly boring. Routine. Sober. Grim.

Basically, I was forty-five going on ninety-three. I hadn't had a date in so many years I couldn't recall how long it had actually been. Three, or maybe five or six years ago.

Sad.

My life had slipped by me and I'd done nothing to stop it. Hell, I hadn't even attempted to slow it down. I had no hobbies, no general interests outside of work. Which brought me to the job that I didn't enjoy—not anymore. I was a workaholic but had nothing better to do so I was the first one in the office and the last one out and I worked weekends. Because, yeah, I had no friends.

No, I did that because five men depended on me to stay alive.

My life was not sad, it was utterly dreadful.

It was a toss-up whether my life could be categorized as a Greek or Shakespearean tragedy, but, nonetheless, it had all the basic elements to be classified as tragic. It was so shitty someone could write a book about a sad, lonely little girl who grew up to be a sadder, lonelier woman and it still wouldn't touch my life.

And now, I could add sniveling, whiny twit to the list of things I was.

"Layla?" Kevin called, pulling me from my pathetic thoughts.

And that was why I worked every waking minute of the day. So my mind didn't wander where it wasn't supposed to go.

"I'm sure I haven't been to a county commissioner meeting recently. Though I wouldn't be surprised if there was some decree that ugly, beat-up vehicles had to have a special permit to enter the county. But I use the Lexus to blend in. An older model car would be noticed in an upper-middle-class neighborhood."

A black SUV two cars back caught my attention.

"I think we have a tail," I told Kevin.

"The black Suburban?"

It wasn't surprising he noticed.

"Cliché, isn't it?" I mumbled.

"Just a little," he returned. "You wanna have a little fun?"

Fun?

As aforementioned, I wasn't entirely sure I knew what fun was.

But I was all-in for something other than boring as all hell.

"Sure."

"What's in your go-bag?"

That question didn't sound like a precursor to fun and if he thought there was something in my bag that would lead to a good time, he'd never met me.

Duh. Of course, he's never met you.

"Nothing that would constitute fun."

There it was again, another throaty snicker that I couldn't deny was definitely a chuckle.

"Do you have pants? Shoes?"

Yeah, Kevin needed a lesson in fun, too.

"Yes. Why?"

"Can you change while I drive?"

I was not particularly modest. I'd spent years in war-torn countries without a lot of privacy but hell to the no, I could not change in front of Kevin. There was a multitude of reasons why, the first being he was quite possibly the most gorgeous man I'd ever seen. Period. He was not hand-some or beautiful. His jaw was too square, his features too sharp. Kevin was attractive in a way that his magnetism called to you. It pulled you in until you were in his orbit—floating around all of his goodness hoping that his gravita-tional force kept you where you were. Forever. But beyond that, the possibility of him catching a glimpse of my white panties, which by the way were not cute bikini cut but instead full-bottom-grannie-panties with flying cherubs was too mortifying to chance. And there was no discreet way to change out of a tight-fitting pencil skirt. If I'd been wearing a cute boho chic skirt (something I didn't own), sure. Even a stylish maxi dress (I didn't own one of those either) I could shimmy on my pants without Kevin's corneas being blinded by the ugliness of my undies.

"I can put on shoes," I offered.

I sensed Kevin's gaze on me and turned in time to watch his eyes go back to the road.

"I won't look."

Well, I was looking at him, and I could clearly see he was smiling.

I was contemplating the voracity of his statement when his phone rang and he reached for the device he'd stowed in the cupholder. On one hand, he was a man, and I didn't think there were many men who wouldn't sneak a peek at a scantily clad woman sitting next to him. On the other hand, Kevin struck me as a man of his word. And if he was on the phone, he'd have less attention to spare. I was still weighing my thoughts when Kevin answered the call.

"Got anything good for me?" Kevin asked.

"Police are on scene. One DOA. White male in his sixties. GSW to the forehead. Neighbor heard noises coming from the apartment but didn't think anything of it.

A few minutes later the same neighbor said it sounded like someone was setting off fireworks." A man who I knew was Garrett Davis stopped talking and cleared his throat before he went on. "Cops also got called by Layla's neighbor. The PD's got two teams going over both crime scenes. I'm guessing you didn't have time to wipe down your prints before you left."

"Negative."

"Doesn't matter anyway, building is in her name. I see you moving. Do you have a destination in mind?"

It wasn't surprising Garrett, Zane's intel specialist, had found the corporation that owned my homes including the apartment building. He was damn good at his job. I wondered if Garrett had ever shared who he was working for when he left the Navy before he went to work with Zane. I'd bet he kept those years to himself. I'd bet he had no idea that the men he'd used to work with were still worried about him. Garrett had cut off all contact with his former brothers, but they had never given up on him. I was shocked Garrett hadn't already put two and two together. He would though. And when he did, I hoped that he would finally be able to let go of years' worth of guilt he should've never been carrying.

But could he forgive me for keeping the truth from him? Would he believe that I wanted to tell him, but I'd promised the guys I'd never reveal what I knew? Doubtful. Garrett would likely view my silence as a betrayal.

"Depends," Kevin said.

There was a lot of information packed into those exchanges. A man was dead. An innocent man. A man who was likely relaxing in his apartment after a day of work, minding his own business, maybe watching some TV, took a bullet to the forehead. Beyond that, the men's calm interaction spoke volumes about the work they did. One man dead, my apartment shot to shit with us in it—just another day at the office. And lastly, neither of them seemed surprised we'd taken fire.

"You don't sound surprised," I noted.

"Surprised?" Kevin asked.

"That we were shot at," I clarified.

"And you are?"

He had a good point. I was actually surprised it had taken so long before someone tried to kill me. I'd been cautious with Theo, with my entire team. Or as cautious as one could be when someone was feeding you sensitive intel from the field. I'd always known there was a chance someone would figure it out, and my guess was it would be one of my former colleagues.

And tonight proved that true.

"Speaking of getting shot at," Kevin continued. "You recognized a voice."

"Eddy Stallone."

"Is he CIA?"

"I don't know his current status, but yes, I worked with him."

"Garrett?"

"I'll look into it."

Kevin sped up as the light at the intersection in front of us turned yellow. I looked to my right then my left and held my breath. He wasn't slowing down.

My breath whooshed out and I sputtered, "You're not gonna make it."

The light turned red just as Kevin gunned it. My hand went to the dash, my gaze went to the right, and my life flashed before my eyes as the fast-approaching headlights of a car blinded me.

"Black SUV at the intersection of Coventry and Old Branch. Run the plates."

I was too angry to look at Kevin after narrowly surviving a second near-death experience in the space of thirty minutes.

"You're a maniac," I grumbled.

"Change your clothes, Layla. The fun's about to start."

Kevin didn't slow his speed and since a high-speed crash was likely in my near future, I decided I wasn't climbing out of the burning wreckage without shoes. I mean, the man drove like he was dodging roadside bombs in Jalalabad, not navigating early evening traffic in Clinton, Maryland.

I was reaching for my bag on the floorboard between my legs when Garrett spoke, "Federal fleet."

"Gathered that. You got facial rec?"

"Working on that now."

That was good. If Kevin got a hit it would be sent automatically to my team.

I pushed my cargo pants to the side and dug deeper in the bag, looking for my socks.

"What can you tell us about Stallone?"

I assumed Kevin's question was directed at me, so I answered while I rummaged through my pack.

"I don't know him well, but from what I do know he's respected. When I left, he'd been with the agency about seven years. Our paths didn't cross much. His area of operation was Africa and I was Asia and the Middle East. I saw him at Langley if we were both there at the same time, though that was rare. He was always friendly with me but he hated Theo."

A little too friendly.

"Why'd he hate Theo?" Garrett asked.

I found my socks and leaned forward to slip them on but stopped when Kevin abruptly swerved.

"You're gonna get pulled over," I complained.

"No, I won't."

Whatever. It was points on his driving record, not mine. I had clean identification in my bag and the car was registered in the same false name. Kevin would get his ticket, maybe arrested for reckless driving, and I'd be on my merry way. It wouldn't be the first time I was on my own in a tight spot and it certainly wouldn't be the last.

"Theo?" Garrett prompted.

"Theo's a by-the-book type of guy. Everything's very black and white for him," I explained.

"Not a good fit for an organization that deals in gray."

Kevin's offhanded—and very true—remark made my stomach tighten.

"No, Theo was not a good fit. I remember when he started. Six months after college graduation, ready to serve his country and fight the good fight. He didn't understand that in order to do that you had to sell your soul. He went from gung-ho to disheartened. He complained and wasn't afraid to share his opinions when operations went south. But mostly Eddy hated Theo because Theo despised Eddy. Eddy only sees the gray, he has tunnel vision and blurs lines. The problem is, Eddy's effective. He produces results. He's a master at building networks and keeps his sources on the string even after the operation is done. He never burns a bridge and lies through his teeth to keep everyone happy."

Edward Stallone was also a royal dick with grabby hands and had a hard time understanding the word no. Another reason Theo hated Eddy. Theo was none too happy when he caught Eddy following me through the parking lot after work one night. This was after Theo had heard me tell Eddy if he touched my ass one more time, I was going to break his fingers. Eddy being the dick he was tried to say he didn't mean anything by it. He was treating me like one of the guys and he wasn't touching my ass, he was *patting* it. As if there was a fucking difference. And if he and his buds wanted to play grab-ass with each other that was on them. I, however, didn't want to be touched.

Though, I was keeping that tidbit to myself.

I finished with my socks and went to work pulling out my sneakers.

"Garrett, you got any idea where my tail went? I don't see them."

"No. I lost them after the intersection. There's not another traffic cam until Woodward. Are you coming in?"

"No. I don't want to lead them to the office."

"Are you going to the Cape?"

"Yeah."

"What's the Cape?" I asked and sat up.

Kevin's head turned ever so slightly to check his right mirror and when he did his gaze flicked to my legs and he smirked.

"Not gonna change?"

"No. What's the Cape?" I repeated.

"Who's going to pick up the car?" Kevin asked instead of answering my question.

"Zane and Owen are on their way now. Pray the new Nav isn't riddled with bullets."

Garrett chuckled but it was Kevin's laugh that had me enthralled. The sound was rich and warm like he laughed often. Full-bodied. It was stupid but I watched until the laughter died down then I continued to watch because he was smiling. It was unlike the ones he'd given me when he was teasing me. This one wasn't a meager tip of his lips, it was a full-blown smile that made the corner of his eyes crinkle.

It was the most beautiful smile I'd ever seen so I quickly averted my eyes.

A man who smiled like that was not meant for me. Not that I was in the market for a man, but if I were, I knew better than to hope for someone like Kevin.

"Are you kidding?" Kevin started. "Zane would love any excuse to crawl up agency ass. Besides, he'd tell Ivy to tack on twenty percent to the repair bill for his time and irritation."

"Thanks for the visual," Garrett grumbled.

"Did you call Tex?"

"Yeah. He's up to his ass in something he's got going on with Annie Fletcher. I'll call in Shep if I need backup."

"Cormac Fletcher's daughter Annie?"

"Yep. Her and her man caught some trouble. He's out of pocket until the situation's resolved."

I knew John Keegan, better known as Tex. Well, I didn't know him personally, but I knew of him—everyone in the intelligence community did. Former SEAL, current information broker. That was, if he liked you and the information you sought and your reasons for needing it fit his moral compass. Which as far as I knew pointed true north and didn't deviate. And since he didn't bend his integrity or ethics, he was useless to the CIA. Though if they could get him on board they'd jump at the chance. Something else about Tex—his loyalty was as fabled as Zane's. If Tex couldn't make time to help, something had gone seriously wrong for this Annie woman.

"Shit." Kevin changed lanes then continued. "Does he need manpower?"

"Right now, he says no. But he'll call us in if he does."

There was a beat of silence before Kevin angrily spat, "I don't like this."

"Neither do I, brother. But if Tex says he's got it under control, then you know he's got it under control. If he needs us, he'll call us in. And on that note, I gotta run. Z's calling."

"Later."

Kevin tossed his phone back in the cupholder.

The car filled with an uncomfortable silence. I could have asked one of the thousand questions I had about where we were going, but that would force me to acknowledge I didn't know where he was taking us because I wasn't driving. And that would lead to me having to consider how easily I'd allowed Kevin to drive my car. Something that my inner control freak never let happen. I'd been in many scuff-ups with GBers and GRS operators about insisting that I drive. Confrontations that sometimes led to two cars being driven to a rendezvous point because some Ground Branch or Global Response operator refused to get into a vehicle I was driving. Such is the ego of a hot-blooded alpha male in a war zone. I didn't have an ego; I had a fear of not being in control. Period. Whether that be a car or a situation.

Yet, I let Kevin drive without argument.

I wasn't going to think about that. Just like I wasn't going to think about his smile or how pissed he was to learn one of his friends was in a tight spot or how easily he'd handled himself or how he handled me. Further from that, asking questions would mean opening myself up to Kevin asking his own.

"Tell me something."

Fuck. Shit. And double damn.

He hadn't exactly made a query as such, it sounded more like a request.

I can ignore a request, can't I? If I continued to stare

mutely out the window, he'd get the hint I wasn't going to bite, and he'd drop it.

Right?

"Layla?"

Wrong.

Shit.

"Yeah?"

"What state were you born in?"

A maelstrom of unwelcomed feelings invaded. Lies and more lies topped with bigger lies that made up my life rushed to the forefront of my mind. The ones that I hadn't had to recall in years. The ones that had kept me safe in the field, but more so because if I was living the lie, I didn't have to live the truth. An ugly truth that I was all too happy to forget.

"Minnesota."

The moment the lie slipped past my lips the air charged, the atmosphere disintegrated and chilled. Anger rolled off of him in waves. And, again, I acutely felt Kevin's disappointment grating my skin.

What the hell was wrong with me?

"Oregon," I corrected.

"Thank you."

It wasn't lost on me that Kevin knew my first answer was untrue. Nor did I miss how his disappointment had prompted me to tell him the truth. Something else I wasn't going to think about. I was better than this. Other people's moods did not control mine. Never in the history of my life had I changed an answer based on someone else's emotional reaction to it.

Not professionally. Not in my personal life.

I gave one answer and didn't deviate. If need be, I made the lie become truth.

"Do you want to know where I was born?"

I already knew. I had a file three inches thick on Kevin Monroe. As I did with all the men Zane Lewis employed. I never walked into a situation unprepared.

"Is this your idea of fun? Because I have to tell you, learning things about you I already know is gonna be pretty boring."

"Sorry, Layla. Your friends didn't feel like playing and backed off. I was planning on a high-speed chase and impressing you with my superior evasion tactics but now we'll have to settle on something else to occupy the next four hours."

"Four hours?" Which begged the question, "Where are we going? What is the Cape?"

"Cape Charles. We have a safe house there."

Cape Charles was a beautiful small village near the mouth of the Chesapeake Bay on what was considered the eastern shore of Virginia though it was on the west side of the peninsula.

"Zane has a safe house in a quaint seaside community?"

"Yep."

Why didn't that surprise me?

"We'll spend the night there," he went on. "And tomorrow we'll head to Annapolis and brief the team."

Briefing the team sounded good. Spending the night with Kevin, not so good.

"Does that mean you're willing to help me?"

"Not my call."

I stopped watching for a tail through the side mirror and whipped my head to the left to look at Kevin.

"What do you mean it's not your call? Zane told Myles it was his team, his choice to help me. Myles asked you to look over my intel, leaving that call up to you."

"It's still not my call. Myles will take my opinion into consideration, Zane will, too. But the choice is not mine. At the end of the day, it's Zane who will decide if he sends a team to look for Theo. I'm not trying to be a dick, but, Layla, after what just happened you better brace there's a good chance Zane's gonna say no."

Right.

Kevin had been at my house and had been shot at.

Zane cared about his men, I knew this about him, too. As stated, his reputation preceded him, and part of that reputation was his temper. Zane Lewis got cranky when his men were in danger. And that was because, unlike Uncle Sam, Big Daddy Zane loved his family.

The man had made it abundantly clear he didn't like me, didn't trust me, and thought I was still working for the CIA. I doubted there was anything that would sway his opinion.

Now, I'd be enemy number one.

I'd be going at it alone.

That was okay. I was used to it. And besides, I had contacts in Armenia I could use though none of my contacts had the firepower Zane had. If I was lucky Easton would be back in the area and he'd rally his team to help. Maybe. They were on the CIA's payroll and outside of Easton I wasn't sure who I could trust.

I might just be up that creek Kevin mentioned. In other words—screwed. A solo rescue op was my last resort.

A suicide mission.

My life for Theo's.

"Consider me braced," I muttered and turned back to the window. "I'm sorry my shit leaked, and you were in danger."

This time when the air charged with Kevin's mood it

was biting and aggressive. I disregarded the icy shiver and shoved aside the hurt.

Rejection was my old friend—sometimes it felt like it was my only friend. A constant companion I couldn't get rid of.

Such was life.

6

FOUR HOURS AND TWENTY MINUTES.

Of deafening silence.

Layla hadn't spoken a word.

I'd waited and waited and then waited some fucking more for her to say something. Argue. Yell. Plead her case. Beg for help. Nothing. Nada. Zilch.

The woman was stone-cold.

But that wasn't what pissed me off. It was her opening up—even if that opening was a sliver it was still huge—then slamming the door shut again and freezing me out.

She told me the truth. Not only that, but by telling me she was born in Oregon she knew how quickly I could unravel her cover and find what she wanted to keep buried. Just the state she was born in, that was all I'd need, and she damn well knew it and gave it to me anyway.

She gave, then she took.

Now she was in the only bathroom in the cottage, and I was staring out the window seeing nothing in an attempt to calm down. I had no real reason to be angry. However, irritation seemed to be the theme of the day. I knew I wasn't being fair to Layla; she didn't owe me anything beyond the facts. My only job was to analyze the intel Theo had sent. I hadn't gone through all ten years' worth of data—that would take Garrett days—but there was no doubt what I'd found was disturbing.

Bad business.

But when the CIA was involved it normally was.

I heard the bathroom door open and a moment later I caught her reflection in the window. She was a beautiful woman. Her professional getup was sexy—the tight pencil skirt showed off her curves nicely. The heels had been insanely hot and highlighted her delicate ankles. Regrettably, those heels were back at her apartment. *No, not regrettably. Thankfully.* However, there was something sexier about her in jeans and a t-shirt. My gaze dropped and I tilted my head to get a view of her feet. Back to bare. For some strange reason, that was sexy, too. I wondered if when she was home alone she lounged in jeans and tees or if she was the type of woman who got tricked out even if she wasn't leaving the house. The first impression she gave me was that she was high maintenance. But now I was rethinking my earlier assessment. Layla wanted to give off the appearance of propriety. She wanted the people around her to view her as in control, qualified, skilled. She hid behind decorum to keep people from getting close. She wanted people to think she was unapproachable.

The thing was, Layla was naturally qualified and skilled. I'd seen her keep her cool, I'd watched her move—with more interest than I should've. Yet she still put up a front.

Why?

Two reasons: it was by habit—a leftover from her time at

the CIA—or a defense mechanism. My guess was the latter. Layla was consciously or unconsciously protecting herself.

The question remained: why?

"Sorry I took so long, I needed to wash the tar off my feet from the roof."

Her quiet words sent my blood boiling.

After four hours and twenty minutes of silence, that was what she had to say to me? Her fucking feet were dirty and she needed to wash them?

What in the fuck?

"Who do you work for?" I asked, going back to my question.

Layla jerked to a halt and blinked. Her gaze went to the window to find my reflection.

Without missing a beat, she answered, "An NGO."

"A non-government organization? That's it? That's all you're gonna give me?"

When she didn't answer me right away, I turned to look at her. If she was going to bullshit me, I wanted her to do it directly to my face.

"I don't know what you want me to tell you."

"How about the truth?" I supplied.

"Why?" She threw her arms up in exasperation until she caught herself and quickly lowered them. "I don't get it. You said it yourself, Zane's not going to help me. So why would I risk exposing ten years of work? My mission is to rescue Theo, but I cannot put the whole operation in jeopardy."

That was Layla's problem; Zane would never send any of us into an unknown situation.

"What's the scope of your operation?"

Silence.

"Who do you work for?" I tried again.

More silence.

"Do you know Theo's location?"

Layla didn't answer that either. Not surprising but frustrating as fuck.

"What do you know about Bronson Williams?"

"Bronson is Theo's half-brother. He owns a small business—mobile detailing. No criminal history. His parents are still married, fairly well-off. I also know Bronson's lucky Zane's been preoccupied with other events or he would've already flown to Canada to put him down."

Of course, she answered the question I already knew the answer to.

She wasn't totally wrong in her assessment of why Bronson hadn't been dealt with yet but she wasn't fully correct either. I would've been the one to go to Canada, not Zane, if I hadn't been sent to Guatemala to help Myles and Delilah. We tended to keep Zane out of the field as much as possible. Zane didn't mind messy, and his brand of mess was hard to clean up.

"How did you know that Theo's brother had been threatening Zane?"

"We always knew there was a possibility someone would figure out Aaron faked his death. As carefully as the plan was executed, as cautious as we've been over the years, there's always a chance someone from an operator's former life would recognize him."

"And the easiest way to flush him out would be to use his family," I surmised.

"Correct."

"So, you kept tabs on Aaron—or Theo's—family throughout the years."

"Correct."

That was a smart move. Something I would've done as well if I were Theo. But there was more.

"So the two of you hatched this plan to fake Theo's death and he was going to do what? Go rogue warrior and investigate the CIA payouts on his own?"

I could swear I saw a flash of apprehension before Layla schooled her features.

"Theo suspected someone at the CIA was dirty," I continued theorizing. "He'd work his contacts in his previous areas of operation. You, being the jilted former officer, would help him. But something's missing. He didn't have to fake his death to do that. Someone threatened him. Not his family, that's too easy. They had something to hold over him. He fucked up in the field and someone had proof."

"Theo didn't fuck up."

Interesting. She was quick to vehemently defend a man who was supposedly only a colleague.

My level of frustration neared the red zone. Nothing added up. With every statement she made the field of questions grew larger. Not to mention, we were wasting time. If she was so worried about saving Theo's life, why hadn't she come clean?

"His family thinks he's dead," I said. "His mother, his brother, his stepfather. That's a lot of pain to dish out on the people he presumably loves. Only a desperate man goes to those lengths."

"When Theo wouldn't back down about wanting an investigation, he was threatened," she replied. "He stopped officially requesting an investigation, but he never stopped looking into what happened. Unfortunately, Theo didn't understand how deep the corruption went and asked the wrong people questions."

Corruption, at the CIA, you don't say.

"Who made the threat?"

"A station chief at headquarters."

More evasive answers.

"What'd they threaten?"

"To expose a situation that would harm someone Theo respected. Not only harm but the evidence when taken out of context would ruin this person's life. We're talking rendition and confinement for the rest of this person's life."

"Is that person you?"

Layla jerked back like I'd punched her.

It wasn't her.

"You're right, Theo was desperate. So desperate, his options were to hurt his family or be the reason a good man would be accused of something he didn't do. He opted to fake his death. Allow the station chief to think he not only backed down but was dead so he could follow the few leads he had while protecting an innocent man."

Man, not person.

Another slip.

So it would seem when pushed Theo *could* deal in gray.

"If you won't tell me who he's protecting then will you tell me what situation he wanted covered up?"

Layla shook her head. "Theo didn't want anything covered up. There was nothing to cover. The operation had been on the up and up. But, again the situation taken out of context would be damning. And I'm not going to tell you about the situation."

"Why not?"

"First, because it was a top-secret mission—"

Is she for real?

"Layla, do I need to remind you that everything we're discussing is top secret? It is now and it was back at the

White House while you were openly breaking your oath. In front of the POTUS," I added for good measure.

"I need not be reminded, Kevin," she snapped.

"Okay, then who was Theo protecting?"

"I'm not telling you."

"Why not?"

"Because I promised I wouldn't tell anyone."

Her words were cold as ice, unmovable. Unfortunately, they did nothing to cool the fire in my gut.

"Tell me the truth," I demanded. "Who's Theo to you?"

"A friend."

I didn't believe that, or was jealousy clouding my judgment?

"You lost your job because of him. And for the last ten years, you've been playing his handler. That's a long time, Layla. Ten years taking risks, putting yourself in potential danger, loss of a career. All for a *friend*?"

"Yes, I gave up my career for a friend."

I knew it was uncool before I did it, yet I did it purposefully and willfully and I almost instantly regretted it.

"Liar."

Total. Shutdown.

It happened the moment the word came out of my mouth and had the opposite reaction I wanted.

"If you think that's an insult, you're wrong."

Yes, Layla was qualified and skilled and it pissed me right the fuck off that even though I knew I sank a verbal blade into her heart her facial expression and voice remained cool and calculated.

"I think you're smart. I think you know who took Theo. I think you know exactly where he is. I think you're looking for an extraction team and you thought you could keep us in the dark like hired mercs. You thought you could manipulate the situation and now you're coming to realize the flaw in your plan. You've backed yourself into a corner. You have one option available to you and you're not going to take it. You're gonna keep your secrets and your friend's gonna die. But hell, you'll be able to visit his grave and know you kept your promise, right? Those lies roll off your tongue so fucking sweetly, but the truth that'll save your *friend* gets locked down. You need *my* help but your inability to trust me is what's gonna get Theo killed."

"I came to you, remember?"

"No. You went to Zane. Not *me*."

What the hell was I saying?

"And there's a difference?"

In general, no. I worked for Zane.

But for Layla there was.

"I can't help you unless you trust me," I ground out.

The look on her face was set to bland, uninterested, indifferent.

Jesus fuck, this woman!

"I don't trust you," she confirmed. "And seeing as you've called me a liar three times it's clear you know you shouldn't trust me. I needed Zane's help but if he's unwilling, then he's unwilling." Layla shrugged like it was all the same to her.

Needed—past tense?

There was a pregnant pause. Layla sighed, then continued. "I never should've approached Zane."

"Why did you?"

"I told you why. I needed help and Zane's the best."

"That and you thought his connection to Theo—however small, would appeal to him."

Layla walked to the couch and sat, a move that would put me in the dominant position. It was strategic, meant to make me think she was nonthreatening, maybe even agreeable.

"They teach you that in spy school?" I asked when she kept her gaze on the coffee table in front of her.

"No, Kevin. I'm tired and I wanted to sit."

"Who told Bronson Williams that Zane killed his brother?"

"Bronson will tell you a man named Liam Martin who claimed to be with the FBI approached him and told him a story about how Zane Lewis is a terrorist and sabotaged the plane Aaron was on. As far as Bronson and his family knew Aaron worked in textiles and frequently traveled overseas to purchase materials. Liam Martin produced photographs of Zane in Cyprus at the airport."

More CIA, fake name, cat-and-mouse shit.

"Please for the love of God break this shit down in an easy-to-understand CliffsNotes version."

"Shall I write it all out for you on color-coded index cards, too?"

Damn, it sucked that she was funny when I was pissed. With a great deal of effort, I kept my smile at bay.

"If you got the time that'd be appreciated. Maybe you can arrange them on a bulletin board and add arrows so I can follow along."

"A man's life is on the line." Apparently, Layla had lost her sense of humor.

"Yes, your *friend* Theo's." I didn't miss the flash in her eyes, so I pushed. "He's lucky he lasted ten years in the field alone before he was snatched. And I have to tell you, I'm not stupid and I still don't understand exactly what he was doing and why. I can kinda understand faking his death to protect someone he cared about or respected or if his family had been threatened. Though, by doing that he actually left them unprotected. And that brings us to you. He left you swinging in the wind towing his line and you gladly participated. That doesn't say friend. That says something more.

"Just to clear something up, Zane's gonna turn you down, but not because I was shot at. Unfortunately, that's in the job description. He's going to tell you no because there is nothing he hates more than bullshit. The CIA burned him, burned his brother and his sister-in-law."

"I know what happened to Jasmin and Zane in Russia."

"I'm sure you do," I allowed. "I'm sure you also know that Zane, Jasmin, and Linc aren't the only ones who work for Z Corps who have been fucked over by the agency. It is no secret that's why Zane left SAC and when he did, he nailed that door shut. The man has integrity and that violently clashes with CIA missions. It will take more than a loose connection and some asshole who detonated a pipe bomb and is currently keying cars, leaving stupid notes on the windshields of women's cars, and throwing rocks at houses to motivate Zane to deploy a team to Armenia. As I told you, I think you're smart. So what I can't wrap my head around is that you thought you could manipulate Zane into helping you by dangling a pissant like Bronson Williams in front of him. When we take Bronson down this is over for us."

"You're right."

"I know I am."

"But then Zane would never know who had the balls to fuck with him. And something tells me Zane likes to know he's got the biggest pair in any given situation."

She was not wrong.

But still...

"I see you think you know Zane Lewis, but you don't. A man who *knows* he's got the biggest pair in the room doesn't allow himself to be led around by his dick. He's got nothing to prove to anyone. And if you think Zane needs help tracking down Liam Martin, whoever the hell he is, you're not as smart as I thought you were."

"Okay."

"Jesus Christ!" I exploded.

A stone-faced CIA officer I was not. But still, I never would've thought it'd be me who broke. However, it was happening. My temper flared to life and red-hued my vision. I didn't give two fucks that I was laying my cards on the table face-up for Layla to read. I was fresh out of patience.

"You're in danger," I told her.

"I know."

Expressionless.

Callous.

What in the hell was wrong with this woman?

"That's it? You know? Back at your apartment, I thought you were a little crazy the way you ran across the room with no regard for cover. A little crazy and maybe a little out of practice. Now I see you just have a mother-fucking death wish. Someone's got Theo. They know you have his intel. If they got to him, they sure as fuck can get to you. You admit you need help. I'm offering you help and to get it all you need to do is tell me the goddamn truth in simple, easy-to-understand terms, yet you sit there totally fucking blank, giving me nothing."

"You want the truth?" she asked incredulously.

Out of everything I'd said, she latched onto that.

"For fuck's sake, Layla, are we playing out a scene from *A Few Good Men*? Is this where you tell me I can't handle the truth? Or are you gonna switch back to it's top-secret so I can't tell you? No, wait, I forgot—you can't tell me the truth because you promised your *friend* Theo you wouldn't tell anyone how he was being blackmailed and why."

"You're an asshole."

Finally!

"I haven't begun to be an asshole yet."

"The truth is, I made a mistake. I never should've approached Zane."

"Well, you did. So you might as well make lemonade. Start squeezing those lemons, darlin', and fill in the blanks."

"I think I'll pass."

"So you're okay with Zane sending me up to Canada to take down Bronson? He's annoying but escalating. I need to remedy that. And say while I'm up there, he decides he's feeling frisky and pulls a gun on me. Either he pulls the trigger and I'm dead, or the alternate, more likely scenario is I take him out. Now I got a deep mark on my soul knowing I had to put down a man thinking he was doing the right thing by his brother, who before that was going about his life not bothering anyone. By all accounts a good guy. The brother of your friend Theo. A man who is being used as a pawn in a game he doesn't know he's playing. For the rest of my life, I'll get to live with that on my conscience. But, Layla, that shit will be on you."

"Bronson's not in Canada," she hissed.

"And you know this how?"

"Because I have him."

"Say again?"

"I have him. I nabbed him right after his last stunt leaving rocks on Max Brown's car in the parking lot of Lowe's."

I didn't take my eyes off Layla as I walked around the chair, taking my time to calm my racing thoughts.

Layla nabbed Bronson more than a week ago.

"Did you kill him?" I asked even though I didn't think that was the case.

Her head jerked to the side and her eyes narrowed. "Seriously?"

Those pretty, troubled eyes remained locked with mine.

Was she playing me?

The beautiful woman sitting across from me would know a man like me would respond to the hurt she exposed. I'd bet her skillset was varied in such a way she knew the right plays to instigate at precisely the right time. She knew when to pivot, duck, move, and run. She'd know when to make herself vulnerable, when to set the trap, and the patience to wait for her victim to submit. And she'd know when her target had underestimated her, and she'd go in hard.

But this was not that. Something else was happening. Something beyond Theo. Some internal struggle. She wanted to unload the truth. She wanted to tell me her secrets. As a matter of fact, I'd bet she was dying to unburden herself.

Layla was intelligent, cunning, shrewd. But everyone had a weakness. I just had to find hers.

Time to switch up tactics.

What was the old saying, you can't play a player?

Game on.

7

THE LONGER I held his stare the more curious I became. The more fascinated.

That was a mistake. I shouldn't have been curious about Kevin beyond what his file outlined and how I could use that information. I should not have been fascinated, period. And I really shouldn't have been wondering how it was possible a gorgeous forty-five-year-old man with a great smile and beautiful eyes had never been married. I should not have been mesmerized by the way his forearms bunched under the folded cuffs of his dress shirt. I shouldn't have been thinking about anything other than how to best exploit his weaknesses.

Did Kevin have any weaknesses?

I had every detail about Kevin memorized. I'd done a deep dive into his service, his military deployments, and his family. I knew at one time the Blue Team specialized in maritime security and until Zane stopped taking those contracts Kevin had spent a lot of time on cargo ships. I wondered if his work had prohibited him from committing to a woman or if he was a typical Teamguy and preferred his sexual encounters fast and loose with busty Frog Hogs who threw themselves at him. *And why do I hate the idea of hot women fawning all over him?*

Then I wondered how I'd become the type of woman who'd look at a good-looking man and study him for weaknesses to manipulate.

Fear, that was how I'd become her.

I was scared of everything and everyone.

My work with my former employer was the excuse I allowed myself to use—the reason why I'd become her. The lie that it was part of my training, it was part of the craft, it was who the agency had made me. But that wasn't the truth. I was self-aware enough to understand that I hid behind the excuse as a way to give myself permission not to change. Because change would mean I'd have to remember who I really was. I'd have to face my past and the person I'd been and since I didn't like that person very much, I was all too happy to forget her and where she came from.

But I wasn't happy.

I'd never been happy.

On that thought, my stomach clenched.

Yes, thinking about Kevin as a man rather than my target had been a huge mistake.

Thinking about my life and the ways I'd screwed it up was an even bigger mistake and I knew it when Kevin called my name in an exasperated way, like he'd been doing it awhile.

"Sorry. What?"

"Where'd you go?"

To a place I needed to forget.

"I was thinking about Bronson," I lied.

"Right," he clipped, knowing I was being untruthful.

Without meaning to I held my breath and waited for him to sink a verbal knife into my stomach.

Liar.

I was one so why did it hurt so bad?

"Where is he?" Kevin asked.

Where was who?

Oh, Bronson.

Damn. I needed to get my shit together.

"With a friend in West Virginia."

"Does your friend have a name?" he barked.

Or was that a growl? A growly-bark that signified just how done he was playing games.

"Kira Winters."

"Kira Winters?" Kevin's head tipped to the right and his gaze went over my shoulder as if he were trying to place a face with a familiar name.

And this was where my plan was going to go to shit.

"Maybe you know her brother, Finn Winters," I begrudgingly shared, ignoring the painful pinch in my chest. "He was a Unit operator who—"

"Was beheaded on a livestream," Kevin finished. "Yes, I worked with Finn a few times on joint operations. And I met Kira at his funeral. Last I heard she was a software engineer. Why is she guarding an HVT?"

Well, I wouldn't classify Bronson as a high-value target; more like a moron who needed to be taken into custody for his own protection before he did something really stupid like injure one of Zane's men—or worse, one of their wives. There would be no coming back from that.

Lies. You hijacked Bronson to interrogate him. You're using him as a means to buy your way into Zane Lewis's good graces. If there were such a thing.

Kira wasn't just a software engineer, she was the brains

behind the cyber division of Patheon. Or more accurately, she *was* the cyber division. There was nothing Kira couldn't find. She'd had a lock on Theo within twenty-four hours of him going missing and was monitoring the situation from a safe house in West Virginia along with running intel for the other five operatives we had in the field. The woman was a multitasking genius.

"I see you over there plotting." Kevin's accusation pulled me from my thoughts. "Assessing risk, pondering how much you're going to need to reveal to keep me on the hook. Contemplating the pros and cons of feeding me more bullshit. Let me help you with that—no more bullshit."

"How'd you know?" I blurted out.

I instantly regretted my question, but it was too late; Kevin was back to staring directly at me. His eyes had latched onto mine and he looked...pleased. Maybe even a little satisfied. It was disconcerting and uncomfortable.

The corner of Kevin's mouth twitched. It was a tiny tic but I didn't miss it nor did I miss the way his shoulders relaxed.

"Now why would I go and do something as stupid as telling you how I know when you're conniving?"

Was he teasing me? It sure sounded like he was. Kevin had missed his calling. He should've joined the CIA, not the Navy. Not that he wasn't an excellent operator, but the agency could've put his observation skills to good use.

No, they would've turned a good man into a soulless liar like they tried to do to Theo.

Focus, dammit!

"I recruited Kira. After her brother died, she was poking around in places that could've gotten her in trouble. I found out and offered her a job."

"Explain that."

"She was digging up information about the terrorist group that killed her brother. She was dangerously close to setting off some big alarms. I stopped her before she found herself locked up in a CIA detention site."

Kevin sat quietly as he contemplated my flimsy explanation. The longer the silence stretched the more uncomfortable I became. Kevin was right, I was backed into a corner. I was on the verge of losing everything we'd worked for, and Theo would die. After years of sleepless nights and sacrifice, we'd finally set the board, all the pieces were in place, all the players identified. Well, most of them, but that last piece would click into place during the opening move. We were days away from making a clean sweep. The house would crumble, and the corruption would be exposed. But it all hinged on Zane Lewis helping me extract Theo. I couldn't pull any of my men from their assignments. I couldn't risk going to anyone else outside for help.

"Layla?"

"Give me a second."

It was now or never.

Either I trusted Kevin and told him the truth, or I needed to walk out the door, scrap the mission, and pull my guys in for a rescue. No, that wasn't an option. Theo would never forgive me.

We'd all agreed: mission before self.

I'd already broken my oath, I'd gone to an outsider for help. I'd alerted the president there was a shadow team working off the books. A team that was buried under so many layers of secrecy the POTUS didn't even know we existed. My time with Patheon was done. I'd be cut from the team, likely brought up on charges, and spend the rest of my life in one of those CIA black sites I'd kept Kira from inhabiting.

"Layla—"

"I need to explain."

Before I could go on, Kevin barked out a laugh followed by a few chuckles.

"Ya think?"

I found myself whispering, "Don't do that."

"And what is *that*? Pointing out the obvious?"

"Don't make fun of me."

God, could I sound any more like a five-year-old?

Kevin's smile died a quick death and his brows pulled together.

"I'm not making fun of you, Layla. I can be an ass when I need to be but I'm not a dick."

I wasn't sure what the difference was between an ass and a dick—well, I knew the literal difference. But right then I didn't have it in me to ask Kevin to explain the variances between the two. If I was going to betray my team I needed to do it now before I changed my mind. I had to tell Kevin everything and hope for the best. Hope that Theo and the others understood why I revealed the truth.

I closed my eyes and pulled up a mental image of Theo. His tawny eyes with long spiky lashes. The last time I saw him he had laugh lines around his eyes that had started to turn into deep grooves of worry. The stress of the job had taken root. Ten years later I wondered if those grooves had gotten deeper. Had he grown a beard? Did he now have gray streaks at his temples? Did he still have a comical appetite for pizza or had ten years in the Middle East and Asia cured him?

Kevin's phone rang, snapping me back to reality with a jarring slap.

I opened my eyes as Kevin unlocked his phone using his

thumbprint then he tapped the screen a few times before answering, "Yeah?"

"Is she talking?" Zane Lewis's voice boomed through the speaker.

No hello. No pleasantries. Oh, no, not Zane. He cut straight to the point and did so in a not-so-happy tone.

"Working on it," Kevin replied just as unhappily.

"Work faster," Zane griped.

I clenched my teeth and took a few deep breaths.

Theo, I reminded myself.

All of this is for Theo.

"She says she's got Bronson in a safe house in West Virginia," Kevin told Zane. "Says she nabbed him outside of Lowe's after he fucked with Max's Jeep. And get this, Finn Winters' sister Kira is babysitting him."

She says.

Did he not believe me? Why did that feel like he'd sucker-punched me in the stomach leaving me gasping to catch my breath?

"She did what?" Zane roared and I flinched. "I swear on Finn's grave if Kira's in danger I'll strangle you myself."

Kevin pinned me with a stare and raised his right eyebrow. I guessed that was his silent way of telling me he wanted me to engage with the pissed-off lion. The man wasn't even in the same room as me but that didn't mean I couldn't feel his anger pressing on my chest.

And you know what?

That pissed me right the fuck off. Not so much at Zane but at myself for allowing fear and weakness to dominate my thoughts once again.

Fuck that.

I was no longer that person. I'd never again be that sniveling woman.

"Kira is sitting with Bronson because she works with me. I recruited her after her brother was murdered."

I could hear Zane's swift inhale. I could feel the tension ratcheting up another notch and I wondered if the cool, calm, collected operator's face was red. Oh, what I wouldn't give to see the high and mighty Viper lose his legendary façade of indifference. Okay, so, I could safely wish that seeing as I was far away from Zane's blast radius.

"I swear—"

"You know," I interrupted Zane. "It's rude to swear on someone's grave. And I'd highly recommend you not saying that in front of Kira unless you want her to slice your throat. She loves her brother and doesn't take kindly—"

It was Zane's turn to cut me off by grunting, "Kira Winters? Finn's sweet baby sister? Her? She's gonna slice my throat?"

Ah, yes, sweet Kira Winters. People liked to underestimate her, and she used it to her advantage. She was the shy, sweet wallflower who went unnoticed. It was amazing how she could blend in and make herself mousey and small. Most people looked at her as inconsequential therefore they didn't guard their words around her. For months, she and I worked on tradecraft. I taught her everything she needed to know about intel gathering. But like any good big brother, it was Finn who'd taught Kira how to protect herself. I had no doubt if she wanted to cut Zane's throat and leave him to bleed out, she'd find a way. And it would start with Zane thinking she was still Finn's sweet baby sister.

"People change when they watch the only family they have get murdered," I told him.

"Jesus," he spat. "You found her and exploited her and what, turned her into a spy?"

"No, I found her and saved her from finding herself in a

CIA black site, or worse, in the hands of the terrorists who killed her brother. I gave her a mission. I focused her anger and gave her what she wanted—a way to take down the cell that took her brother from her. I made it safe for her to do what she was already doing."

"The asset," Zane muttered. "The Al-Qaeda leader."

And there it was, Zane proving he needed very little to put the pieces together.

"Yes, Yaser Said," I confirmed. "We were hunting the same man. It was her intel that finally led a GB unit to take him out."

Per our orders, we'd anonymously turned over our intel to the CIA. Within forty-eight hours a Ground Branch team from the agency's Special Activities Center was deployed and Said was taken out. A terrorist responsible for the murder of a Delta operator and the bombing of a convoy taking out a good number of U.S. troops was a fortunate secondary operation, but not our primary function.

However, I needed to move the conversation away from the ground unit that took out Said. That was a topic I wasn't prepared to discuss. Zane was too smart; it was only a matter of time before he connected the dots back to Garrett and I needed Theo safe before that happened.

"Yeah, see, that doesn't make sense to me." Zane sounded thoughtful, more relaxed, he'd shed some of his anger and was in Tier One mode. Which was a dangerous mindset when I was trying to keep the truth from coming out too soon. "Why would she hand over intel to the very people you wanted investigated?"

Shit.

Shit.

"We went to the OIG."

"You just what? Called up the Office of the Inspector

General and asked for a meeting and he cleared his busy schedule for a former CIA officer and a software engineer?"

More sarcasm.

"Pretty much," I told him, leaving out a chunk of the truth. "Would you like the address of my safe house?"

There were five seconds of silence. I knew because I counted them. Each second felt like an eternity. I felt it even before Zane opened his mouth and dropped the bomb I never saw coming. The hair on the back of my neck tingled. My stomach fluttered the way it did when I was in the field and danger was approaching. A feeling that had saved my life more than once. It was too bad that flutter had failed me before Theo's last op. Because now I had a feeling I was totally and thoroughly screwed.

"No. Garrett will find it." Zane's voice had gone icy, and I braced for his denial. He was going to tell me I was on my own. "The only thing I want from you is a reason why I shouldn't have Kevin haul your ass back to Washington and turn you over to the dumb fucks. Which, I have to tell you, the only reason I waited hours before I made this call is I kinda like knowing the agency's running around searching for you. It makes me warm and fuzzy inside when I have something they want."

That was a problem I hadn't allowed myself to think about. Eddy Stallone. Why was he in my apartment tonight and who had sent him?

"I didn't know Eddy was after me or I never would've gone to that apartment. Hell, I don't even know why he'd bother with me."

More silence, and when I lifted my gaze from the phone in Kevin's hand to his face I wished I would've kept my eyes averted. Everything about him had changed. There was no sign of his earlier annoyance. His eyes held understanding.

His posture was relaxed and non-threatening. He looked exactly how I would if I'd been the one attempting to recruit an asset.

I was being played. That was the only explanation for Kevin's change. He was smart, he'd switch up tactics. His attempts of hurting my feelings and being an asshole hadn't worked so now he'd play the sympathetic good guy while Zane played the growly bear with a thorn in his ass. Though I didn't think Zane was actually playing a role, I figured that was his normal disposition.

"That's easy, your name's on the top of the CIA's most-wanted list. Congratulations, you made the Matrix."

Smartass.

The Disposition Matrix was a database of HVTs. The agency's version of a kill list, but of course, they'd deny the Matrix existed and those who knew about it would call the list a necessary precaution to keep the U.S. safe.

It was a good play on the agency's part. If I'd been in the room planning the takedown of a target on American soil, I would've suggested that very thing, ensuring every government agency would be after my mark.

"What's she on the list for?" Kevin asked.

"War crimes and treason."

"War crimes?" I breathed, finding it hard to well...breathe.

There was any number of ways to make me look guilty of violating international treaties. It would take me less than five minutes to create a fake case file against an officer. I was not one of the fortunate officers who'd never had to draw a weapon in the field. I'd had to defend myself, resulting in the loss of life. How easy could the agency turn those situations into willfully killing a civilian? The answer was, very easy—so damn easy I was positive all of my kills would be listed as murders. There would be a notation that I was armed and dangerous and should be taken out, not captured.

Fuck.

Outplayed by the very book I lived by.

"It's interesting that you didn't ask about the treason," Zane noted.

Fuck. Him.

"I think you were in the room this morning when I broke my oath. Beyond that, I have never betrayed my country. And it's debatable if me trying to save one of my men and a ten-year operation can be considered treason. I think you of all people would agree with me."

"*One* of your men?" Kevin scoffed. "I think it's time for you to start filling in some holes, Layla."

Damn it all to hell!

8

I WATCHED as Layla's eyes darted around the room. It was an interesting sight to see—her mind working double-time to come up with a solution to her latest problem.

It was a good maneuver on the agency's part. Not only would the authorities be gunning for Layla but now the CIA had a reason to go after Z Corps. Specifically Zane, seeing as after all these years, they still had a hard-on for him. And being seen at the White House with her handed them the keys to the castle. They'd question Zane about Layla and if he didn't turn her over, we could be charged with aiding and abetting.

I was sure the CIA had a stack of evidence against her. Likely Zane had already been privy to what the agency had compiled. The good news was, if Zane had believed any of it, he wouldn't have called. I would've received a text to take Layla into custody and I'd be on my way to Langley to hand her over.

And it was good that Zane didn't buy the bullshit because I didn't either.

"Layla?" I prompted.

She peered at me from under her lashes. A flash of righteous indignation glittered in her hazel-green eyes. The sight of her obvious insult and anger made me want to smile. Not because there was a damn thing funny with an innocent woman—or man for that matter—being accused of something they didn't do. But the determination I saw spark to life made my chest compress.

Right before Zane called, I saw resignation; she was going to tell me who she really worked for and what her mission was because she was out of options.

I had to admit I liked seeing this version of her better.

"I need to make a call," Layla responded.

"You can't turn your phone on," I reminded her.

Layla leaned forward with her eyes narrowed. But before she could smart off she thought better of it and blew out a breath then relaxed her shoulders.

"I have a burner in my bag."

"Zane?"

"It's her ass," he answered. Then to Layla, he said, "I hope you trust whoever you're calling with your life because if the spooks come knocking, I'm ordering Kevin to stand down. You're on your own."

For once Layla didn't attempt to hide her response. The corners of her mouth turned down into a frown and sadness coated her expression.

"Nothing new," she mumbled, then stood.

Once Layla was across the room rummaging through the backpack she'd grabbed out of her attic, I took Zane off speaker and asked, "Has anyone contacted you?"

"Talked to Graham. He's not buying it, but without proof, he's not gonna stick his neck out for her. I also got a call from a unit chief, Harrison Washington. Now he had a lot to say about Layla."

A CIA unit chief offering up intel on an active and ongoing case? If that didn't reek of shit I didn't know what did.

"How much?"

"Too much. He offered up the charges without me asking and before I could press him on specifics, he told me he'd already sent the intel to Garrett."

"Convenient," I muttered.

"What's your take on her?"

That was a loaded question.

"She's like a wounded animal caught in a trap."

"You mean a wild animal caught in a web of agency fuckery."

She was that, too.

"Right before you called, she told me she nabbed Bronson, and about Kira's part. I think she picked up Bronson as a bargaining chip. But she's gonna want to guarantee his safety before she hands him over. She knew we've been busy and that was why we haven't put much effort into finding him ourselves. She's either been following us or more likely Kira's been digging in places where she shouldn't be. You might have Garrett check our systems."

Zane blew out a frustrated breath.

"I have faith in Garrett, but I'll tell him. What's your gut say?"

I found Layla standing across the room staring down at the burner phone she'd retrieved from her bag. One of the few possessions she now had since the CIA would seize the rest of her belongings.

"I think she wants to unload but she's duty-bound. She's struggling with what to tell us, hoping to get by with the bare minimum. She's got more than Kira and Theo; she said *one* of her men. Which leads me to believe she's the team leader the way she's sticking her neck out. And side note, the woman has zero regard for her personal safety. As in none."

"Do you trust her?"

"Fuck no."

"Good. I was worried your little head had already taken over."

And that didn't take long.

"Lucky for you, boss, I don't have a little head and my brain is fully functional."

"Hey, it's me." I heard Layla say.

"I'm putting you back on speaker," I told Zane.

"I know." Layla stopped pacing and nodded. "Yes. I had no choice, sir, he's my best shot. I need—" She abruptly stopped speaking, her eyes cut to mine, and she held me hostage with her pleading gaze.

Good Christ.

Please tell me your secrets.

"No, sir, that's not my call to make, that's why I'm asking. There are lines I'm willing to cross to save Theo, and Kira gave me her permission to tell Viper. Finn trusted him; he told her if anything ever went wrong to go to him. I'd say we're at mission-critical, he's our only chance. But again, the call is yours. I can walk out now and..." She paused again and I wasn't sure if she was letting that hang or if she'd been interrupted. "Yes, I, um, trust him."

Her response might've been an answer as to whether or not she trusted Zane but her eyes glued to mine told an entirely different story.

Layla trusted *me*.

And why did that make my heart pound in my chest?

"Copy that. Give me twenty minutes to explain. But I'll tell him to expect a call from you."

Layla disconnected the call. Her eyelids slowly lowered as she exhaled a relieved breath. And when they opened, she asked, "Are we on a secure line?"

"Yes."

Then with her shoulders back, chin tipped up almost defiantly, and a fire in her eyes she launched in. "I'm the team leader of a group called Patheon. After Theo approached senior leadership and was shot down, he went to the Inspector General. Ashcroft agreed there was a need for an investigation, but he wanted an outside team brought in. While Ashcroft was in talks with the POTUS, the threats Theo were receiving intensified—"

"Stop!" Zane interrupted. "President Adams or Tom Anderson?"

Tom Anderson won the White House when President Adams's term was up. Depending on the timeline ten years ago could mean the end of Adams's presidency or the beginning of Anderson's. Tom and Zane were friends. Not only that but Tom was the uncle of Zane's sister-in-law, and Colin, one of my teammates, was married to Tom's daughter, Erin. If Anderson had authorized a shadow team Zane could make one call and have all the details.

"President Adams." *Damn!* "He gave Ashcroft the okay to form a task force to investigate Theo's claims. While the team was being briefed, I was fired. Ashcroft approached me at Theo's recommendation. I was brought on as the lead intelligence officer."

"And you thought the best way to protect Theo from the threats he'd received was to fake his death?"

Zane didn't sound impressed, likely because his thoughts had gone to where mine had; Theo faking his death left his family and friends exposed.

"It was the only way to protect everyone involved."

"That day in Cyprus," Zane started then stopped.

Layla turned away to face the windows. But I didn't miss the panic before she hid her face from me.

"Why were you there?" I asked Zane when he didn't continue.

"I was supposed to meet an asset, but he never showed. I was working at the airport as a baggage handler. Did you set me up?"

"No!" Layla turned. "Theo wanted you brought in. He wanted you on the team, but I found out you had a brother. All the men on our team with the exception of Theo have no siblings and were either already estranged from their families or their parents were deceased. Ashcroft was adamant about this. No immediate family. But by the time I found out about Lincoln you were already on your way to Cyprus. Due to your presence, we had to delay the operation until you left. It was too risky with you in the area."

Goddamn spy games.

"You wasted three hours of my life waiting around the airport. Actually, you owe me two fucking days seeing as I had to leave South Africa and get my ass to Cyprus. And people wonder why I won't work with the agency. Y'all are a bunch of life-stealing bloodsuckers," Zane grumbled. "Who died in the plane crash?"

"No one."

"What do you mean no one? There was an explosion."

At my reminder, the corners of Layla's lips slowly curved up into a sinful smile. The transformation was instant, the power behind it stole my breath, the beauty had me wondering if I'd unintentionally lied to Zane. My brain momentarily blanked and suddenly Layla wasn't a former spook—she was a stunning woman I wanted to get to know.

All of that from a smile.

No, not just a smile. Everything about her had changed. She looked excited, and maybe a little proud of herself. But mostly she looked accessible and unguarded. The change in her was extraordinary and I couldn't help but return her grin.

"Did you know that Theo was a pilot?" Her smile grew as she continued. "And he was a master at low-altitude jumps."

Smart but risky. Theo takes up an empty plane, ditches it, then detonates it when he's out.

"The passenger manifest was easy to create. Backstories about fake passengers that no one was going to look into, easier. Our only worry was the CIA, so we made sure Theo's DNA was all over the plane in the hopes that something would survive the explosion and they'd be satisfied he was dead." She finished with a shrug.

"I'm not sure if I'm impressed or disturbed," Zane mumbled.

"How about you go with impressed and agree to help me?"

"How about no. And you finish explaining to me how you're the leader of a team I've never heard of that was created by a man who no longer works for the government and was authorized by a man who is no longer POTUS, and the existence of your team wasn't told to Anderson after he took office, or Graham after he took the White House. And speaking of Graham, did you tell him who you really are, or are you lying to the President of the United States?"

Layla's smile faded and I wanted to kick Zane's ass for breaking the spell.

"I wasn't completely forthcoming with the POTUS."

"Jesus."

"Ashcroft is calling him now."

"That should be an interesting conversation. Speaking of interesting, I'm dying to hear all about how you managed to keep your team together through two presidents and with no oversight. If I knew that was a thing, I would've been doing this on good ol' Uncle Sam's dime instead of bleeding money as I ridded the world of scumbags."

Zane was so full of shit. He didn't bleed money, he made it hand over fist and he charged the government for his services, plus he tacked on a charge for mental anguish.

"Yes, well it seems Ashcroft's smarter than you," Layla shot back.

"Or maybe I'm just honest and don't want to risk spending the rest of my life in a foreign jungle locked up with terrorists playing hide the soap."

"You must think highly of yourself to assume they'd like your ass enough to stick something in it. After spending ten minutes with you my orifice of choice would be your mouth."

Layla's cheeks turned pink almost incautiously when she realized what she said. I heard Zane's burst of laughter and mine was soon to follow.

"I mean your mouth to stuff a sock in it," she huffed.

"Sure." Zane laughed.

"I'm serious. I'd stuff a sock in your mouth, not soap in your ass."

I couldn't take it; I bent double, holding my stomach as tears formed in the corners of my eyes.

"Holy shit," I choked out.

"Good thing you don't want to stick things in my ass, Miss Cunnings. My wife tends to frown upon that."

"Can we stop talking about your ass, please?"

I stayed crunched forward and laughed harder at Layla's pissed-off demand. The woman was hilarious without meaning to be. And the blush on her cheeks made her look carefree and adorably cute. She probably wouldn't like to be described as such but there was no denying she was cute and unconsciously funny.

"I don't know, are we? If you'd like to move on to other parts of my anatomy, we—"

"I'd rather not," Layla snapped. "You seem to have a large head—"

My burst of hilarity cut off the rest of what she was going to say.

"Are you really that immature?"

Was she talking to me or Zane? Both of us were laughing so it was hard to tell, but I fielded the question.

"When a beautiful woman is digging herself into a hole and her pretty cheeks turn rosy while she's doing it, yes. When I've had a shit day and been shot at, yes. When humor's the only way to cut the tension, yes."

"And on days that are mundane and boring, do you still find ass funny?" Her hands were on her hips, her face severe in a failing attempt to be chastising.

"Yes."

"Right."

Then it happened, her lips twitched. She tried to fight it, probably worked hard, but in the end, she couldn't pull it off. Her brilliant smile was coupled with a shake of her head.

I noticed two things at once. The first and most important was Zane was no longer laughing. The second was that the cottage was dimly lit, giving the room a romantic vibe. Floor-to-ceiling windows took up the back wall. Of course, the glass was a three-inch-thick silicate and polymer material that would withstand multiple blasts from a five-five-six rifle. The furniture was meant for comfort, not style, the décor was beach-themed—Zane's wife's doing no doubt. The lighting was meant to be calming. Not too bright, a yellow hue cast over the space.

An unexpected, unwanted, wholly inappropriate mental image of me fisting her long brown hair popped into my head. A tug would tip her head back, giving me access to her lips. The maneuver would expose her delicate throat. It would be a toss-up which I'd taste first. Start at her neck and tease my way up to her mouth or go in for a kiss that leaves us both breathless. A mind-stealing kiss that would make us forget the events that had brought us together.

"Kevin?"

My dick twitched at the sound of her soft voice.

What the hell was wrong with me?

"Yeah?" I coughed to cover up the roughness in my voice I was positive Zane would pick up on.

The guy was a bloodhound; even through the phone, he'd pick up on the tiniest inflection in my tone. He'd sniff it out and exploit it.

"What'd I miss?" Garrett's voice pulled me out of my thoughts.

Focus.

"Layla was getting ready to tell us all about the super-secret spy organization she runs," Zane answered with his customary sarcasm.

"How super-secret?" Garrett inquired, playing along.

"The secret kind where she gets to run amuck with no congressional approval."

"Ah," Garrett muttered. "So the illegal kind."

I watched Layla's body become tenser and tenser through Garrett and Zane's banter, remembering when she'd mistaken my smartass comment as making fun of her. I'd obviously touched a nerve and she'd called me out on it.

"How about we let Layla finish telling us about Patheon so we can move this along?"

Layla blinked, her body jolted but before I could get a read, Garrett spoke and she looked completely deflated.

"Patheon?" Garrett asked.

Did she know Garrett? No, he would've mentioned working with her in the past and even if she was using a fake name now or had used one in the past, he'd seen her picture. And there was no doubt Layla was the kind of beautiful you didn't forget.

"You've heard of it?" Zane asked.

"Patheon is the facial rec software I use." I almost heard Garrett's eye roll at Zane's question.

I didn't need to prompt Layla to explain. She, too, seemed to want to get out the rest of her story and move on. She was probably thinking about Theo. And why did I get a knot in my gut when I thought about who he really was to her?

"As Zane pointed out we needed a way to operate under radar totally in the black. And we needed to do this through power shifts. Our mission's too important to be subjected to politics. So our team became a line item in the DoD budget. On record, Patheon is nothing more than a sophisticated facial recognition program. We needed government funds to operate, but more we needed access."

"Access to what?"

Layla's eyes went back to darting around the room, something she did when she was debating what to say.

Please tell the truth.

"Patheon amasses all the data the users collect. Every face that's been run through the software gets sent to us. Kira developed a program that now uses two hundred forty reference points—local feature analysis, surface texture—

but she was also able to advance the program to use vein matching. That's the part of Patheon that's not available to the end-user. The patterns of blood vessels underneath the skin are unique to each individual. With the data we collect we are able to build a database and track people even if they attempt to disguise their face."

"Who's Kira?"

In a flash, all the blood drained from Layla's face. All the pretty pink in her cheeks disappeared, leaving her ghostly pale.

What the hell was that about?

And was that fear in her eyes?

9

I WAS FAIRLY certain I was going to vomit listening to Zane explain to Garrett that Kira Winters worked for me and why. Garrett was already working for a CIA SAC unit when Finn was captured. It was Garrett's Ground Branch team who had searched for Finn. But the rescue attempt went bad, and Finn was murdered. The fuck of it was, Garrett blamed himself even though he was going off of bad intel. Intel that Garrett didn't know Zane had provided.

That deployment was also Garrett's last. After Finn was murdered, he got out and word was, he went totally dark. No one had seen or heard from him for over a year. When he reemerged he took a job at Z Corps.

To say Zane was my only option was the understatement of the year. If there'd been anyone else who could've helped me, I would've never approached Zane.

He was my *last* resort.

Not because it was Zane's asset who had turned traitor. Zane would get that; he understood the world of espionage. What I never wanted was for Garrett's past to be dragged to the present. He already blamed himself for Finn dying. I didn't want him to doubt Zane.

What a damn mess.

So many secrets. Lies that kept piling up.

From what I'd heard about Garrett, he was a good, solid operator. A good man. And now because of me, he was being slapped with Finn Winters' death all over again.

"Finn..." Garrett croaked then cleared his throat. And when he spoke again his voice was dripping with malice and I was thankful I wasn't in the same room as him. "What do you know about Finn? Who the fuck are you really?"

Kevin went on high alert and stood. Yeah, I'd bet Garrett worked hard to keep that temper in check. Further, I'd venture to guess Kevin hadn't ever heard Garrett sound murderous if I went by Kevin's startled expression.

"I'm sorry."

The whispered words popped out before I could think better of them. Garrett deserved to know the truth, but it wasn't my place to tell him. That was up to Easton, Cash, Jonas, and Smith. They'd vowed to tell Garrett as soon as the operation was over and they got to come home. It was Theo's place to tell Zane the truth about why he really faked his death.

God, how had ten years slipped by in the blink of an eye?

I promised I'd never tell.

Yet there I was asking Zane for help.

Did you really think you could outsmart Zane Lewis, you idiot?

At Theo's demand, Kira had scrubbed all evidence of Zane's involvement in her brother's murder. Evidence that could paint Zane as a traitor. Witnessing Kira go through the intel had been painful. But never for a moment had she believed Zane had turned on Finn. The pain came from Leif Robinson using Finn's death as a weapon to blackmail Theo.

"What exactly are you sorry about?" Garrett snarled.

It was happening. Everything I hoped wouldn't happen until Theo was safely home and the rest of the guys could talk to Garrett.

Kevin hadn't moved except to stand, and I appreciated him keeping his distance. If he got close, I was worried I'd do something stupid like tuck myself to his side and bury my face in his chest. What would it feel like to have Kevin's strong arms around me? What would it feel like to have someone comfort me when I felt like my whole world was coming apart?

And why now, when everything was imploding was I thinking about how it would feel to be in the arms of a man I didn't know?

I was the last person on earth Kevin would want to comfort.

Alone, like always.

I had to get through this, then I was done. No more missions. No more lies. No more saving the world. I just wanted to disappear into obscurity and live a quiet life.

"Ashcroft put together a five-man squad to deploy. Kira is the brains behind our cover. And I serve as the team's TL."

I held my breath knowing what the next question would be.

"Who's on the team?"

I shook my head, needing to tell Kevin first that I couldn't answer before I denied Garrett the information that would send his life further into a spiral.

"I'm not at liberty to say. And before you call bullshit,

please know I wish I could. I'm not prevaricating, I'm not trying to deceive you. I am bound not to disclose the identities of the men who I work with. Not bound by oath, bound by loyalty."

"That loyalty doesn't extend to Theo? You dropped his name," Garrett accused.

I tore my gaze from Kevin and focused on the coffee table that separated us. I was being a coward but for some reason, I couldn't look at Kevin while I admitted how weak I really was. Or was it that I was so accustomed to lying that I knew I couldn't look a good man in the eyes while being honest?

"I know what I'm doing is unforgivable," I whispered. "But I don't have it in me to let Theo die. I thought I could do it. Hell, if this had happened a year or two or five into the mission I might've. We all knew going into this that there was a possibility one or more of us wouldn't survive. We agreed, all of us, that mission success was top priority. But now I can't do it and that's why I broke Theo's trust and came to all of you for help." I sucked in a breath and told Garrett the only truth I could offer him. "I did it knowing your connection to Finn and how deeply you felt his death. I know it was a shitty thing to do, getting you involved in something that is so closely related to him, but I did it anyway. And you need to know as sorry as I am I'd do it again if it saves Theo's life."

"So you know," Garrett ground out.

"I know," I confirmed.

"Then I know," he rasped.

Fuck!

This was the worst-case scenario.

"What the fuck are you two talking about?" Kevin's inquiry slammed into me, and I closed my eyes.

This was it.

Garrett would tell Zane and Zane would take Garrett's back—as he should. Zane was as loyal to his team as I was to mine. He'd be pissed on Garrett's behalf and tell Kevin to cut me loose, meaning I'd made a huge mistake—costing Theo his life. My team would be disbanded, Ashcroft would be questioned, and if the President wasn't feeling altruistic the former IG would find himself in a cell somewhere deep in the Nicaraguan jungle. And I was now marked for death. I wouldn't find myself spending the rest of my life in blissful anonymity—I'd be six feet under.

Ten years down the toilet.

"Her team. I know who they are," Garrett said.

Yep.

I was right.

Garrett was too damn smart.

"Is this why Easton reached out to me a few years ago? Four years ago, to be exact?"

Easton reached out to Garrett? That was against the rules. My team was to have no contact with anyone in the U.S. besides me and Kira. They didn't even communicate with Ashcroft. I was the go-between.

What happened four years ago?

Damn.

We lost our main target, Leif Robinson.

"Maybe," I told him. "Though I didn't know he broke protocol and tried to connect with you. But the timing would make sense. I mean, if he was going to break rank it would've been then."

"I didn't take his call, was he in trouble? Is he still alive?"

There was a hint of alarm in Garrett's tone. I shouldn't have confirmed I knew Easton and I really shouldn't be engaging in any further conversation about him but I couldn't allow Garrett to think something had happened to his former teammate. Besides, he'd already figured out who was on my team, that much was clear.

"He's alive. Four years ago, we were ready to wrap up our operation when our target was killed. If I had to guess, I'd say he reached out to you because it had taken longer than we thought it would, and after Leif Robinson was killed, we had to start over—meaning he'd be in the field for even longer."

"Christ."

I heard a crash then a mumbled curse from Zane that would have me blushing if the situation wasn't so screwed up. It had to be noted the guy was seriously creative with four-letter words.

"Do not let her out of your sight," Zane ordered. "Chain her, cuff her, tie her up, or pin her ass to the ground. Whatever you have to do to contain her but she's no longer free to leave. And if the spooks show up, have some fun but she does not leave with them."

With that, Zane disconnected and Kevin pocketed his phone.

I couldn't remember when I'd opened my eyes and didn't remember the journey they'd taken to reach Kevin's, but I was staring at him. God, he was back to looking at me like I was the devil.

"I mean Garrett no harm," I told him.

"I believe that." My relief was short-lived when he continued, "But you fucked up. You should've told me there was more of a connection to Garrett. And if not me you should've warned Zane so Garrett wasn't blindsided."

He was right.

However, I was walking a tightrope. One I desperately

wanted to jump off. There would be no safety net below me. The fall would be freeing but the landing would leave me a mangled mess.

Does it even matter anymore?

"How bad is this going to fuck Garrett up?" Kevin's question reminded me how close these men were.

Brothers.

Just like Garrett had been with the guys on his old team before he bailed on them. The same men who were now on *my* team at Patheon.

"Do you know what Garrett did before he joined Z Corps?" I asked instead of answering.

"Teamguy, then he did a few years with...*fuck*." Kevin's eyes sharpened. His muscular arms came up and both hands tore through his hair before he crossed them over his chest. "He doesn't talk about it. *Ever*. He's never even mentioned anyone by name. I take it he worked with Easton. What about Theo? Did he work with him, too? Was there a falling out?"

No.

Garrett went off the rails, blamed himself for Finn's murder, and he bailed on his team and life in general.

I shook my head, not trusting myself to answer verbally without telling Kevin a story that I'd promised I wouldn't reveal.

"The rest of your guys, are they connected to Garrett?"

"Four of them. Theo's the only one who never had direct contact with Garrett."

"But Theo has a connection to Zane."

"Yes."

"And that's the real reason you came to us. You thought if Zane wasn't inclined to help, Garrett's connection to your team would seal the deal."

I could see how Kevin would come to that conclusion, though it made my chest ache that he thought I would be so callous. The opposite was true. I'd done everything I could to protect Garrett from his painful past.

"Actually, no. It was stupid of me, but I'd hoped that I could get through this without Garrett learning the identity of the other men. But I couldn't tell you about Patheon without revealing Kira Winters. I knew she'd be the link that Garrett would need to piece everything together."

Kevin dipped his chin, and I took that as him accepting my answer as the truth. Which strangely made me feel good —or maybe not so strange since I wanted Kevin to believe me.

"You didn't mention the threats that Theo received."

His statement felt like I'd been plunged into a bucket of ice water.

Things were going from worse to seriously FUBAR.

Nothing had gone right.

If I was lucky Ashcroft would be on the phone with Zane doing his best to convince Zane not to turn me over to the CIA. I had a contingency plan, but it would only work if Ashcroft agreed to scrap the mission and allow Kira to contact the rest of the team for an extraction. But we'd lose everything. Which in my opinion would be worth it to save Theo.

"Theo was protecting Zane." Kevin muttered the truth.

Tears of frustration filled my eyelids. I couldn't remember the last time I cried. My mother's funeral maybe? Before that, the day my dad left us. God, it had been so long I was a little surprised my tear ducts still worked.

"That's what you promised not to tell," he continued.

Unable to look at Kevin any longer I turned my back to him and dropped my head. I was so, *so* freaking tired.

Utterly exhausted. Ten years' worth of stress and worry settled into my bones causing fresh tears to roll down my cheeks.

I startled when Kevin's hands landed on my shoulders. The warmth of his palms did nothing to stave off the chill that had fallen over me.

When his thumbs dug into my shoulder blades, I couldn't contain the moan that slipped out. I was beyond concealing my emotions. I was totally and completely spent. If Kevin used my weakness to his advantage, so be it.

I had nothing else to lose.

Except Theo.

"Tell me something."

I hummed hoping he didn't expect more than that while his strong fingers kneaded the tension that had knotted in my shoulders and neck.

"Is there anyone you trust, or do you carry this mountain of burden yourself?"

There were a few people I trusted. Kira was one of them. I trusted Theo, Easton, Smith, Jonas, and Cash. Then there was Ashcroft; he was like the father I never had.

But that didn't mean I would unburden myself on one of them—especially one of the guys. They were kicking in doors, putting their lives on the line every day. Kira was fierce but still had a fragility to her. It was bad enough I'd recruited her; I wouldn't put more on her than was necessary. And Ashcroft was over seventy; the man had done his duty, he deserved as much peace and quiet as he could manage. So while I trusted them all with my life, I didn't trust them with my burden.

"I carry it alone."

"So strong," he muttered and worked his thumbs deeper.

"How can you say that when I'm standing here crying like a—"

"Like a woman who carries unimaginable stress. A woman who has managed to run a covert operation for ten years. Which is damn impressive. A woman who is worried about a teammate. You cannot keep everything to yourself. At some point, you have to debrief, unpack all the weight or you'll be buried under it."

How hard would it be to tell Kevin the truth? Start from the beginning and tell him who I was and how I became Layla Cunnings. Tell him how disappointed and angry I was when I found out that my dream job had been tainted by reality then by corruption. I had once been like Theo, bright-eyed and hopeful. I believed we were doing good work, until I learned what went on behind the curtain. How difficult would it be to show him the truth? Let him read the unredacted files. Five human intel assets collecting data for ten years—needless to say, there was a lot of damning evidence on a lot of high-profile people. And not just men and women who worked for the government. Wealthy civilians who pulled strings like puppet masters.

It would be overwhelmingly hard.

It would mean I'd have to admit I wasn't really Layla Cunnings. It would mean trusting someone with the real me. It would mean admitting to myself I wanted Kevin to understand how I became this person. The secret keeper, the liar, the failure. Everything had gone wrong, I had nothing left to lose and if that was the case, what was the harm in telling Kevin the truth? Unburdening my thoughts. Just once, what would it feel like to open up and share something about myself that no one knew?

"My name's Layla Brower. I'm from Bend, Oregon. I was in my junior year at UCLA when my mother died. I hadn't been home to visit her since I'd graduated high school. I left Bend and swore I'd never go back. I was pissed at her, and I missed saying goodbye because I'm stubborn and selfish."

Kevin's hands had clamped down on my shoulders after I'd told him my real name, and loosened until I admitted my biggest regret.

I'd allowed anger to overshadow the years I could've spent with my mom.

And since I'd started, I didn't stop the words from flowing.

"I joined the CIA because I was afraid of life. I was alone and adrift. I wanted a purpose. I thought I found that with the agency. And I did. I excelled at my job. I was a damn good intelligence officer. I was good in the field; I was useful when I was back at headquarters. I'd been to a dozen countries, worked hundreds of agents, I'd never questioned our mission in any of the places I worked. Until I worked under Leif Robinson while I was in Pakistan. He'd leave the compound without a Scorpion for protection. He'd be gone for hours. At first, I thought he was a maverick, an old-timer who didn't like to follow safety protocol. But when one of my assets showed up to a meeting wearing a gold watch I'd seen on Leif's desk a few days before I became suspicious."

My stomach churned as visions of Hamza's dead body invaded my mind. So young, and like me, hopeful. He wanted to help. He didn't believe in the radical ideology that was being forced on him and his family. All he wanted was to escape. Instead, he wound up dead.

"Layla?" Kevin gently called.

"I asked him where he got the watch. He apologized to me, thinking I was mad he'd accepted a gift from someone who wasn't me, 'another American' as Hamza put it. Then when he failed to show up to our next two meetings, I took a Scorpion and we went to search for him. Nineteen, the kid had so much life to live but it was beaten out of him. I had no proof that Leif had met with my asset, no reason to think that my chief of base would kill an agent, yet my gut told me he did. Something wasn't right. I finished up that assignment and was sent back to the U.S.

"I'd been working at headquarters for four months and was getting ready to spin up again when Theo got back from Spain. He was red-hot pissed, armed with cables proving Leif Robinson had signed off on the payouts to Yaser Said, and he was demanding a probe into how a terrorist was on the CIA's payroll. But it was a few weeks later, the day that Finn Winters was beheaded, that shit went nuclear. Reports came in that Said's cell had claimed responsibility and Theo nearly choked the life out of Leif in the conference room. The next day Leif showed Theo the..."

My heart was pounding so hard it felt like the organ was going to explode out of my chest. I thought back to something Kevin had said, *but you'll be able to visit his grave and know you kept your promise.*

I'd never broken a promise until this morning.

I'd lied, I'd skirted the truth, I'd misled, but I'd never made a promise I hadn't kept.

But Kevin's words held merit. Which was worse? Breaking my promise or saving Theo's life? And if he didn't forgive me, at least he'd be alive to hold a grudge.

I could not and would not visit Theo's grave.

10

LAYLA WAS SHAKING SO BADLY it was a miracle she was able to keep her feet. And her shoulders were so tense I didn't know how she didn't have a throbbing migraine. Hell, maybe she did. It wouldn't surprise me to learn she walked around all day every day with her head throbbing and her muscles spasming from all the stress she was under.

I wanted to scoop her up, carry her to the couch, and hold her until the worry ebbed from her body.

Wait, where did that come from?

"What did Leif have on Zane?" I asked when she remained silent.

"Did you know that from time to time Zane was pulled from his platoon to work with the CIA when we needed to get someone into an area that was considered impossible to infil?"

There was no such thing as impossible to infiltrate.

"Yes, I know about what Zane did with the CIA and with SAC."

"Zane left Egypt; that was where he and Theo were working together. A week later Finn was captured. It was

Zane's intel that led to the agency deploying a team to take out an HVT. The intel was bad; it was an ambush. Zane caught wind of the situation and asked to go back to Egypt to talk to his asset there, the agency let him. He got his guy to talk and give up Finn's location, Zane reported it back to Washington, and the GB team—Garrett's GB team went in for a rescue. The location was wrong, and that night Finn was murdered. Zane's cables were intact, but he never named his source—which isn't abnormal—but out of context it looked like at the very least Zane was giving bad intel. Leif threatened to take the reports to the seventh floor and demand Zane be brought in for questioning. Normally this wouldn't have been an issue; Zane would've named his source and he would've been cleared. But his source, Abrax Salah, was dead. And Leif had made insinuations that Zane had killed him to cover up Zane turning into a double."

Holy fucking hell.

I wasn't sure who was shaking worse, me or Layla.

I was vibrating with anger, and she was trembling with anxiety.

"And Garrett left his GB team after Finn died?"

"Yes."

Her answer was either whispered softly or the roaring in my ears was making it difficult to hear. Whichever way her answer was delivered it felt like a blow.

Layla's body sagged forward. I quickly wrapped an arm around her waist and pulled her back against my chest.

"Baby, let's sit," I suggested.

Her body bucked and a deep groan that sounded like it emanated from her soul tore from her throat.

"I tried so fucking hard," she gasped. "We were so close. Fuck Harrison Washington. Fuck him and all his dirty—"

"Unit Chief Harrison Washington?" I interrupted.

"Yes. Him and his network of lying, thieving shitbags."

Oh, fuck.

"Layla baby, Harrison is the one who called Zane about you being on the most wanted list."

Layla baby?

Had I lost my mind?

"Of course he did. He's the one who found out that Theo is still alive. We tracked his payment to a group of wannabe terrorists in Armenia. We were so close, and with this added piece of evidence, Harrison was fucked. Theo didn't want an extraction, he thought he'd be safe. We were wrong. So f*ucking* wrong."

She knew Harrison Washington was on to her, that was why she wasn't surprised she was on the Matrix list. She wasn't surprised and she wasn't concerned.

Did she possess one ounce of self-preservation? She'd called herself selfish when talking about not seeing her mother before she passed, but I couldn't see it. Sure, maybe she'd made a mistake and regretted her choice now, but I would be shocked if the decision was made out of self-centeredness.

"What about Eddy? Is he a target?"

"Eddy's a pissant with grabby hands and an inability to comprehend the word no. But I can't see Harrison trusting him, he's too stupid and too full of ego, to be in Harrison's inner circle. Eddy was following agency orders hoping to be the one to shoot me in the head and drag my lifeless body back to HQ so he could get his atta boy and brag later about how he took the kill shot. I wouldn't put it past him to write a tell-all book about how he singlehandedly took down the CIA's most wanted criminal."

Layla was rambling. I was impressed she'd pulled herself together enough to use humor to explain who Eddy was. However, I was stuck on one piece of information that needed clarifying.

"Grabby hands?"

Layla went from melting into me, trying to eliminate any space between her back and my chest, to stiff as a board and on alert.

"He's just an asshole."

"An asshole with grabby hands?"

"Yes."

"And these grabby hands, did they touch you?"

Alert turned into high alert. When she tried to pull herself free I kept her pinned to my chest.

"You've got no reason to be afraid of me and no reason to be ashamed if that fucker touched you." I lowered my head until my mouth was level with her ear and as gently as I could manage, which was to say, not gentle in the slightest, I rumbled, "But mark this, Layla, if that fucker put his unwanted hands on you, he'll soon find himself without hands."

"Theo took care of it," she whispered.

Ah. The real reason Theo hated Eddy.

"Are you sure you don't want to amend your answer about Theo being just a friend?"

That was the wrong thing to ask. Layla was out of my arms and two steps away when she whirled around. With a face full of thunder she bellowed, "You know what? Yes, I'd like to amend. Theo is more than just a friend. He's my teammate. He's Patheon. He's mine. He's one of my men and right now he's being fucking tortured and I'm standing around having a goddamn pity party because I'm tired and stressed and so damn sick of people disappointing me I could scream."

I wisely didn't point out she already was screaming. Instead, I homed in on something she hadn't said until now.

"People disappoint you?"

"They don't disappoint you?" she returned.

"No."

"Then you're lucky. I have seven people I can count on. *Seven*. That's it."

"A cynic."

"A realist," she corrected. "One of my former colleagues tried to kill me today. Another one gave him the order. If that's not disappointing then I don't know what is."

She had a point. But my chest still burned with rejection. I didn't have to ask to know I wasn't included in the seven people she trusted. Not that I could blame her; she'd known me all of a handful of hours and for someone like Layla I suspected it would take years—and lots of them—before she would begin to trust.

Yet she told me her real name and where she was from.

That was something, right?

A baby step.

I didn't necessarily need Layla to trust me to rescue Theo. Which I was going to do with or without Zane authorizing the rest of the team to go.

I wouldn't be one more person who let Layla down. And I knew Zane—once he knew the truth and understood the depth of Theo's loyalty to him, we'd be wheels up in a few hours.

"Maybe try a new job. One where the requirement isn't scoring a hundred on deception 101."

There was a ghost of a smile but before Layla could commit to the emotion my phone rang.

I made no move to pick up the call, not wanting Zane or

Garrett to intrude...on what? Our moment? We weren't having a moment, not since she'd pulled away. But there had been one, hadn't there? I wondered if Layla realized she'd been the one to press herself against my chest even if I was the one to pin her there. *She'd* been the one to wiggle closer.

"Are you going to get that?"

No.

Yes.

Maybe.

I took a step, then another one. The distance between us was such that she had to tilt her head back to look into my eyes. "Tell me something."

"What do you want to know?"

Why did her voice sound like my proximity stole her ability to breathe? If that was the case it would only be fair seeing as she stole my good sense. I shouldn't be thinking about anything beyond her troubles.

But there was something about her, an unknown emotion that took over, a feeling, a reaction, a whisper, a connection I couldn't ignore. A tightening in my stomach that had always been reserved for the battlefield. That sixth sense warned of impending danger.

"If Zane had turned you down, would you have gone to Armenia alone?"

"Yes."

No regard for personal safety.

But I understood.

Her loyalty and bravery overshadowed common sense.

A combination with deadly consequences.

My phone stopped ringing only to start again.

"As soon as you answer that I guess we'll know if this is a solo—"

"You're not going anywhere alone. No matter what, I'm going with you."

I pulled my phone free, tapped in my code, and swiped the screen to connect the call.

"Kevin—"

"Yeah?" I greeted.

"Wheels up at oh-six-hundred," Garrett started. "I'll check her intel on the plane."

"You're rolling out with us?"

It was rare Garrett left the office. He preferred to be behind his many computers. It wasn't due to a lack of tactical knowledge or skill. He never voiced his reasons, and I respected the man enough not to push him to talk about why he preferred staring at a screen over kicking in a door. Now I was thinking I should've pushed.

"Unfinished business."

"Your team—"

"*You* and the rest of the guys are *my team*."

Fuck yeah, I should've pushed.

Actually, if his hoarse tone was anything to go by, we all should've pushed Garrett to open up a long time ago. Ten years was too long to keep pain buried.

"Copy that, brother. I hope you know we got your back. Whatever it is you need."

"I just…" Garrett stopped and blew out a long breath. "Did she tell you?"

That felt like a loaded question.

"She filled in some blanks. But there's a lot you and Z need to know."

My gaze lifted to Layla. As soon as our eyes met, she quickly looked away.

Was she hiding or did she feel guilty?

"You need to talk to Layla," I told him.

No sooner had the words come out of my mouth when her shoulders hunched forward and her eyes closed.

A few hours ago that move would've been construed as a play—a way to gain my sympathy. But now, I saw it for what it was—her blocking out the pain. She tended to close her eyes when she didn't want to face something.

"Tomorrow."

"Brother—"

"I can't." Those two words sounded like that'd been wrestled from his lungs. "Not yet. I need to...there's...just give me until tomorrow. We'll talk on the plane."

He disconnected without giving me a chance to argue.

"Why'd you allow Garrett to think he fucked up Finn's rescue?"

Slowly, so fucking slowly. Infuriatingly slowly, Layla opened her eyes.

"Look at me, Layla, and tell me why the hell Garrett thinks Finn's dead because of him."

She didn't look at me.

As a matter of fact, she turned her back on me and walked to the wall of windows.

"Layla!"

"You have to understand," she began. "When we started, we thought we were only looking at Leif and maybe a member of the support staff at HQ. But once we started digging, we realized it went deeper and we broadened our scope. Then we started to doubt that Leif was the tip of the spear, evidence was suggesting that Leif was taking orders from someone, but we couldn't make a connection. But we still thought it would take a year, two, tops. Easton and Cash wanted to talk to Garrett and explain before they went dark, but Garrett had already left SAC. And let's just say when Garrett doesn't want to be found, no one's finding him. Not me, not Kira, not even our best tracker Smith could get a lead. Garrett went underground and my guys needed to get started so they agreed to wait and find Garrett when they got back. As you know, a year or two turned into a lot longer."

Motherfucker.

For ten years Garrett thought he'd fucked up and gotten a teammate killed.

Ten goddamn years.

"Nine months after my guys left, Garrett's back on the radar," she softly continued. "And what does he do? Goes to work for Zane Lewis. The man who'd been given the wrong intel. I thought Leif had gotten to Garrett and lied to him, shown him the intel that he'd threatened Theo with. So, I had Kira monitor the situation. It became clear that Zane and Garrett were close, so I did what I promised my guys and I didn't approach."

"You seem to make a lot of fucked-up promises," I noted.

"It wasn't supposed to take this long," she attempted to defend herself. "And when time started to pass what was I supposed to do, go to Garrett and tell him that he didn't fuck the location, that his good friend and boss did? Was I supposed to rip everything away from him for a second time? I had no evidence proving Zane had been played. We'd deleted everything we could find, but we didn't know if Leif had other copies. If Garrett would've looked into what happened he would've found exactly what Leif wanted him to find and with Easton, Cash, Smith, and Jonas out of the country undercover, there would be no way for me to stop the fallout. I couldn't take the chance that Garrett would believe that lying piece-of-shit Leif. So I let it lie. I kept my promise and kept my mouth shut."

Anger rolled through me until I was dizzy with it. I so badly wanted to lash out at Layla and blame her for something that wasn't her fault. The injustice of the situation made saliva pool in my mouth. I knew Garrett, there was no way he'd taken a year to lick his wounds then resurfaced a new man free of guilt. He'd feel Finn's death every day. It'd be an ache he couldn't get rid of.

An uneasy feeling knotted in my stomach. There was a missing piece.

"What else aren't you telling me?"

"Nothing. A lot. You have to be more specific."

"There's more to the story," I prompted.

"There's always more, but again, what are you asking?"

Fuck. I didn't know what I was asking.

I didn't know what fucked-up mess to start with. Leif using Zane to threaten Theo. Some of the guys from Garrett's old GB team being the operatives Layla was in charge of. Layla *being* in charge of a team of former Special Forces guys. How a mission to flush out a traitor had turned into a ten-year operation, even after that traitor had been eliminated.

There was too much to process. Mental fatigue and the need for answers warred in my head.

I checked my watch and decided to wait. If we bedded down now, we'd have three hours of rack time before we had to be on the road to make it to the airport. Some sleep and time away from Layla would do me a world of good.

"How about we hit pause on this conversation and hit the sack? We leave for Armenia at oh-six-hundred."

With that, she spun around.

Her relief was palpable. A living, breathing entity that filled the space between us. And it was then I realized how much she'd been holding back.

No, she'd been holding *on*. And by the look of her, just barely. I'd seen her desperation. I knew she'd only divulged her information because Theo was running out of time. But I had no idea just how hopeless she'd felt until right then when she dropped the layers of pretense she'd hidden under. The tough intelligence officer façade was gone. The secretive team leader of a shadow organization had vanished. The woman I'd met in the White House briefing room was nowhere in sight.

The Layla who stood in front of me was going to be a problem.

A beautiful problem that I was fairly certain would break me.

I hated liars but I was a sucker for a complicated woman.

I'd known her a handful of hours and I already knew she was the most complicated woman I'd ever met. She'd captured my attention from the moment I'd clapped eyes on her and since then she'd pissed me off, frustrated me, lied to me, made herself vulnerable, opened up, smiled, cracked a few jokes. She was competent, strong, and smart. If that wasn't complicated, I didn't know what was. But the bottom line was Layla made me feel to the extreme.

So, yeah, she was going to be a problem.

"Thank you."

As much as I wanted her gratitude, I didn't deserve it.

"Don't thank me. It was Garrett."

And cue the guilt.

"I'll make it right," she whispered. "With him, I mean. I'll explain everything when I see him."

I wasn't sure she could ever make it right. Which made my chest ache. The situation being what it was, Layla's direct involvement with Garrett's pain made her off-limits.

Garrett was more than a teammate, he was a close friend, a brother. Rendering the connection I felt with Layla void.

Isn't that a bitch?

I resisted lifting my hand to rub the spot over my heart that now burned.

"You take the bedroom. You'll be safe in there. The windows don't open and they're blast-proof. I'll take the couch."

"Kevin..." she started but trailed off.

"What?"

"Nothing. Never mind."

I should've let it go. We needed to get some sleep. Tomorrow was going to be another long day filled with mystery and CIA intrigue. I needed a clear head to deal with that kind of bullshit.

Yet for some reason going another round with Layla was a compulsion I couldn't control.

"Don't do that. You had something to say, say it."

Was that insecurity I saw flash in her eyes before she covered it up?

"I was going to say I'm sorry."

Well, that wasn't what I thought she was going to say.

"Sorry for what?"

"For everything. For not telling you the whole story. For not telling Zane the truth before I dragged you all into this mess. But mostly I'm sorry I made promises I shouldn't have made. I could've denied my team's request not to approach Garrett without them. I could've saved him from feeling responsible for Finn's execution. I'll never forgive myself for that. I told you I'd make it right, but I know that's a lie. I can try but there's nothing I can say or do that will erase what I've done to Garrett. That's my cross to bear, the guilt I'll carry for hurting a good man. I know Garrett will never forgive me, not that I'd ask him...or you, or Zane for that matter. I just hope it's enough for you all, knowing I'll spend the rest of my life regretting my decisions."

With that, she strode to the bedroom. It took control —*extreme* control—to lock my legs and not follow her.

I didn't want her to feel guilty. I didn't want her to bear a cross of remorse and shame when the promises she'd made were born out of loyalty.

But it wasn't my call. It wasn't me she'd fucked over; it was Garrett who would need to absolve her of her sins.

And wasn't that a goddamn bitch?

11

KEVIN WAS DRIVING—AGAIN.

I hadn't even put up a weak fight when he opened the passenger side door for me to get in. I simply obeyed the silent order like a good girl.

More like a whipped puppy.

I was blaming my current lack of fight on sleep deprivation. It had been a solid twenty-four hours since I'd slept, and it was doubtful I'd be getting rest for the foreseeable future. Especially since I'd be on a plane with Garrett, Zane, Kevin, and whoever else would be accompanying us to Armenia. I was ninety percent positive Zane wouldn't murder me inflight for keeping him and Garrett in the dark for ten years. Though there was a hundred percent possibility I'd die a slow painful death when I came face-to-face with Garrett. Sure, it might take thirty or forty years but I'd die a little more each day knowing I'd concealed the truth that would've set Garrett free.

I deserved nothing less.

Every ounce of regret I felt now would increase tenfold

when my team learned I'd betrayed them, too. Which reminded me.

"I need to check in with Kira."

"Lincoln Parker is on his way to West Virginia to pick up her and Bronson."

I wasn't surprised Garrett found my safe house, and since I didn't make it a habit of asking questions I knew the answers to, I skipped over asking how Zane's brother knew where to go and focused on Bronson.

"He's not gonna—"

"Kill him?" Kevin supplied.

My head whipped to the left and I was relieved to see Kevin smiling.

He was teasing me.

"And you didn't ask how Garrett found your safe house," he noted.

"I have a rule."

Don't ask questions I know the answers to.

"Just one rule? Singular? Not a list of them?"

Kevin turned to look at me and when he did his full-fledged smile felt like warmth and sunshine after being trapped in the darkness for so long. Last night I'd done my best to ignore how good it felt to have Kevin's arms wrapped around me. But it didn't stop me from lying awake thinking about how perfectly I fit when tucked against him. How for the first time I felt protected. I'd even tricked myself into believing I wasn't all alone.

All too soon the harsh reality came crashing back in when Kevin asked me about Theo. His question served as a necessary reminder that he didn't trust me, and I needed to keep my distance.

"Oh, I have a whole book of them," I finally answered. "I keep it tucked under my mattress near my diary."

Kevin's eyes went back to the road, but he was still smiling when he quipped, "I think I'd pay good money to read that."

"The diary? Spoiler alert, it's boring."

"Somehow I doubt that. But, no, I prefer to puzzle out my women. The game's more fun that way. Though your rule book would be an interesting read."

I opened my mouth then quickly clamped it closed. What the hell was going on? Did he say *his* women? Was he still teasing? Was this banter or were we flirting?

Holy crap, my life was so sad that I could no longer tell the difference between a man flirting with me or only joking.

"Is that another rule?" Kevin asked.

"Is what another rule?"

"No fun?"

"Rule number seven, no fun in the middle of an op," I deadpanned. Then for some reason, I tacked on, "For the record, I think I'm offended on behalf of the sisterhood that you view women as puzzles that need to be solved."

"Like a lot offended or just a little offended?"

I ignored his jab and his chuckle.

"And besides, sometimes there's no solution."

Now why did I say that?

"In my experience, there's always a solution. It's all about how much time you're willing to invest to find it. It's also my experience that the more difficult the problem is to solve, the bigger the payout."

"Is that what I am, a problem?"

I was, of course. If I was around and there were issues to be had, there was a good chance my presence was the cause.

"Yep."

"So you're trying to solve—"

"Nope, I'm not *trying* to do anything."

Damn. That hurt. Just like when he'd called me a liar, I felt his quick denial straight in my chest.

I tore my eyes from his profile and fixed my gaze out the side window.

"Were you as easy to read when you were a CIA agent?"

"Officer," I automatically answered.

Kevin's chuckle filled the small space and I forced myself not to look at him.

No more staring. No more jonesing for a smile. No more thinking about Kevin, period.

"You didn't answer my question."

Oh, right.

"I'm not easy to read."

"Babe, you're an open book."

Babe? "No, I'm not."

"Okay." Kevin drew out the two syllables.

"Fine. If I'm so easy to read, then what I am thinking?"

I just couldn't help myself, could I? What I should've done was feign sleep until we made it to the airport, delaying further conversation.

"For starters, you wish you hadn't asked me what you're thinking. And you looked away from me because I hurt your feelings. You didn't ask why I wasn't trying to solve the very complicated puzzle that is you. Instead, you turned away because you thought I didn't want to invest the time it would take to find the solution. It never occurred to you that I wasn't trying because I'd already solved it. Which tells me *you* don't think you're worth the time and effort. And you close your eyes when you don't want to face me or answer a question."

Kevin barely took a breath before he continued. But I

was gasping for air or maybe I was trying to hyperventilate so I'd pass out and not have to listen to how easily he had indeed read me.

"And in case you're wondering, the pieces started to fit when I called you a liar and I saw how badly that hurt your feelings. Just to make sure I wasn't seeing what I wanted to see I called you that two more times. And I wasn't wrong; all three times you flinched then closed down. Which at first I found odd since that's part of your craft. But it dawned on me, you don't want *me* to think you're a liar. You want me to understand the difference between you protecting your mission and operation security and you lying. So, I'll confirm, I understand the difference.

"Which brings us to last night—"

"Please stop talking."

"Actually, we need to talk about last night."

No, we didn't.

We didn't need to talk about anything.

"Why'd you tell me your real name?" Kevin quietly asked.

A rush of panic came over me so quickly I actually felt queasy.

"Hey." Kevin's hand landed on my thigh and gave it a shake. "Layla, hey, look at me."

Was he looking at me? He should've been paying attention to the road.

"I need..."

Shit, what did I need? A moment? A few minutes? A year? To get my head examined, that was what I needed to do. I'd officially lost my marbles. It was a damn good thing that I'd already planned on telling Ashcroft I was done after we got Theo back. Kevin being able to assess and dissect my thoughts so easily was proof I'd lost my edge. I couldn't do this anymore. I was useless to my team if I couldn't keep my shit together.

"You can have whatever you need after you explain to me why you're pale."

Great. Not only was I a basket case, I was pale to boot.

"I've never told anyone. After I assumed Layla Cunnings, I mean. My team doesn't even know my real name. I guess I just wanted you to know the truth."

Kevin allowed the silence to stretch for so long I thought I was off the hook.

"Thank you."

I closed my eyes. Not because I couldn't face him, like he'd accused.

I couldn't face the world I'd created where a man like Kevin would thank me for telling him my real name.

———

I FELT lips travel from my jaw up to my ear.

Not soft but firm as they skimmed the sensitive skin.

Not slow or fast but just right.

"Are you ready?"

I tipped my head and looked into Kevin's eyes. The brandy color had deepened, pupils dilated.

There was nothing gentle about Kevin. Not the way his large hand cradled my cheek. Not the way he looked at me. Not the way he held me.

Every touch, movement, and look was done with purpose. Controlled and commanding.

But there was kindness and understanding.

"Ready for what?"

"To give me everything."

"Yes."

Suddenly Kevin's face was gone, and I was alone in the darkness.

So dark.

I shivered.

So cold.

I shook.

"Layla."

Kevin was back. His voice was far away. I needed to find him. I didn't want to be alone in the cold darkness.

Fear ticked up my spine. He was close but I couldn't see him. I couldn't reach him.

I needed to get to Kevin.

"Layla! Wake up!"

I jolted and my eyes opened.

It was still dark outside the car but I could see airplane hangars off in the distance.

Airport. Armenia. Theo.

I'd fallen asleep.

"I'm awake."

"Didn't want to wake you up but I couldn't have you moaning and twisting in your seat when we meet my team."

Moaning and twisting in my seat?

What the hell?

"What are you talking about?"

"Babe." He chuckled. "Either that was one hell of a good dream, or you were being murdered."

I felt my cheeks heat as bits of my dream filtered through my mind. Kevin kissing my neck. His big body on top of me. But he had clothes on, didn't he? Surely if I dreamed of Kevin naked those mental images would be seared into my memory for all time.

"I was being murdered," I lied.

"Sure you were."

Kevin stopped at a chain-link gate, unrolled the window, and punched in the code. A few seconds later it slid open. My gaze landed on three black Navigators parked in the lot and my anxiety skyrocketed.

"Who's coming with us?"

"Zane, Garrett, Cooper, Owen, and Gabe. Myles is staying back to deal with Bronson."

"Deal with Bronson how?"

Which reminded me I'd fallen asleep before I'd called Kira. I needed to do that and warn her Lincoln Parker was on his way. The last thing we needed was Kira shooting Zane's brother.

I reached for my bag but halted when I caught sight of Garrett and Zane standing next to one of the SUVs. Each man was deadly in his own right but together they made an imposing pair. Both were tall, though Zane was taller than Garrett by a few inches. Both had their feet planted wide, arms crossed over their chests, identical frowns. They looked like the tactical version of the Brawny paper towel guy with the plaid button-down shirts. Zane's was blue, the top few buttons undone. Garrett's shirt was red and his was completely unbuttoned, exposing the black tee under it. Both had on black cargo pants and boots.

Tactical lumberjacks.

My gaze went to Kevin. Navy-blue long-sleeved cotton shirt. Black cargos, and I couldn't see them, but I knew he had on black combat boots.

"You're out of uniform," I teased.

Kevin smiled as he pulled into a parking spot.

"I was thinking the same thing. I'm sure the guys already gave them shit for being twinsies."

There was something funny about hearing big, bad, tough Kevin say "twinsies". So much so I couldn't stop myself from laughing despite the seriousness of my current situation.

Garrett.

Theo.

I sucked in a breath and my laughter died.

"Everything's gonna be okay."

"Sure, for you," I muttered.

"Just be..." Kevin paused, likely searching for the right word.

"Honest," I supplied.

"I was going to say, just be yourself."

Myself?

At this juncture, I wasn't sure who *myself* was.

"Right, because I'm so charming and likable. Zane looks like he's ready to rip my head off and I'll be lucky if I make it onto the plane without Garrett shooting me."

"They would never hurt you." The vehemence in Kevin's tone took me by surprise.

"I didn't mean literally. But this isn't going to go well for me, and it shouldn't. I deserve every blow Garrett's going to deliver. His anger is justified. So is Zane's, and yours for that matter. I didn't mean for everything to spiral out of control, but I won't make excuses. This is my fault and I take full responsibility."

Kevin's mood shifted. The best way to describe the switch was that he'd gone into operator mode. I was familiar with the change. When I was in the CIA, anytime I left the compound, I'd been escorted by Scorpions—SEALs that were on special assignment. It always amazed me how quickly they went from smiling and having a good time with one another to being fully operational. The same with the Ground Branch guys I'd briefed. They jackassed around right up until the gate opened and they went outside the wire.

I lacked that ability. When I was in the field I was "on" twenty-four-seven. I couldn't switch on and off like they did. I knew the guys I worked with thought I was uptight and bitchy. I'd never allowed myself any downtime. From dawn to the middle of the night I was on the go working. There was always new intel to go over, cables that came in or needed to be sent, assets to work.

Can you say burnout?

"Are you ready?"

Didn't he ask me that in my dream?

"Yes."

And wasn't that the same answer I gave him when my dream Kevin stared into my eyes?

Unfortunately, right then his brown eyes weren't full of tenderness and lust.

They were full of concern.

Nothing was going to be okay.

Garrett would never forgive me, which meant Kevin wouldn't either. He'd take his friend's back—as he should—and when this was over, I'd walk away.

Alone.

That was if I was lucky and survived.

12

AN UNEXPECTED CLENCH of affection followed by a strong urge to pull Layla into my arms came over me.

With every foot the Gulfstream G280 Zane had chartered climbed, the tension in Layla's body mounted.

No one had spoken to her when we'd entered the hangar. A tactic I was sure she was familiar with, one that was meant to keep her unsteady. But it wasn't the silence that seemed to bother her, it was Garrett. And when he'd sat in the club chair facing us, Zane taking the seat next to Garrett, I didn't miss the way she'd clasped her hands in her lap. Nor did her stiff posture go unnoticed. She was braced, waiting for Garrett to unleash.

I wanted to reach over and grab her hand and tell her I'd protect her. I wanted to tell Garrett and Zane to stand the fuck down and give her a break.

The plane leveled out right before the captain came over the coms informing us we were at altitude and could move about the cabin.

"Tell me about Easton, Smith, Jonas, and Cash," Garrett demanded.

"What would you like to know?"

Her voice was soft and noncombative. So very different than the woman who went head-to-head with Zane yesterday. When my gaze went to Zane, I was not surprised to see him studying her closely.

"Where are they?"

There were a few moments of silence and the longer it stretched, Zane's careful study of Layla turned into heavy scrutiny. I turned my head to look at her. The color in her face had drained, her lips were pinched tight, and her indecision was clear.

For some reason, I felt like everything hinged on her making the right decision. I needed her to open up and be honest. Not for Garrett. Not for the sake of the mission.

For me.

I needed her to prove I was right about her. She wasn't the hardass, remorseless intelligence officer she portrayed herself to be.

"Cash is in Argentina. Smith is in Brazil. Jonas is in Somalia. Easton is in Ireland."

"What?" Garrett rasped. "Why the hell haven't they been pulled from their assignments?"

"Mission success—"

"Is a priority," Garrett growled. "You already explained that. But if Theo was captured, did it cross your mind that the others are compromised, too?"

"There's no indication that Harrison Washington knows about Easton, Cash, Smith, and Jonas."

Garrett's knee started to bounce, something he did when he was close to hacking someplace where he shouldn't be. 'The thrill of adrenaline' as he put it. Though in this case, I figured it was worry for his former teammates.

"You're willing to risk their lives—"

Layla abruptly leaned forward, her seat belt only allowing her upper body to pitch forward.

"We're here, aren't we?" she snapped and lifted her hand using it to indicate the cabin of the plane. "So, obviously I'm not willing to risk anyone's life. But they are. They're willing to risk everything to nail Harrison, and before him, Leif. But *you* know that already because *you* know *your* brothers. They never stopped fighting and they won't until the truth comes out."

Garrett jerked back like Layla had slapped him. Her raised voice garnered the rest of the team's attention. Owen, Gabe, and Cooper made their way aft and stood behind Zane and Garrett.

Layla didn't spare them a glance; her gaze was firmly locked on Garrett.

"But *I* did? Is that what you're saying? I quit and gave up the fight?"

"I didn't say that, Garrett." Layla softened her tone. "I know—"

"You don't know shit. That's the goddamn problem. They should've left it alone."

"Time to get naked." Zane clapped his hands together and smiled.

Layla leaned back in her seat. Her gaze shifted through the men, finally landing on me.

Yeah, it was time to get naked; unfortunately, it wouldn't be the fun kind that would lead to multiple orgasms. It was the bare your soul kind of naked.

And it would seem Zane was going to start.

"After Finn was captured, I went back to Egypt. I had assets there that were reliable. Some I'd turned at the request of the CIA, some were loyal to just me. I met with Abrax

Salah; he was eager to tell me all about the captured American. He had details, he had a location, he had too fucking much. I paid him for his time and happily slunk away. After I was fed that bullshit I sought out a woman who had no ties to the CIA but her brother was a soldier for a local arms dealer. She told me there were rumors Yaser Said was in Egypt and she was worried her brother was going to seek him out. He wanted to join Said's group. I followed him that night and sure as shit, he met with Said. Abraham was invited to join Said and to prove his loyalty to the cause it would be Abraham who killed the American. I called my contact—*Leif Robinson* gave him the correct location. Wrote my report which unfortunately was thorough and included Salah's false intel along with a note that Abrax Salah was no longer an asset and should be considered a double agent."

What in the actual fuck?

Layla swayed and her mouth dropped open. When she regained her composure she asked, "So, did you know that Leif threatened Theo with that report?"

"Come again?"

"Leif showed Theo your report. But there was nothing in there about the woman or her brother. Nor did it have your thoughts on Salah. Leif's spin was that you purposely gave false intel on Finn's location. He threatened to have you brought to Langley for questioning. And with Salah dead, Leif was quick to pin his death on you and threatened to present you as the double. The charges might not have stuck but your reputation would've taken a hit and your clearance would've been pulled. That's why Theo went undercover. That's why he faked his death. To prove Leif was dirty and protect you."

Zane sat frozen. Except his icy blue eyes sparked fire.

"I knew it was a bad idea to let Zane off his chain," Gabe mumbled. "DEFCON 1, here we come."

"Who else?" Zane's voice was deceptively cool.

"Who else what?"

"Besides Leif Robinson and Harrison Washington? Who else is involved?"

"Too many people for me to rattle off but my reports are thorough and intact for Garrett to go over." Which meant she was going to give Garrett unredacted versions of what she'd shown me. "Though Gold Team did screw us over when they took out Prince Mohammad Al Issa. We'd been tracking him for two years. He was stealing and selling ancient artifacts. We were after one of his buyers and lost him when you took out Al Issa."

My team wasn't involved in that takedown, but I was well acquainted with the case that had been the starting point of Gold Team dismantling Omni. A group of the wealthiest individuals on the planet who controlled everything from the price of oil to financial markets around the world. It was a good day when they crumbled.

"That wasn't the first time we screwed you over," Garrett mumbled.

"What's that mean?"

Layla's question drew my attention back to her. She looked no less on edge than she had when she first boarded the plane but now that the exchange of information had started she seemed to get some of her bravado back if her snapping at Zane was anything to go by.

"Do I look like the kind of man who likes to get fucked?" Zane barked.

"Well..." Owen started but didn't finish.

"According to your wife..." Gabe piped up and shrugged.

Layla's scowl deepened, not appreciating my team's humor.

"So you figured out Leif fucked you?" Layla surmised.

"Oh, yeah, he straight-up fucked me and when he did, he forgot the lube. That shit stung, Layla. So much so I wasn't going to let it go. It might've been Yaser Said working the blade at Finn's throat, but it was Leif Robinson who killed him. I gave the exact location Finn was being held. There was drone footage confirming my intel, a GB unit in the area ready to roll out. And that motherfucker altered my cable back to HQ. Then someone at the CIA deleted all of the digital files. It took me six years and a shit load of markers to get hard copies of my original report and the proof I needed to take that asshole down. Six long years of me knowing that asshole was breathing while Finn was in the ground."

Layla looked like she was going to be sick.

Garrett's jaw was clenched, clearly pissed but not in shock.

"You knew?" I asked him.

"I knew. Zane found me in Wyoming and told me what happened. I took the year, cleared my head, and when I was ready Zane hired me." Garrett paused before he turned to Layla and asked, "Did Kira scrub the files at the CIA?"

She mutely nodded her answer.

"Yes, but the cables she deleted were the ones that Leif had obviously altered. Though at the time we didn't know Leif changed them; Theo was adamant that Zane would never turn. Kira also scrubbed all of Leif's reports, the ones that accused Zane of killing Salah to cover up his connection to Said." Layla stopped, looked over at Zane, and swallowed. "Your original report wasn't there. We never would've deleted that. Theo wanted to protect you, not hurt you. He never believed you withheld Finn's real location, neither did Ashcroft. Theo swore there was an explanation for the screw-up and he didn't believe that you were the one who screwed up. We never...I didn't...damn."

Layla's hands trembled as she unbuckled her seat belt. Her legs wobbled when she abruptly stood.

"I need a minute," she whispered.

It was painful watching her stumble her way past Zane and Garrett only to have to face a wall of unfriendly men. I kept my eyes on her as she pushed through my teammates and made her way down the aisle to the lavatory. And for the first time since I'd met her, her steps were clumsy, unsure, gawky. A far cry from the competent woman I'd spent the last twenty-four hours with.

My first instinct was to go to her. Comfort her. Reassure her.

Indecision clawed at my insides.

I needed to get to Layla, but I needed answers. I couldn't help her if I didn't have the full picture.

"All the secrets, all the bullshit, and the lying and hiding for no fucking reason," I mumbled.

"Now do you trust her?"

"Yes."

No hesitation. Her reaction was honest and raw. There was no faking her guilt and fear.

"Do I smell love blossoming?" Owen mumbled.

"I think that's your pits," Gabe returned. "Did you forget your deodorant, again?"

Owen dipped his head and made a show out of sniffing his armpits and I was grateful Layla wasn't present for his show of stupidity. "Nope. Old Spice fresh."

I ignored the idiots and asked Zane, "What else don't we know?"

"About Leif Robinson, nothing. I tracked down the intel I needed and now he's in hell."

"But you didn't need the intel, you knew what really happened."

"I knew. Leif knew. But I wanted Leif to read my report —word for word to Garrett before he bit it. Demons have a way of sneaking up on a man when he least expects them. It took me six years but now I know my brother knows—no doubt, no questions, no second-guessing he didn't fuck up the rescue mission. I didn't give bad intel. Leif's lies killed Finn and the last thing he did was admit it."

One could say Zane's sense of justice had no gray, unlike the world he lived in. Retribution and punishment were black and white. Guilty was guilty.

Which begged the question of how he viewed Layla.

"Theo did what he did to protect you," I reminded Zane.

"I'm not a man who needs protection."

Fuck.

"I know that, but Theo thought he was doing you a solid and Layla thought she was, too."

"By not coming to me? Fuck, Kevin, she thought Garrett was holding on to some fucked up notion he got Finn killed by botching a mission and she let him feel that."

"He's right."

Goddamn, how did I not see Layla approach?

"There's no excuse." The wobble in her voice felt like a knife to my gut.

Loyalty to my brothers was at war with some crazy feeling inside of me that screamed at me to grab onto her and not let go.

"There's nothing that will make it right, so I won't insult you with a bunch of reasons why I made the promises I made. But, please, I'm begging you to try to understand why Easton, Smith, Jonas, and Cash wanted to tell you themselves. Face-to-face. When you left them the way you did, they were worried. Easton took leave to try to find you. And as soon as Ashcroft approached them, they quit the CIA. No question, they were all in. They gave up everything to make this right. No one thought it would take ten years, but it did."

There was pleading in her tone—not for Garrett to forgive *her* but her *team*. Hell, she wasn't even asking him to understand why she didn't tell him, but she didn't want him to hold a grudge against his brothers. Men who by the sound of it did give up everything to go after the man who was responsible for the failed rescue that had killed Finn. Those men tried to clear Zane's name.

When she was done speaking sadness clung to her like a second skin. She wasn't concealing a single emotion. Layla was laying herself bare. I respected that, admired it, found it immensely appealing.

"Why did it take you ten years?" Owen asked.

"It took us six years because the more we uncovered the more questions we had. We could've taken out Leif but that wouldn't've dismantled the operation. We thought there was someone above Leif, or if not above him then someone else at the agency had turned. I would buy information from an agency source, and we'd wait for the money to hit one of Leif's accounts, but it never did. And Kira couldn't find who the accounts belonged to. Then Leif died and we thought we were done. We had all this evidence, a strong case, and it was useless. My guys were wrapping up a take-down of gun traffickers that worked for Leif when suddenly there was intel out of Russia that Leif's contacts there were on the move. Jonas went to Russia and Harrison Washington was there meeting with Leif's contacts. Using Patheon's facial rec software we started tracking him. Harrison slid right in and was up and running using Leif's network."

"I gotta message from Linc," Zane announced, looking at Layla. "Kira needs to talk to you. She says it's important."

"I'll get a secure line set up for you," Garrett said and pulled out his laptop from the case at his feet.

"Sit down, Layla." I motioned to the seat next to me. "Unless you need privacy."

Layla was no more stable than she was when she'd excused herself as she made her way back to her seat.

"I think I'm well beyond OPSEC and the need for security. Besides, a secured line doesn't mean that Garrett would be securing my communication from him."

She wasn't wrong, and Garrett didn't bother hiding his smirk. He'd had every intention of recording her communication with Kira.

"Yo, G, I don't know how you work in this pig sty." I heard Linc say. "Are you a closet hoarder? I'm thinking an intervention is in order."

"Don't touch my shit," Garrett returned.

"You've got case files on your desk from five years ago. I didn't know we still had paper copies of SITREPS."

"Don't move anything."

"Repeat after me, brother—filing cabinet. That's a real thing, you know. It's this piece of furniture that's pretty nifty. It can—"

"Where's Kira?" Garrett interrupted.

Lincoln was almost as bad as his brother when he got on a roll. He could bust balls for an hour if you didn't reel him in and keep him on task.

"Sitting next to me," Linc started. "Well, more like in

the corner. I put her in the naughty chair since she tried to shoot me."

"I didn't try to shoot you," Kira huffed.

"You pointed a gun at me."

"And?"

I felt movement next to me and glanced at Layla. Her shoulders were shaking. Was she laughing?

"And I don't like guns pointed at me."

"My finger wasn't even on the trigger."

"Where's Bronson?" Zane cut in.

"In the conference room. Myles went out and bought a bag of landscaping rocks. The team's taking turns going in there and throwing them at him. Seems fitting since we can't kill the fucker."

I waited for Layla to protest, say something on her friend's brother's behalf but she said nothing.

"May I please speak with Layla?"

"Keep Kira away from my desk," Garrett ordered. "I'm passing the computer to Layla."

"I'm not going to snoop in your office, One. Though the big Viking's right, you need to clean up. Follow me into the digital world and save a few trees."

One?

What the hell did that mean?

Garrett had gone stone cold. Layla jerked and I felt like I was missing something big.

Or I should say, more somethings since I still felt like there were holes in the big picture.

Wordlessly, Garrett shoved the laptop across the small space separating him and Layla.

She mouthed *sorry* to him before she took the computer and turned it to face her. I glanced over and Kira Winters' face filled the screen. An older version of the girl I'd seen at Finn's funeral.

I tried to recall what I knew about the girl who was now a woman. She'd been twenty when her brother died, still in college though I couldn't remember what university she'd been attending. At the time she had her blonde hair cut into a short bob that barely brushed her chin. Now it was much longer and pulled into a ponytail. She bore a striking resemblance to her brother.

"Good to see they didn't stone you to death," Kira muttered.

"Are they really throwing rocks at Bronson?"

"Yep. And let me tell you, if the big pissed-off beast hadn't snatched my phone, I'd record it for you. I know he's Drifter Two's brother and I should feel bad, but seriously, that guy's a pain in the ass. All he's done since you've been gone is bitch and moan. I had to gag him, and I don't feel bad about that. It's like Two was adopted. There's no way he shares blood with the sniveling idiot."

"I'm the big pissed-off beast!" Linc yelled from off-screen.

"Two will..." Layla trailed off as her gaze sliced to Garrett. "He'll deal with his brother when he gets back. Sorry I didn't check in last night. What'd I miss?"

"Drifter Six called in. The sale went through and he was ready to move in. Five had his target. Mission was executed."

A ghost of a smile played on Layla's lips when she asked, "And the weapons are secured?"

"Side ceased all weapons—"

"Side?" I inquired.

"Secretariat of Intelligence," Layla clarified.

"Oh. SIDE."

SIDE was an acronym for Argentina's version of the CIA. Back in the seventies SIDE had instigated a honey-trap. The setup was known as Operation Marilyn. SIDE had recruited blonde women to get close to Cuban diplomats in Buenos Aires. The operation was a bust and no relevant intel was gained, but SIDE learned a valuable lesson about the power of a beautiful woman.

"The Minister of Defense is taking credit for the seizure," Kira went on. "Five and Six are en route with targets to SO One."

There was a lull in the conversation and I used the opportunity to clear up the call signs the women were using.

"Who's Drifter Five and Six?"

Again, Garrett went solid, Layla shifted in her seat, and when Kira started to speak, Layla's gaze locked on Garrett in a way that communicated apology.

"Two's Theo. Three's Easton. Four's Jonas. Five's Smith. Six is Cash," Kira told me.

And that meant Garrett had to be One.

Drifter was his team's GB call sign and his team had not only continued to use it but they hadn't replaced him as One.

"Five and Six are mission complete," Kira continued like she hadn't rocked Garrett. "I think it's time we route them to Armenia."

"Hold that," Layla denied. "That's not our call."

"No, you're right, it's not *our* call. But it is your call as Ghost One."

"Fan-freaking-tastic," Linc huffed. "*I'm* Ghost. She stole my name. It's like I never even existed."

"You didn't, jacknuts. Hence the name Ghost," Zane ribbed his brother.

Layla ignored the banter, focusing solely on Garrett.

"It's One's call." Then to clarify. "Drifter One."

"It's been too long. Two needs—"

"I know what Two needs." Layla's gaze snapped back to the screen. "But this is not up to me. One...I mean Garrett... or actually, Zane's team can handle the extraction. Where are Three and Four with their targets?"

"At least she remembered who's in charge. That's progress," Zane mumbled.

"I think we need to talk about this," Kira pleaded.

"*I* think I'm done fucking with people's lives," Layla hissed. "End of discussion, Seven. SITREP on Three and Four."

"Copy that," Kira mumbled.

"Shit. I'm sorry," Layla whispered. "You didn't deserve that. You know I value your opinion."

"Since we're discussing me and I'm sitting right here how about I participate in the conversation?"

All eyes went to Garrett.

Well, not Layla's, she'd closed hers.

And I couldn't stop myself from reaching over and grabbing her hand off the leather arm rest she was white-knuckling.

After I'd perpetrated that act of insanity, I upped the madness and threaded my fingers through hers.

When her eyes didn't open, I gave her hand a squeeze. I wasn't sure what message I was sending. Support, comfort, or something more. But I could no longer allow her to think she was alone.

If Garrett had a problem with her, I'd talk to him. I'd find a way for both of them to get what they needed. And in doing that maybe I'd figure out why I was so drawn to a woman I shouldn't have been.

13

WHY WAS Kevin holding my hand?

And why couldn't I let go even though I knew it was wrong?

So damn wrong.

But the rightness of it made it impossible for me to pull away. Just once I wanted someone—no, not someone. It was Kevin. I'd never wanted or needed anything from a man. I was wholly self-sufficient. But Kevin was different.

He *felt* different.

I did not feel peace when I was around him. Kevin didn't give me butterflies and delusions of hearts and unicorns. He made my skin heat and my heart pound. He was lightning and thunder. A storm I wanted to dance in. A rain that would cleanse my past. A tornado that would sweep me clear off my feet. A sandstorm in the desert that left me blind and gasping for air.

He was a challenge. Not in a bad way. In the sense he'd challenge me to be the person I was too afraid to be, he'd challenge me to be open and real. He wouldn't allow me to hide. He'd bring me into the light.

He terrified and excited me.

I wanted his arms around me again. I wanted his support. I wanted to hold his hand and never let go.

But he wasn't an option. Not after everything I'd done. Not after what I'd done to Garrett.

Kevin would help me get Theo back then we'd part ways, and everything would go back to the way it was before.

You've known him twenty-four hours, I reminded myself. And at no point during any of those hours had I made a good impression. *And why am I thinking about this?*

I started to pull my hand away, but his grip tightened. It was unfortunate we had an audience and me yanking my hand any harder would draw even more attention to our clasped hands.

"Well?" Kira's snappy question pulled me out of my crazy thoughts.

"Well, what?" I asked.

"I was talking to One since he wanted to participate but he hasn't said anything beyond that."

I wanted to apologize for my teammate. Sometimes she forgot that speaking to real, live humans was different than when she mumbled at her computer screen when a program wasn't working the way she wanted it to.

"I think I like her," Zane remarked. "She's my kinda people."

"The rude kind?" I asked, staring at Kira through the screen.

"I'm not rude," Kira argued.

"She's totally rude." Lincoln's face came onto the screen. "She actually reminds me of Kevin. Neither of them has a filter and say whatever pops into their brains. She actually asked Bronson if he shit his pants on the drive over. It sounded like he had some gas, but come on, the man was zip-tied and gagged. Let the guy *shart* without calling him on it."

"Gas? He ripped one and I nearly choked. Common courtesy is to at least give some warning to roll down the windows." Kira made a vulgar sound and shook her head.

"He had your bandanna in his mouth, how was he supposed to warn you? And who taught you prisoner care? Bread and water only. You feed a man tacos, what do you expect?" Kira opened her mouth to argue but Lincoln put up his hand. "Nope. I saw the Taco Bell wrappers and if you try to tell me you ate all that food by yourself then I'm calling you a liar. Unless it was you who *sharted* in the car."

"I don't fart!" Kira shouted. "I'm a lady."

"And that's why ninety-nine percent of women are bitchy," Zane cut in. "They need to fart. But instead of letting it fly they hold it in and give themselves a stomachache. Then they get irritable because they have cramps. Just fart. Who cares?"

Was this happening?

All of the men added in their two cents, which was to say, they agreed.

I turned to look at Kevin only to find him already staring at me.

"Is this real?" I whispered.

"Yep."

"So, they're really talking about farting?"

"Yep."

"Y'all need a rule book," I muttered. "Number fifteen, no discussing flatulence on a mission."

The corners of Kevin's eyes crinkled. His lips turned up into a smile. This one was new, a devil-may-care grin that was far sexier than any he'd given me thus far.

Yesterday when I'd met him, he was clean-shaven, today he had a five o'clock shadow. I hoped I was still around tomorrow to see if that scruff filled in. Then I hoped I was around the day after that to see what he looked like with a full beard. And maybe the next day, too, to see him smile a few more times.

"We have an employee handbook," Kevin told me.

"Clearly it needs an addendum."

"It covers the basics," he said with his lips twitching.

"And those are?"

"Eh." He shrugged. "You know, the normal stuff."

I couldn't help but return his smile.

"No, I don't know what Zane Lewis would consider normal stuff."

"Rule number one, no falling for a woman involved in drama," Zane snickered. "Rule number two, no falling for a woman who will cost me money—you fall under this category by the way. This little jaunt is seriously cutting into the Prophylactic Fund. Number three, or maybe this is rule number one, I'm in charge of said woman until the mating ritual is complete and she's claimed. Number four, no glove, no love. Or if you'd prefer—"

I fell under rule number two—no falling for a woman who would cost him money?

And what the hell was a Prophylactic Fund?

Kevin was in no danger of breaking the rules. I might be, but thankfully I didn't work for Zane thus his handbook didn't apply to me.

"Please make him stop, my ears are burning," Kira butted in.

And again, I'd forgotten she was still on the line, but I still couldn't tear my eyes from Kevin.

"Better your ears than your vagina," Zane tossed back. "Another reason to wrap it before you tap it."

"You're like a walking, talking, breathing lawsuit waiting to happen."

"Better a lawsuit than a bunch of fire-breathing vaginas."

"Yes," Kevin whispered and leaned closer.

"Yes, what?" I breathed.

I watched with avid fascination as Kevin's eyes flared then the brown was eaten up by the black of his pupils. *Amazing.* I'd never seen anything like that before. Right before my very eyes Kevin's had changed, the sight had me mesmerized.

"I forgot what I was going to say," he admitted.

"I don't know what's being piped into the cabin of that aircraft, but can the alpha pheromones get dialed back until I disconnect? You know I haven't had a date since 1998."

"You were like two in 1998."

"I was six."

Kira and Lincoln blathered on; the sound of their voices muted by the static that was clouding my mind. I needed to look away, break whatever spell I was under. Concentrate on work. Theo. Garrett. A hundred other things—important things. But right then, nothing seemed more important than savoring the way Kevin was staring at me.

I was in such deep contemplation that when the plane suddenly dipped, Garrett's laptop started to slip off my lap and I made no move to save it.

Thankfully Garrett did.

The spell was broken.

At least it was between me and Kevin because Garrett was staring at me funny. He was no longer eyeing me with suspicion and skepticism but instead with curiosity. His gaze went to where Kevin was holding my hand, then to Kevin, before it came back to me.

"Finish up with Seven so we can go over your intel."

Right. Ten years' worth of intelligence that would land Harrison Washington in a cage for the rest of his life and take down all of his buddies who think their money makes them untouchable.

"And for now," he went on. "Let's hold off on troop movement to Armenia. This mission needs to run smooth. The reunion can wait until after Theo's safe and you're no longer on the most wanted list."

Did that mean he was going to forgive the guys for making me promise not to approach him?

"Oh, yeah, I heard Dickhead Extraordinaire made you number one on the HVT list. Congrats, Bosslady, you now outrank Alejandro Castillo."

Just what I'd always wanted, to be ranked with the world's worst criminals.

"Maybe you can throw me a party if I don't die," I teased, and Kira beamed a big, beautiful smile that made her look like a teenager instead of a cyber mastermind.

"We're totally having a party when the team gets stateside. Four already called in his order—a double cheeseburger with extra bacon. Last I heard from Two he said he just wants beer and pizza. Hard to believe that none of them have been in the U.S. for ten years."

Well, there you had it, Theo still had a hankering for pizza.

"Speaking of Four, did he find the money?"

Jonas had been tracking the money that Easton had marked before a drug buy.

"Yes, ma'am. Four will have his mission wrapped up in the next twelve hours. Money less Dickhead Extraordinaire's cut, which of course was sent direct to Harrison's account, and smugglers will be taken to SO One. Our issue is Three."

SO One was our outpost where we were holding our targets until Harrison Washington was locked up.

"What's the issue?"

Please don't let it be major.

"Sheep Dog doesn't want him to engage with Irish."

The Irish had purchased a shit ton—literally a ton, two-thousand pounds—of meth, cocaine, and pills from Somalia. Easton was supposed to intercept the drugs, meaning we'd have the money, drugs, buyer, and seller in custody.

"We need the Irish, he works for Harrison."

"Risk outweighs the reward. We have enough on Harrison without the Irish."

This was new.

"I don't like last-minute changes," I grumbled. "Did he say why? And when did he tell you this?"

My mind was swirling around different reasons why Ashcroft would suddenly change his mind about taking down a drug deal in Ireland. Sure, the Irish wasn't the largest outfit in Limerick, but he was working his way up the food chain, and it'd be nice to take him out before he got bigger, and besides two-thousand pounds of product was going to hit the street.

"This morning," Kira answered. "And he said taking down the Irish might have a political impact. The drugs are in Ireland and not our mission. We just needed the money to exchange hands and tie back to Harrison."

I wanted to override Ashcroft's order but technically he was the boss. While taking down the Irish and preventing two-thousand pounds of drugs from hitting the streets wasn't our mission it was one of the side benefits. Tons and tons of drugs had been destroyed over the years. Guns, ammo, RPGs, bombs, and bomb-making material, all seized and taken from criminals and terrorists. Ten years' worth.

"Pull Three and tell him to meet the team in Canada. Oh, and do me a favor and show Bronson a picture of Harrison and Eddy. We need to figure out who Liam Martin is. I don't think Harrison would trust Eddy with something that sensitive, but we can't leave that thread loose."

"I'll get on that as soon as the guys here run out of rocks."

Right. I forgot Zane's employees were having some fun with Theo's brother. Good Lord, I hope he understood when he got home.

"Please don't let them kill him," I begged.

"You do remember reading their files, right? Plus, there's kids running around this place like a daycare center. This little black-haired kid who looks a lot like the big pissed-off Viking threw a handful at Bronson and stuck his tongue out. Next thing I knew a second one ran around the corner and flipped him the bird. He got in trouble for that, but still, if they're gonna kill him there's nothing I can do."

I peered at Zane in hopes that he'd give his brother the order not to kill but all he did was shrug.

"Those are my nephews," Zane proudly announced. "Robbie and Asher."

Upon saying his nephews' names Zane smiled. A real and true smile that lit his whole face.

"Christ," Lincoln rasped. "He's smiling, isn't he?"

"Woman down," Gabe muttered.

"Maybe someone give her a tissue to wipe her drool."

Oh, shit. I hoped I wasn't drooling like Owen said but

good God, Zane had dimples. Deep impressions in each cheek that ratcheted up his good looks by a hundred.

I lifted my free hand and Kevin tugged the one he was holding.

"Babe, Owen was joking."

"Oh, right."

Thank God.

"What's happening? All I can see is Layla's face and Mr. Hot Guy next to her."

Mr. Hot Guy.

Kira and her nicknames.

Shoot me now.

"Zane smiled," Lincoln informed her.

"So?"

"Dimples. The minute he shows his dimples women... never mind."

"Turn the camera, I wanna see!" Kira demanded.

I glanced back at Zane and sadly his dimples were no longer on display.

"Too late, he's back to Scary Zane."

"Well damn. Next time take a pic."

"That's not happening," Kevin growled.

A chill raced up my spine followed by a tingling sensation that I vaguely remembered as being desire. When was the last time I was turned on by the tone of a man's voice?

Yesterday when your nipples tingled after Kevin tackled you.

Right.

Yesterday felt like forever ago.

"Alrighty then, no picture for me. I'm off to make my calls. Be safe."

"Always. I'll check in when I can."

"Copy that."

The screen went dark and I awkwardly handed Garrett back his laptop.

I really should've already let go of Kevin's hand, but I really liked the way it felt to be connected to him.

"Before we start, I want to talk to Layla. Clear the air."

Kevin's fingers tightened around mine. Did he not want to leave me alone with Garrett or did he not want to stop holding my hand?

God, please let it be the hand-holding thing.

I squeezed Kevin's fingers hoping he understood that I'd be okay. Whatever Garrett had to say I'd listen. I owed him at least that.

Men started to shuffle back to their seats. Zane unbuckled and stood—well, he didn't stand to his full height, he was more like hunched over since he was so tall—but he didn't move.

Instead, he narrowed his eyes and said, "I'm gonna say this once. I was wrong about a few things. I had you pegged as one of *them*." By them, Zane meant the CIA. "I understand loyalty. I don't accept anything less from those I'm close to and offer mine back ten-fold. There is nothing I wouldn't do for one of my men, including keeping a misguided, fucked-up secret. But if I was in their shoes, I wouldn't have allowed you to have a conversation with one of my men that I would want to have with my teammate directly. So, in the end, the secret you kept wasn't fucked-up. At least not in my book. We'll get Theo for you, you have my word on that. But the rest is up to Garrett. And if he chooses to walk away from them, you control that and keep your team in check."

"I will."

"I want your promise."

"I promise."

With that Zane nodded and walked away.

The moment Kevin let go of my hand coldness crept in. Icy cold that I couldn't shake.

"I'll be…" Kevin paused and smiled. "Guess that's not necessary since I can't go anywhere but two rows back."

He threw me a wink and walked away.

Alone with Garrett.

My heart hurt looking at him.

"Before you say anything, may I?" Garrett jerked his chin, so I continued. "I already promised Zane but if you'd prefer as soon as Theo's safe, he and I will leave immediately. If you don't want to see or hear from them again, I swear, Garrett, you won't. They mean you no harm and will respect whatever you decide."

"Why didn't Easton take Drifter One? He was my number two."

His call sign?

"Because you're One. Easton wouldn't let anyone use One and when I'm on the radio he calls me G-One, never just One. That's you."

Garrett's eyelids slowly lowered. The sight was painful to watch but I'd venture to guess it was more painful for him.

"How are they? Aside from Theo, I mean. And I haven't said this yet; I'm sorry Two was taken."

Two was taken.

Theo.

My stomach tightened.

"Thanks," I croaked. "But…um…the rest of them are good. Or as good as they can be while being homesick and globetrotting."

"They've been out there for ten years, no R and R?"

"No rest for the wicked." My joke fell flat so I rushed to

continue. "No R and R. No travel back to the U.S. We didn't want to take any chances that someone at the CIA would catch on. They're out there alone."

Alone.

Them. Me. We had each other yet we were still alone. The only person from the team I saw was Kira and that was because Patheon was a legit program. It was a calculated and necessary risk. But I never met with Ashcroft face-to-face.

"I shouldn't have left the way I did. And when they all reached out I should've been man enough to answer. My head was too fucked-up and by the time Zane found me I just wanted to move on. Them, too. I didn't want to be the reminder that Finn died. I wanted..."

I sat back in the plush leather seat and kept my eyes glued to Garrett while he unburdened his guilt. Not over what had happened to Finn—he knew the truth about that. But guilt over how he'd turned his back on his brothers. I listened and while I did I prayed he'd let them back in.

14

I'D TAKEN the aisle seat, diagonal from Layla. Zane was in the window seat next to me, Owen and Gabe directly across. Cooper on my other side across the way. Conversations were going on around me, but all of my attention was on Layla. She'd lounged back in her seat, her gaze parked firmly on Garrett, and she hadn't said a word in at least five minutes. Which meant she was listening and as the minutes had ticked by her eyes had turned gentle and were now full of concern. Her hands clasped together in her lap, knuckles white, and I wondered if she was holding herself back from reaching for Garrett. Her pink, pouty lips were downturned into a frown and her shoulders were stiff. It was clear she was struggling not to interrupt what he was saying.

The longer I stared at her the harder it became not to get out of my seat and go to her. It was like a compulsion I was fighting against. Which didn't make any sense. Was this what Gabe felt when he first saw Evette? I'd heard her tell the story a hundred times, how when she first saw Gabe in the lobby of Z Corps she just *knew*. She called it kismet. Gabe had told a similar story, one that I'd thought was bullshit because no one fell in love at first sight. I'd seen plenty of beautiful women. I'd had my fair share of sweet, sexy, smart women and none of them had ever stirred any emotion other than lust. I'd dated, spent time with, and bedded enough women to know that when it was time to walk away, I walked away. But the thought of Layla walking out of my life after we rescued Theo was unfathomable. Never had my chest ached with fear at the prospect of losing something that wasn't even mine to begin with. It was the *something* I couldn't figure out. The nagging, persistent feeling that if Layla left, I'd lose something big.

Was this what Myles had felt when he finally found Delilah in Mexico? This overwhelming need to keep her safe. Was this why when Delilah went with us to find her research scientist, he looked like a cross between a murdering psychopath and a scared five-year-old? Delilah, too, had been marked for death. Had Myles wanted to take Delilah and disappear like I wanted to do with Layla? My team could sort out the rest of her operation—rescue Theo, take down Harrison, bring the rest of her team back to the U.S., then clear her name. All the while she and I could be safely hiding out.

"You got it bad, brother." Gabe kicked the toe of my boot and chuckled.

"You know she can't leave without a parachute, right?" Owen added. "She'll still be in the plane if you look away."

Shit.

Here we go.

With a great deal of effort, I tore my eyes from Layla to look at my team.

Did they expect me to say something? Explain what the hell was wrong with me? Why I couldn't concentrate on the operation we were in the middle of planning?

"How many...I mean..." I scrubbed my hands over my face and bowed my head. I was fucking this up. Which was not like me. I was the level-headed one. I was the one who had no time for bullshit. I was to-the-point and single-minded when we were planning a mission. There was too much at stake to fuck around and allow my mind to wander. "What the fuck is wrong with me?" I muttered, hoping one of my brothers had the answer that would snap me out of my fog.

"In general, or right now?" Cooper asked.

I flipped him a rude gesture that unfortunately didn't offend him, or if it did it didn't prevent him from laughing.

"You've got a simple case of batter on the brain," Owen told me. "Right now, you're at the beginning stages of the buildup. The part when you fight like hell to keep your distance. The next part is when all the excuses run out and all you're left with is a whole lotta messy emotions that accumulate until they explode all over the place. P.S., that's the fun part and if you're lucky and she's caught a case of the feels, too, then all that tension will be worked out hopefully when your team's not downstairs listening. But along the way, your brothers will have your back. Of course, it'll come in the form of torture, as you well know."

I did know. I'd well and truly fucked with Owen while he and Natasha were working their shit out. And the team had indeed been downstairs while their tension had exploded, as he called it. Though none of us heard as much as we'd told him we had.

What's a little fun between brothers while stuck in a cabin in the middle of nowhere, Idaho?

But that was not this. I wasn't falling in love.

I was fascinated, sure.

I was absolutely attracted to her. Unlike what I told

Zane, my dick had definitely taken notice and I was having a hard time keeping my reaction to her in check.

But love? No way.

"Brother, you've lost your edge if you think I'm falling in *love*." But the denial felt like a lie as I said it. "We should have your head checked because it is broken."

"There's not a damn thing wrong with my head. All the signs and symptoms are present: trouble concentrating, puppy dog eyes, elevated heart rate."

Puppy dog eyes? No question, Owen had bumped his head.

"Christ, what is this, preschool?" Cooper asked. "Or is Nat keeping your balls in her pocket because I know what you really wanted to say was, he can't keep his eyes off her ass and we all saw him adjust his hard-on as she walked up the stairs onto the plane. Not to mention the hand-holding thing. Don't know if that's love but he wants to—"

"Don't," I cut in.

"And that right there is the proof. If she was just some hot chick you wanted to bang you wouldn't sound like you're ready to take my head off at the mere mention of you wanting to throw her over your shoulder and find a bedroom. Or a wall. And a condom, don't forget the condom."

Great, now Cooper was getting in on Zane's mantra.

Exchanging blows with Cooper while on a plane wasn't on my list of top ten things I wanted to do. On the other hand, it would relieve some of the stress that had built over the last few hours.

"I'm not especially concerned about where anyone puts their dicks—"

"You're so full of shit," Gabe interrupted Zane. "You designed a handbook around that exact topic."

Zane's unapologetic shrug followed by his eyes coming directly to me made me brace.

"You wanna play hide the Tootsie Roll with that woman, that's your business." Obviously, Zane's comment was directed at me. "But when she's not in your bed, I'm in charge. Period, end of story." Zane stopped and smiled. It was then I knew he was getting ready to piss me off more than he had. "That means if I kit her out and put her on point, that's my call to make. She has an issue with strapping on a vest to rescue her man then that's up to her to tell me."

First, Theo wasn't her man. He was her teammate. Secondly, I knew Zane was pushing my buttons by threatening to put Layla in danger. I'd seen this scenario play out before. Yet, I couldn't stop the fear and anger from mixing together at the thought of Layla infiltrating a terrorist compound.

That wasn't happening.

"She's not strapping on a vest."

"Not your call."

"The fuck it's not. Even if you and Garrett sit out, we got a three-man team to get Theo out. A team that's worked together on countless operations. We don't need a distraction—"

"Seems to me the only person who'd be distracted is you," Zane pointed out. "And you know damn well I wouldn't send anyone in unless I was goddamn confident they won't get themselves killed or one of my men killed on my watch. After our meeting yesterday, I did a deep dive into her deployments with the CIA. Made a few calls. By all accounts, the woman has her shit together and is good in a firefight."

I didn't want to think about Layla in the middle of a firefight. I'd witnessed her reckless disregard for her own safety once and that was more than enough to give me nightmares for the next twenty years. And further, why the hell was I engaging when I knew if Layla wanted in on Theo's rescue there wouldn't be a fucking thing I could do or say to talk the stubborn woman down?

Unless I used Zane's suggestion from last night and cuffed her to my bed. Which at this juncture would be a very bad move on my part unless I wanted her to claw my eyes out. *Better that than her dead.* I'd have to find a way to reason with her, or better yet find a way to exhaust her until she was so boneless, she wouldn't think about rolling out with us.

What I wasn't going to do was fall victim to Zane's head games.

I gave myself a moment to recover after my unfortunate show of emotion.

"It's up to her," I said, knowing I had no intention of allowing her to come. "If she wants to go with us, I can't stop her."

And after I fed my boss that line of shit, I fought the urge to rub the ache that had started in my chest.

"Liar."

Zane's word choice only made me think of the times I called Layla that and the hurt I'd purposely inflicted to get a reaction out of her. Damn, I was a monumental asshole.

I ignored my boss and asked, "What do we know about the cell that's holding Theo?"

"Nothing, until she shows us her intel."

Fucking hell, I was off my game.

"Right."

"Really? You got nothing else to say on the subject?" Zane's tone was downright incredulous. He'd expected me to throw a holy shit-fit like the others had done when he'd pushed them on matters of the...*Christ, I was actually going to think it...* heart.

Without meaning to, my gaze moved back to Layla. She looked tired. Not physically, not even mentally—her fatigue went deeper.

Soul deep.

She'd given up her career, put her life on hold, and had supported her team. And not for a little while, she'd done it for ten years. Remained loyal to the men she worked with, steadfast in their mission.

I admired that kind of commitment. Respected her dedication.

Layla wouldn't quit until her mission was successful. I understood the sense of duty she felt. I also knew the toll it took.

Seeing the exhaustion, finally understanding what it meant, I had to force my body not to go to her. Garrett was speaking too softly for me to make out the conversation, but whatever he was saying was painful for her to hear. Yet, she was sitting there quietly.

She'd already convinced herself she was the villain.

Wait. Wasn't she?

Was there a villain in this story or just a whole lot of misinformation? Did Garrett get to be pissed at Layla for doing what his old teammates had made her promise to do? And Zane had been right—not that I'd tell the man that, his head was already so big it was a miracle he could walk through a door without getting stuck. But if I had been in that situation and the mission had gone sideways, no one but me would explain things to my teammate.

Guilt assailed fast and heavy. Even thinking that felt like a betrayal. Garrett had the right to feel any way he wanted to. Layla had kept the truth from him and Zane. It didn't matter they'd known about Leif. She had known, too, and hadn't come forward.

Murky.

That was what the situation had become—muddy and murky and fucked-up.

"I got no control over that," I said, not turning away from Layla. "I can't—"

I couldn't finish my thought; I couldn't say it out loud without getting more pissed off than I was that Layla was sitting alone with a frown on her face and sad eyes. Unlike Owen, Myles, and Gabe I didn't get to claim Layla as mine. I didn't get to argue and throw a shit fit when Zane pushed my buttons.

Layla couldn't be mine.

Garrett deserved my loyalty, and if he couldn't forgive her then I had to walk away.

Jesus Christ. The thought made me want to vomit.

"You can't what?" Gabe pushed.

That was the million-dollar question. What couldn't I do? Believe that I felt some insane, instant connection to Layla? Believe that Gabe and Evette had been right and there was such a thing as fate? Believe that I took one look at Layla and felt down to my bones that she was meant to be mine? That I found the woman I was meant to spend my life with—but, oh, by the way, she'd lied and kept secrets from one of your best friends. Was *that* my destiny? Finding the one woman who set me on fire in ways I hadn't known were possible only to have to walk away from her?

Was that my penance or was it a cruel cosmic joke?

I found the one, but I couldn't keep her.

Fury built until the explosion happened, though I didn't think it was the kind Owen had in mind.

"I can't stop thinking about how wrong I was about her. I can't stop wanting to protect her—from everything and everyone including Garrett. I can't stop from believing that there's something about her that I need. Something special, something real, something that I've been missing my whole fucking life, and when she leaves, I'll never have another shot at happiness because she will have taken it with her. But mostly I can't stop thinking about what a dick that makes me because my loyalty should be a hundred percent with Garrett but it's not. I'm torn between the two and the fucked-up part is a woman I don't know is winning out."

Zane didn't give me a chance to catch my breath before he launched in.

"What the fuck are you talking about? What do you think is going on over there? No, don't answer either of those, I have a better question. Do you think I'm dumb?"

"What?"

Zane lifted his hand and jabbed his big meaty index finger in Owen's direction.

"We'll start with the most obvious. Owen the standoff-ish, I'm never getting married again since my first wife screwed me over, yet he wouldn't allow Natasha out of his sight and demanded she live with him. He denied it but we all saw it. Next up, Gabe." Zane pointed at him. "He was actually the easiest, he didn't deny shit. He walked Evette up to the conference room and that was it, he was a goner. Myles saw a picture of Delilah and that was all it took; he was out on his own and refused to give up on her. And that's just your team. I've seen this shit happen over and over again. I can spot this shit from a mile away.

"So again, do you think I'm a dumbass and I somehow missed how the woman looked like she was ready to jump into your lap and beg you save her from the shitstorm she'd found herself in? Or maybe you think you're better at hiding your emotions. Sorry to say, my man, but you suck at it. Why do you think Myles sent you to go with her?

"Garrett was in shock, not pissed. We'd already taken care of Leif. That asshole is nothing but a bad memory. But his old team is something he still struggles with. He didn't leave on good terms. He feels guilt for that. He was blind-sided and now he needs to make a choice he's not ready to face."

Well, damn.

I didn't know what to say so I said nothing and tried to digest everything Zane had said.

"You never told us about Leif," Owen pointed out the obvious. "Why'd you go at that alone?"

"I wasn't alone, I had Garrett."

Zane paused and suddenly he looked uncomfortable. A look I'd never seen my boss wear. He was always confident, and that confidence was normally just shy of arrogance. He didn't pause to contemplate his words. Zane said what he said and gave zero fucks if what he said was offensive. The man didn't mince words, but right then he was considering his next words carefully.

"I understand her," he started, and I assumed he was referring to Layla. "I know why she kept the secrets she kept. Each and every one of you trusts me with your lives. That includes shit you don't want anyone else to know about. Garrett wasn't ready to share, now he has no choice. I did for him the same I would and have done for all of you."

Out of the corner of my eye, I saw Cooper shift and I wondered if Zane was keeping a secret for him. I had nothing in the past that my team didn't know about. But that didn't mean I didn't respect my brother's privacy. There was a fine line between a friend and pushing someone to talk about something that's bothering them, and prying into someone's life when they don't want you there.

Just one more burden that was Zane's to bear.

"Now, back to the topic at hand. Layla and her kicking in some doors—"

"Not gonna happen," I growled.

Zane's loud and very obnoxious laughter filled the fuselage. Layla's startled gaze came to mine and when it did a few things snapped into place.

As crazy as it was, I believed.

As insane as the notion was, there was something undeniable happening between us.

It would be just my luck that in the middle of chaos and confusion I'd found the one woman who provoked emotions that I didn't know I could feel. I'd find the woman I didn't think I could live without, and was she marked for death.

Complicated.

15

WE'D CHANGED planes in New York and were headed across the Atlantic. Another private jet but this one was larger.

My nerves were shot, and hysteria might've set in. If not full-blown hysteria, then I was certainly having delusions of grandeur.

Zane and Garrett had been going over my files for hours now. Owen and Gabe were snoozing. Cooper was reading a magazine. And Kevin...he hadn't left my side. Something had changed—something big. And that was where my delusions came in. He'd held my hand when we disembarked the last aircraft and hadn't let go until he'd shuffled me up the boarding stairs of the new plane, and back to our seats. And even then, he hadn't let go until Garrett had handed me his laptop so I could get him into my secure reports.

I wasn't sure what to make of Kevin's gestures. I knew what I wanted them to mean but that would be crazy. People didn't form the type of connection I felt with Kevin in a day. It took weeks and months before real feelings started. Hell, maybe it even took years before someone knew the person they were with was the person they were compatible with.

I didn't need weeks or months or years to know I wasn't compatible with Kevin. There was nothing about him that spoke of harmony and synchrony. But I did have a weird feeling that there was a balance between us, and I'd felt that the moment he challenged me. But that had to be wishful, nonsensical thinking brought on by extreme stress.

"Why didn't you go back to visit your mom after you left for college?"

Kevin's out-of-left-field question made me jerk my head from looking out the window into an abyss of blue over to him and I immediately wished I hadn't. Part of the something that had changed was the way his attention had become acute. He'd watched me like a hawk ever since my conversation with Garrett. There was no trace of anger. All vestiges of distrust were gone. I had to be imagining his concern; there was no other explanation for the way his eyes had gentled on me. His expressions were no longer severe and scrutinizing. They were cautious and kind.

His inquiry wasn't the first personal question he'd asked me but unlike the others this time it didn't sound like a test. He sounded like he was simply curious.

I searched for an excuse not to answer. Lying was no longer an option, not to Kevin. But I loathed speaking about my mother. So much so I'd never told another person I felt guilt over not visiting her. Yet, I'd already opened up and told him, I just hadn't told him why. The harder I sought a reason not to tell him the faster my heart started to beat.

Just tell him.

"My mom was an alcoholic. She started drinking when my dad left and didn't stop until she was diagnosed with cirrhosis. And even after that, she fell off the wagon more than a few times. I was seventeen when she finally got sober for good. By then she was in the end stages of liver failure and her only chance at survival was a liver transplant."

The shame of turning my back on my mother always lingered; it wasn't something that would ever go away.

"Did the transplant not work? Rejection?"

The only rejection my mother had incurred was from her daughter.

"She refused to consider a transplant even though she'd been sober over a year and was eligible."

My mother had been adamant. It hadn't mattered that I'd begged her, that the doctors had told her she was going to die without it. She wouldn't hear of it.

Then I left her to die alone.

I went to California and two years later she was gone and I was alone—which was exactly what I deserved.

"Why didn't she want the transplant?"

"She said that there were people on the list who needed a liver. People who hadn't been alcoholics. She told me that she'd selfishly drank her life away and she wouldn't selfishly take a liver from someone else. But what about *me*? What about her drinking *my* life away and now that she was sober giving *me* a chance to have a mother? She wouldn't hear of saving herself. Flat out refused. I was so angry and hurt she was going to let herself die I never went back. I wasted those last two years she was alive too bitter to go home and be with her."

And now that Kevin knew what a raving bitch of a daughter I was, surely he'd let go of my hand and recoil. His eyes would turn hard, and he'd reject me the same way I'd rejected my mother.

"Damn, baby, I'm so sorry."

"Sorry? I did it to myself."

Kevin did let go of my hand but only to cup my cheek. His big palm held me in place as he leaned in closer until there were only inches separating our faces.

"I say this with the preface that I know it might hurt you, but I respect what your mother did. She knew she was going to die yet she stood by her convictions. She knew it would leave you without her, but she still did what she felt was right. She didn't waver when faced with her mortality. I'm sorry you lost time with your mom. Not only the last two years but your childhood. Did she ask you to not go to college and stay with her?"

Not trusting my voice, I shook my head. My mother had wanted me to go to school and I hadn't argued when she practically shoved me out the door.

"Did she ask you to come home?"

Again, I shook my head. I was working part-time and going to school full-time. Summer breaks I worked as many jobs as I could to save money to get me through fall and spring when I couldn't work as many hours. My mother was on disability and couldn't afford to help me financially—not that I would've taken money from her if she'd offered. But she knew how hard I was working and even if she'd wanted me to come home she never would've asked.

"You don't understand. When I left, I was so angry I told her I never wanted to see her again, then I didn't. The next time I went to Bend was for her funeral."

"Words spoken in anger leave scars that never heal," he whispered.

"Yes, they do."

"I wish there was something I could say or do that would heal those scars for you, but I can't, and neither can you. The only thing you can do is take the lesson and not forget it. But I know you already know that."

His honesty hit me square in the chest. He wasn't giving me some bullshit platitudes. He wasn't telling me not to blame myself for acting out in anger and in doing so hurting myself and my mom. I don't even think he was trying to make me feel better, nor was he criticizing me for my deplorable behavior. He was simply talking about it.

Balance.

"I still lose my temper," I admitted. "So obviously I haven't learned."

"There's a difference between losing your temper and lashing out. I think you get that I've paid close attention to you since we've been together. I know there have been times when I was an asshole and gave you good reason to lash out at me, but you didn't. I called you a liar and did that to purposely hurt your feelings to get a reaction. I apologize for that. Three new scars I have to live with."

I didn't want that for him.

"Let that go. It's not worth it to—"

"What you're saying is *you're* not worth it," he interrupted me. His fingers slid into my hair at my temple, the feel of that so sweet I shivered. I knew he felt it; there was no way he didn't when the tremble started in my scalp and moved all the way down to my toes.

"I'm not saying that. All I meant was I don't want you to have to live with new scars. It wasn't a big deal."

"Did I hurt your feelings when I called you a liar?"

Shit.

Was a white lie to save someone from hurt feelings still a lie?

Yes.

Dammit.

Apparently, my hysteria also included talking to myself in my head *and* answering.

"Yes."

"Then it's a big deal. Top that with doing it deliberately, I now bear the consequences of that. That's how life works, Layla. You said something to your mom that you regret. You live with that."

He was damn right about that. I lived with that horrible conversation playing on repeat.

"But that doesn't mean you beat yourself over it for the rest of your life," he continued. "There is something called forgiveness. Keep the lesson and forgive yourself. Stop over-thinking and replaying a single moment in time while the rest of the moments slip by. That's a waste. That means you haven't learned jackshit and you're still letting anger get the best of you. There is no difference between being angry at yourself and angry at someone else. Anger is anger, baby, and it's crippling."

I had a smartass comment ready to fire back to break the uncomfortable conversation. It was on the tip of my tongue. But as hard as I tried to spit it out, I couldn't get the words unstuck. This was too important; Kevin was too important. And I wasn't sure how that happened or what it meant. I just knew that for the first time in my life I wanted to be real, I wanted to be me, and I wanted to trust someone.

"You're right. About all of it. But I don't know how to forgive myself and I don't know how to stop thinking about the conversation. I apologized to her for saying it, but actions mean more than words and I never went back. I'm still angry with myself and at her. She lied to me, after my dad left she promised she wouldn't leave me, too, and she did. She left."

"Baby, she didn't leave you, she died."

"Same thing," I spat.

"Okay," he conceded. "I can see how you'd think that due to the circumstances."

There was nothing in his tone or expression indicating he was being anything but honest. He might not have agreed with me but he was open-minded enough to see the situation through my eyes.

"Thank you."

Kevin tilted my head down and tipped his up. Then I felt his lips on my forehead.

"I'm not sure what you're thanking me for," he murmured there. "But I'm gonna take it when I should be the one thanking you for not pulling away. I saw you struggling but unsurprisingly, you pushed through."

Unsurprisingly?

What did that mean?

"I'm finding that opening up to you isn't all that hard."

No sooner had the last word left my mouth than Kevin went solid. His forehead went to mine and I swear it felt like he was trying to meld us together. I would've thought it was more hallucinating on my part if his other hand hadn't come up so both of them were now tangled in my hair. I would've thought that I'd dreamed that kiss if his lips hadn't branded my forehead.

But it was what he said next that sealed the deal. I was awake and cognizant. I wasn't dreaming or fevered. Though my body had warmed significantly and I wanted to wrap my arms around Kevin so he couldn't ever take himself away from me.

"So you feel it, too?" he asked softly.

I could've played dumb but just like with all things Kevin, I couldn't bring myself to prevaricate.

"I do, but I can't explain exactly what *it* is."

"Right? It's lingering between us. Whatever it is draws

me to you. It's *something*. An unexplainable, unbelievable feeling yet it's the realest thing I've ever felt."

"I thought I was going crazy. That maybe the stress had caught up with me and I'd finally cracked."

And maybe I had cracked. It was the only reason I could come up with as to why I'd opened up to Kevin in the first place. Not even Kira or any of the guys knew my real name. I'd certainly never discussed my mother's death with them. I didn't actually tell them anything personal about myself. I was all work, all the time.

No-fun Layla.

Not that discussing my guilt and anger was fun.

"You're thinking mighty hard over there," he murmured.

"Am I?"

"Yeah, I can feel your brain overthinking."

I smiled and asked, "Through my forehead?"

"No. I feel it in my chest. It starts as an ache. A message of distress. It also happened when you were talking to Garrett. I could feel your pain from across the plane. Whatever he was saying to you was hard for you to hear but you didn't stop him from saying it."

God, he was so right about Garrett. Everything the guy had said felt like a dagger to my heart. The pain he'd carried since he'd left his team was immense. He felt guilt for leaving the way he had. But he'd done what was best for him, for his sanity and he didn't feel sorry for that. He'd said he didn't blame me and wasn't mad I hadn't approached him. He was grateful I'd watched out for Cash, Easton, Smith, and Jonas. But he still didn't want them in Armenia.

"I'm not fishing or asking you to tell me what you and Garrett talked about. That's between the two of you. All

I'm saying is that I physically could feel your mental anguish."

That sounded totally insane, but I knew he was telling the truth. When Zane had laughed and I looked over at Kevin, I saw it. His empathy was written all over him. But more than that, I'd *felt* it. It was because of that feeling I was able to finish listening to Garrett's heartbreaking story of self-discovery. Alone for a year, wandering with nothing but his thoughts.

"I think maybe we're both totally crazy. This doesn't happen. It's impossible."

"I'd agree with you if I hadn't witnessed it firsthand. When we get back, I'll introduce you to Evette and let her tell you the story about how she met Gabe."

I knew their story, or at least the mission that had brought them together.

"The story about Timor Leste?"

Unfortunately, my question made him lift his forehead off mine. Thankfully he was smiling which took some of the sting out of losing contact.

"You did your homework."

"I did. Now it feels kinda creepy I know everything about you and your team."

"You know what would make that less creepy?"

If you kissed me.

"No, what?"

"If you spent the rest of the flight telling me all about you."

There were eleven hours left on our thirteen-hour flight. I wouldn't even need half of that to tell him about myself. Even if I went into great detail, I'd need only a few hours, max.

So very sad.

"There is not much to tell. I have no hobbies. I have one friend, Kira. I work too much and when this op is over, I'm quitting. There's my life."

Kevin's eyes went round and his brows pinched. The surprised expression was so comical I couldn't stop myself from lifting my hand and tracing the grooves in his forehead with my fingertip.

"You're quitting?"

"Yep."

I watched my finger trace the lines until I got to his temple then I did what I'd wanted to do all day and moved my fingertips over his scruff.

"It's softer than I thought it'd be."

I felt him smile and that was a thousand percent better than just watching it happen.

"Softer, huh? What'd you think my face would feel like, a cactus?"

"I knew you'd say cactus and not porcupine," I muttered. "And no, not that prickly. Rough maybe. I don't know. But I didn't think your whiskers would be so soft."

"Do you not like it? Want me to shave it?"

Hell to the no!

"No, I've never kissed a man with a beard."

I should've been shocked I'd blurted out that tidbit or embarrassed at how presumptuous it was that I thought he'd want to kiss me. But I was neither shocked nor embarrassed. I was beginning to wonder if there was no truth I wouldn't tell Kevin.

I'd been so lost in my exploration of his burgeoning beard I hadn't realized he hadn't said anything. I lifted my gaze from my fingers trailing his jaw and saw he was staring at me. No, he wasn't staring—his eyes were ablaze, and he was *staring*.

"Glad we had our talk. But now I need you to stop touching me."

I didn't stop touching him. I ran my knuckles over his whiskers. Back and forth until his eyes narrowed.

"Why do you want me to stop?"

Kevin's hand came up and covered mine, effectively halting my movements.

"I didn't say *want*. I said *need*. I need you to stop before I haul your ass to the lavatory and we share more than our first kiss in a cramped, tiny space with my team twenty feet away."

I didn't see the issue with that. As a matter of fact, it sounded fun and exciting and sexy to get busy with Kevin in the plane's bathroom. The space was so small neither of us would be able to completely undress. He'd have to pin me to the wall with my legs wrapped around him. The sex would be hot and ravenous. But I bet he'd keep his kisses sweet.

"Sounds like—"

"Layla," he groaned. "Please, baby, give me this. The first time—no, any time I have you—I do not want anyone around to hear. The noises you'll make for me are for me. No one else. We have eleven more hours on this plane. Two hours from Qatar to Armenia. Then we're headed out to pick up Theo. It's gonna be a long forty-eight hours until I get you to myself. Please don't make it harder than it already will be."

"How hard is it going to be?"

I didn't know what had gotten into me. I didn't flirt, I didn't talk dirty—hell, I wasn't even sure if I was doing it right. But when Kevin smiled and shifted in his seat, I figured I was on the right track.

"So fucking hard it's taking more control than I care to admit not to show you."

"I take it you're one of those possessive—"

"Straight up, I don't share. Not in any sense of the word. And that goes both ways. You'll have me, all of me. And I'll demand all of you. No secrets. No distance. This is who I am. All or nothing. So you got forty-eight hours to think on that. If you need more time, I can give you that. Something crazy is going on between us. I feel it and you feel it. I'll give you something else. Back at your apartment when that bullet zipped by your head was the first time in my career I lost focus. Everything faded away except for you and the danger you were in, and I felt fear. Bone deep fear of losing you. Of losing something special before I had the chance to really have it. I'm telling you that so you'll understand when I ask you to stay behind when we go in to get Theo you don't think I'm questioning your skills in the field. I'm questioning my ability to do my job if I know you're in danger."

I was still processing the first part of his soliloquy—no secrets, all or nothing. *And finally, I feel it and you feel it.* He was correct, I did feel *it*; whatever that it was should've scared the hell out of me. I should've run from him and the feelings he invoked, especially since I was on the most wanted list and if Harrison had his way, I'd be eating lead soon.

But I wasn't scared, and I wasn't going to run, and I wasn't going to shut down and hide.

I wanted this more than I'd ever wanted anything. A chance at something real and true. Something good and unsullied. Pure and clean with no lies and secrets. After the last ten years, I needed this and if it didn't work out, then I'd go with my original plan and live out the rest of my life alone.

Kevin's honesty freed me—not from my past, nor did it abolish my transgressions. But it freed me to be me. It gave me the strength to give him back what he'd given me—the truth.

"When I was a child, I lived in the shadows hoping no one would discover my secrets. I hid my mom's drinking. I lived in constant fear I'd be taken from her if someone found out how bad it was. Since I graduated college all I've known is deception. I was back in the shadows, only these were darker. I learned how to lie when I was five. By the time I was a teenager I was so good at it, I couldn't remember the truth. When I joined the CIA I was already a master. I'm telling *you* that, so *you'll* understand how much I appreciate your honesty. And the irony isn't lost on me— I'm a trained liar but the thing I desire most is candor. I can't remember the last time someone told me truthfully how they felt."

Still staring into Kevin's beautiful eyes, I hoped I'd get more days and months and perhaps even years to study the flecks of orange dotting the brown of his irises. More time to memorize the length of his lashes. To file away every one of his expressions so I could call them up when I needed to see his smile. I would never get that time if one of Harrison's men found me. Beyond that, Kevin or one of his teammates could get hurt or worse. And that would be worse than me dying.

"I can't go with you to get Theo. It would be too dangerous with my picture already being released. If something were to happen to one of you because of me I couldn't live with myself. As far as the rest of what you said, I don't need forty-eight hours. But I do need clarification about this touching rule. Does that include holding hands? And hugging? I liked how safe I felt when you wrapped your arms around me. And kisses to the forehead. Do I get more of those, or do I have to wait?"

That earned me an easy grin that turned into a sexy smirk. I felt that smile wash over me followed by a thrill of excitement that started in my belly—a quiver, a flood of anticipation. But it was Kevin's lips brushing my temple as they moved up to my forehead that had me squeezing my thighs together to quelch the throbbing between my legs.

"The rule is, I get to touch you," he whispered.

"That doesn't sound like a rule, it sounds like an advanced interrogation technique," I returned and shivered as Kevin's hand glided down the column of my neck. "And I believe torture was outlawed by the last administration."

"Does this feel like torture?"

I would understand his question when his mouth dropped to the sensitive skin below my ear and he pressed his lips there.

"Yes," I breathed, barely holding onto the moan that was fighting to slip free.

"Good."

His warm breath skated over my flesh and since I was fighting to stay quiet, I had no energy left to stop the shiver.

"Why's that good?"

Kevin shifted so his lips were directly over my ear, I could hear and feel his labored breaths, and that, too, excited me. Knowing I wasn't alone in my desire caused wetness to surge. Knowing that Kevin was so affected he couldn't control his breathing caused my pussy to convulse.

And wow, that had never happened to me.

"You get I talk straight?"

I sucked in a breath and nodded.

"Are you ready to hear me explain why I like you clenching your thighs? Why I like you not being able to hide your reaction to me? Why I like knowing all I need to do is kiss your neck and you squirm? Why I like knowing that while my dick is hard and throbbing in my pants, I have no doubt you're slick and wet for me?"

I shook my head, not ready to know any of that, not while he'd imposed a no-touching rule. Not after he'd already told me going back to the lavatory wasn't an option. I was too afraid if he kept speaking, I'd crawl into his lap and do something I'd regret later—like rub myself on him until I found a cure for the ache he'd created.

But then suddenly I had to know. I stopped shaking my head and started nodding.

He pressed another closed mouth kiss under my ear that wasn't chaste, and I was sure he hadn't meant it to be, seeing as he said he liked me squirming and that was exactly what I was doing.

"The torture is waiting," he started. "Right now you want more than just my lips on you. You want to feel my tongue glide down your neck. You want to feel it trace your nipples. You want to know if, when I get them in my mouth, I'll be gentle or if I'll scrape my teeth until you cry out in pleasure. You want my mouth on yours and between your legs and in the next forty-eight hours you're gonna spend time thinking about where you want it first. You're gonna wonder what it will feel like when I get my hands under your clothes, and you're gonna spend time thinking about what it's gonna be like when you touch me. The anticipation of that's gonna drive you crazy."

Holy mother of God.

The mini-orgasm Kevin had inspired was better than any self-induced orgasm I'd ever experienced, and unfortunately, those were the only kind I'd ever had —until now.

"And while I'm going crazy with anticipation what will you be doing?"

Sweet baby Jesus, why did my voice sound so husky?

"I'll be thinking about the reward."

"I think we should stop talking about this."

"Yeah, we should," Kevin agreed.

But he didn't pull away. He gave me another soft kiss, then another, until he reached where my neck met my shoulder, and his tongue came out for a taste.

More torture.

"Forty-eight hours," he growled. "Then I'm gonna devour you."

As far as I was concerned, he could devour me right then and there. Hell, I was on the verge of begging. There was zero possibility I'd be able to hold out.

I startled when Kevin suddenly lifted his head and moved back to his seat. He grabbed my hand out of my lap and rested it on his thigh. All of this was done so quickly I was left dazed and confused.

"Sit back, baby, and tell me about your team."

Was he serious?

"Um."

Kevin gave me an award-winning smile. He knew he'd muddled my head and left me in a state of need. I narrowed my eyes then the bastard winked.

"You suck," I mumbled.

"I'm hoping you do, too."

It took me a moment to understand his retort.

His rule was no touching.

He said nothing about verbal taunts.

And two could play his game.

I shrugged and sat back in the comfortable leather chair. Flying on a private jet really was the way to go. The leg room was especially nice, so I took advantage of it and crossed my legs. Kevin's gaze dropped to my lap, so I made a show of squeezing my thighs together.

"Oh, I do. And I like knowing for the next two days you'll be wondering what it'll feel like to have my mouth on you. You'll wonder if I'll start slow and tease the tip or if I'll glide my tongue down your shaft getting you nice and wet. You'll spend time thinking about how good it's gonna feel like when I swallow around—"

"Layla," he growled a warning.

I couldn't stop the bubble of giddy laughter that escaped. I took a moment to marvel in the knowledge that for the first time in my forty-five years on earth I was actually giddy about something. I smiled and laughed and gloried in the beauty of the moment.

16

"YOU LOOK like you're in pain."

I glanced over to Zane and debated my chances of getting in a solid kick to his balls before he kicked my ass. Normally I'd have a sixty-forty shot in my favor. But right then with the worst case of blue balls I'd ever had, I figured my chances had been significantly lowered and there was a good chance I'd need to ice my dick before we left to get Theo.

"I'm pretty sure you're supposed to seek medical attention for an erection lasting more than four hours," Gabe tossed out.

"He's ten hours past that," Cooper correctly noted. "At this point, he might need a trauma physician to take a look at it."

That might've been the truth.

"Unless he wants his cock to fall off, I suggest not seeking any medical care while we're in the Syunik Providence." Garrett looked up from his laptop and gave me an evil smile. "You're just gonna have to tuck—"

"Can we stop talking about my dick and get back to work?"

Thank God, Layla was upstairs and in the shower and not present for the current discussion.

"Are you going to be able to work?" Zane smirked. "You do know we're headed into a battle and not going to a swordfight, right?"

I resisted the urge to roll my eyes at my boss's lame attempt at a joke.

"But if we were, Kevin there just might win."

Great, now Owen was joining in.

"You know, sometimes I lie in bed at night and wonder if your woman still thinks about my—"

"Swear to God," Owen grunted. "If you say *meat*, I'm gonna punch you in your dick, then we won't have to worry about you poking someone's eye out with that thing."

And with that, my work was done. All attention went back to Garrett's screen, giving me the opportunity to adjust my still-stiff dick without my team staring at me.

"What's the compound look like?" I asked and leaned over Cooper's shoulder for a better look.

"We keep calling it a compound but it's nothing more than an abandoned homestead. Sat images show two intact dwellings and six nearby partial structures."

Garrett zoomed in on the satellite picture. He was being generous calling the mounds of concrete and cinderblocks structures. They may at one time have been houses but now they were nothing more than rubble. It was the two homes still standing that gave me pause. They were completely unprotected at the base of the Artsvanik Reservoir, which was actually a tailing dump for heavy metals. The stench of gray water and toxic waste had been bad at the Kapan Airport and even though we were now more than ten miles away in a house near the Azerbaijan border I could still smell the rotten egg scent that perfumed the air. I could understand why someone would abandon the homestead; the sulfur smell would be nasty at the base of the mountain.

"How sure are we Theo's being kept there?" Gabe asked what I was thinking. "Holding an HVT in that location would be insane. We take the high ground and drop down and there's no stopping us. The ridge to the west of the buildings is a perfect sniper perch. Hell, even Owen could get a clean head shot from there."

Owen didn't bother acknowledging Gabe's jab. As the saying goes, only a little man is worried if other people think he's little. Owen knew he could out-range Gabe with a headshot, thus there was no need to respond.

"All of the intel points to that location. Kira tracked the money." Garrett minimized the sat image and pulled up a file with rows of numbers. "This is a list of Harrison's accounts. Which, I have to say, it's impressive that Kira was able to track these accounts. Five countries, five banks, she hacked them all and cross-referenced the deposits and transfers out and hacked those accounts, too. We have a complete accounting for the last ten years. But Theo's snatch-and-grab was paid in cash, actual U.S. currency. See these numbers here?" Garrett pointed to a column. "Those are serial numbers. Remember on the plane Kira and Layla were talking about Jonas tracking the money? Well, they meant that literally. Not only was Jonas able to tag trackers onto the suitcases, but all the paper notes were scanned."

"How the hell is that possible?" Owen asked.

"It's not as hard as you'd think," Garrett returned. "But it would take time. You know the cash counting machine banks use? Jonas would have had something similar to that; set the notes in the machine and it rolls through. Instead of counting the money, it scans. Kira tracks that money. Harrison paid for the grab with cash that was scanned six years ago. The serial numbers match the money from the sale of drugs from an op in Pakistan."

"Cash is king," Gabe muttered.

Garrett jolted at Gabe's offhanded comment.

"That's what Cash used to say," Garrett said softly. "Before an op, he'd belt out 'Cash is king'. He said it was his good luck mantra."

Garrett shook his head, the movement jerky like he was trying to dislodge the memory. I glanced around and the rest of the team was staring at him with concern. Even Zane looked like he was at a loss for words. There was nothing any of us could say that would make this easier for Garrett. Zane was right; demons always have a way of sneaking up on you and Garrett's were now in his face whether he was ready for them or not.

"Wait. Six years ago?" I asked. "Leif was still alive six years ago. Did Harrison find Leif's stash?"

"Remember Layla said they thought there was someone higher on the food chain than Leif? I was thinking about how easily Harrison slid into Leif's role. So I started digging deeper into Harrison's accounts. I'd bet that cash was Harrison's cut from the op in Pakistan. I think they've had the top dog for the last four years and they didn't realize it."

"We'll circle back to this," Zane cut in. "Verify the location first."

Garrett pulled up a new file and started scrolling through images until he found the one he wanted.

"That's Harrison meeting with Armen Apcar, a low-level terrorist. So low I wouldn't call him and his group terrorists; they're criminals who terrorize in the name of the Justice Commandos of the Armenian Genocide even though JCAG hasn't been active since the eighties. In reality, Apcar and his group kidnap wealthy travelers and make their money from ransoms."

Was it bad luck that Theo happened to be in Turkey at the same time as Harrison or had Harrison known Theo was alive and went to Turkey looking for him?

"So Theo caught Harrison paying Apcar for his abduction," I noted. "Did Harrison know Theo was in Turkey or did Theo know he'd be there?"

"Neither." Garrett scrolled through more images stopping on a picture of crates. "Theo was there tracking a shipment of medical supplies that had been hijacked."

"Why was he tracking medical supplies?" Cooper asked.

"First, I have to say, Layla's intel is detailed. As in so detailed, Harrison is beyond fucked with the four years' worth of dirt she has on him. They have his whole network plotted out and the guy had his hand in everything. If it could be sold on the black market, he sold it. He uses his CIA assets to get him what he wants. The agents get paid from the U.S. government for the intel they give, then they double dip and tell Harrison when shipments of drugs or weapons are being moved. Harrison uses that information and the resources he's built to seize the shipments. Not for the government, for himself, then his assets sell what he stole. He works with warlords in Africa to steal humanitarian aid. That's where these crates of medical supplies came from, Eritrea. Two weeks prior to being in Turkey Theo was in Ethiopia when he got word one of the warlords Harrison was known to work with was on the move. Theo followed him, then marked the crates before they were sold. He followed the medical supplies to Turkey. Harrison happened to be there. Theo reported seeing Harrison but didn't think Harrison spotted him. Layla did some digging and found that Theo was wrong. Harrison did see him and contacted Apcar to take out Theo. She warned Theo but he was sure it wouldn't be an issue and stayed in Turkey. No idea how he actually got snatched but obviously they got the drop on him."

Jesus, I needed the color-coded note cards I teased Layla about. How in the hell had Harrison been able to fly under the radar for ten years? And if she'd been able to amass all this intel why the hell hadn't they taken him down sooner?

"Why wasn't Harrison taken out years ago?" Owen asked the million-dollar question. "Or were they still looking for the top dog?"

"We wanted his whole network to crumble," Layla said from behind me.

I turned and was momentarily stupefied.

The first time I saw Layla she was dressed to the nines. Designer outfit, heels, perfectly styled hair, face full of makeup, and expensive jewelry. Since then, I'd seen her in jeans and a t-shirt, no jewelry, makeup no longer perfect and the same with her hair. But she looked no less beautiful than when she was perfectly put together.

Now she was freshly showered, hair still wet and hanging loose around her shoulders, no makeup, bare feet, another pair of jeans, and a clean t-shirt. She didn't look beautiful, she looked absolutely stunning. This was the real Layla—no armor, no hiding behind her professional getup. Fresh-faced and so damn pretty.

"Feel better?" I asked.

"Yes. Thank you."

Her gaze shifted around the room, none of her normal confidence present. Every part of her called to me—her strength and her vulnerability. Her high-maintenance persona and her innocent girl-next-door look.

I hadn't had a chance to broach the topic of Layla with Garrett but thankfully after their talk he didn't seem to hold a grudge, and if he did, I'd figure out a way to make him okay with my relationship with her. My gut told me, she was my once-in-a-lifetime shot at finding something special. He'd understand that. He had a woman in his hometown he was still in love with—his one and only. Hopefully, Garrett facing his old teammates would finally put to rest whatever was eating him, and he'd go home and get his girl. *That's assuming she's available to get.*

"You chop off the head another grows back," Zane sneered.

"Yes," Layla agreed. "We wanted to make it so no one else could step in and take over. You know, in the beginning, I wanted to believe it was an isolated incident of a case officer paying a terrorist by mistake. Then Leif blackmailed Theo and I still wanted to believe it was one bad apple. But when Theo approached Ashcroft and presented his theory, Ashcroft already had his own concerns. Someone had anonymously sent him footage of an aid drop. The crates were marked Peakon which is an American relief charity. The drop was supposed to be full of MREs and other aid. However, it was a shipment of handguns. And before you ask, no, I don't know who sent the footage to Ashcroft. Not only was it concerning—what was supposed to be relief aid was actually guns—but Peakon's Chief of Operations was a distant relative of Leif Robinson's. A cousin by marriage on his mother's side."

Layla paused and sucked in a breath. When she let it out she locked eyes with Garrett.

"It was a rabbit hole. The more we looked into Leif

the more we found, none of it good. And when we mapped out his contacts our mission shifted. As we collected evidence, we also started working with foreign governments to take out traffickers, dealers, thieves. You name it and Leif was buying, selling, and trading with it. Humans, drugs, water, medical supplies, guns, ammo, missiles, anything that would make him money. It took us longer than we thought but we were doing important work. And each time we took out a cog Leif had to scramble to repair what we'd done. We should've stopped when Leif was taken out." Layla's right brow lifted, and her lips twitched before she went on. "But then Harrison took over and the guys were already in deep, so we continued."

Garrett stood from the kitchen table he'd used to set up his laptop and files and moved to stand in front of Layla.

"I read your reports."

"We should've—"

"Stop saying that. You and your team did the right thing. I'm a little amazed at what y'all accomplished. I already told you I'm not mad. I was shocked and didn't handle that well. It's murky water under a bridge I should-n't've burned. That's on me to repair. Our mission is to grab Theo and get him home. After that, I'll help you tie this up and Zane will handle Harrison from there. You'll bring your team home, and we'll get you off the Matrix. But we need to talk about Harrison."

The guilt I'd felt slid away and relief flooded hearing Garrett tell Layla he understood. It was also good to hear he'd wanted to repair the situation with his former teammates.

"What about him?"

"I think you missed something," he told her.

Layla's eyes narrowed and she shook her head. "I *missed* something?"

No one missed her disdain at the prospect she'd overlooked a piece of the puzzle.

"She kinda looks like she's pissed but I can't tell since she's throwing love vibes at Kevin," Gabe mock whispered.

"I might throw something sharp at you if you don't let Garrett finish."

She didn't deny throwing love vibes my way.

"Damn, killer, no need for violence." Gabe smiled.

"You know, just once I'd like to get through a briefing that didn't disintegrate into useless barbs."

Five sets of eyes swung to Zane.

"Is he joking?" Cooper asked.

"He says that like he's not the one who disintegrates the conversation," Owen noted.

"If I had a dollar for every time he turned the topic to condoms I wouldn't need to work," Gabe added.

"Dude, you're filthy rich and don't need to work," Cooper pointed out.

And damn but that was the truth. Gabe was loaded.

"Yeah, and that reminds me, stop coming to my house for dinner, you freeloader."

"What can I say, your woman's a damn fine cook. Pretty to look at, too."

"You're now permanently cut off."

Layla sidestepped Garrett and came to my side. As soon as she did, I hooked her around the waist and pulled her closer. And since I had nothing to hide, I slid my arm around her and left it there.

It took her a moment to settle in but when she did, she had a smile on her face.

"I see they do this often," she said.

"They do," I confirmed.

"Perhaps Zane should incorporate some of my rules into his handbook. I feel like if he adopted the no-fun rule more work would get done."

I smiled at that.

"It doesn't take long for them to burn themselves out."

"What are you two over there whispering about?"

I looked over Layla's head at Owen and answered, "About how awesome I am."

Layla lifted her hand and patted my chest. The gesture was innocent, nothing more than a friendly slap, yet my heart started to beat a little faster.

I hadn't even kissed the woman yet. I hadn't done more than touch her face and tease her with a few brushes of my mouth. I hadn't seen her naked body or felt it pressed against mine. Yet her hand on my chest set the rest of me on fire.

And if I was being honest, I liked that. Layla was different, infinitely different from any woman I'd ever spent time with. Sure, there was a spark of lust when I first saw her; she was gorgeous. But within minutes it had morphed into something more. And within a few hours, I was fighting to control my feelings.

"He's lying. We were talking about how I don't miss things."

Her head tipped back and I looked down to see her eyes glittering with humor.

I dropped a kiss to her forehead and reluctantly pulled back. The control it took not to dip lower and take her mouth was astounding. Waiting until we got back to the States was going to be more than torture—it was going to take a miracle.

"Hate to say it, but you missed something this time." Garrett brought the conversation back around.

Layla stiffened and asked, "What'd I miss?"

I gave her hip a squeeze, but she didn't take her gaze off Garrett. She wasn't used to messing up, that much was obvious. But the way she'd turned to stone was concerning. What the hell did she think was going to happen?

"Harrison was the senior officer. You didn't look back far enough."

As soon as Garrett stopped talking the stiffness in Layla's body took on a whole new level of rigidity.

"I looked," she defended herself. "We confirmed Leif turned two years before we started investigating him."

"Correct. But I think it was Harrison who turned him. Which makes me wonder if Harrison had someone else in play and something happened, and Harrison was left without his patsy so he approached Leif. Maybe Harrison knew about Leif's connection to Peakon and wanted to use the charity to move product. There's an account you didn't find."

"What?" Layla whispered.

"Woman, you're standing over there clinging to your man like someone's gonna drag you out and strap you to a whipping pole," Zane ground out. "I'm trying to figure out if you're one of those overachievers and that's why you look scared to death or if someone in the past made you think you're not allowed to fuck up."

"I'm not allowed to fuck up," she shot back.

Zane rolled his eyes and smirked.

"Is that one of your rules?"

Layla dropped her head and looked at the cement floor. The house Garrett had found for us was dirty and barebones but was off-grid and secure. Thankfully we wouldn't be there longer than it would take to go pick up Theo. Which would be happening in a few hours when Kira's contact would have a drone up and ready for us to use.

"Yes," she hissed. "That's one of my rules."

"She needs—"

"Nope!" I cut off Zane before he could say something that would embarrass Layla and piss me off.

"I was going to say a day at the spa so she could relax," he lied.

"What account did I miss?"

"Kira marked small transfers out of Leif's accounts. The dollar amounts are low but there are dozens of them a month."

"Yeah, we couldn't figure out where they were going. Leif had a large network; we had to focus on the big picture and not chase down a few thousand dollars here and there that went into separate accounts."

"Right. Totally understandable and that's why I think Harrison was the big dog. Those accounts all belong to Harrison. He's smart. New account for each transfer, then he transfers the money out and closes the account. But I found an account with eighty-seven million in it. The account is eighteen years old. That goes back eight years before your investigation, six years before Leif hit the scene. And when I looked back there were thousands of small transfers into the account along with big ones from other sources. So what happened twelve years ago that made Harrison turn Leif?"

The lengths criminals go to hide their money was dumbfounding. The effort it took to be dishonest was a full-time job which begged the question—how the hell did Harrison get any actual CIA work done? And how in the fuck had he been at this for eighteen years and no one knew?

"I don't..." Layla trailed off then she jerked her shoulders back and shook her head. "No."

"No, what?" Garrett inquired.

"An officer, Louis Patterson, died. He had a heart attack. But that can't be it. Louis was a great guy. Friendly to everyone. Married, five kids, madly in love with his wife. He told anyone who would listen how wonderful she was. Called her Wonder Woman for taking care of the house and kids while he was on assignment. He used to say when he retired, he was taking her on one of those yearlong cruises."

For a woman who worked in intelligence, specifically the CIA, where the building was full of trained liars, she sure did sound naïve. She should've known better than anyone that people are rarely who they seem.

"So what you're saying is, you don't want to find out a great man, a family man with a wife and five kids who tells his co-workers how great his wife is, is really a traitor and corrupt?" I asked.

"Yes, that's what I'm saying," she murmured. "I also don't want to mistakenly accuse someone."

"I'll look into him. And the truth is, the guy's dead, so there's not much we could do. Leif's also dead. And if we only use the last ten years' worth of intel, Harrison's going down. Y'all wrapped him up nice and tight."

"Did I miss anything else?" Layla asked.

The hitch in her voice was telling.

And what it said was, we'd be having a serious conversation about why she was being so hard on herself. No one liked to fuck up. And in her line of work, fucking up could lead to very bad things. But Zane was right; Layla looked like her world had come to an end, or alternately, someone was going to give her a lashing.

"I admit, in the beginning, I didn't want to be, but I'm impressed. Your intel is thorough. Your team in the field took down a lot of bad men. And Kira, she's a shockingly good hacker. But not as good as I am. Which reminds me, she and I will be having a discussion about her fucking around on my system."

Before I could ask Garrett what Kira had done, his laptop started ringing.

"Speak of the devil."

Garrett moved back to the table and the rest of my team followed.

When we had a smidgeon of privacy, I turned Layla to face me.

"We don't have time to talk about it now, but we will be talking about it when we have time."

"Talking about what?"

"How you reacted to missing something."

Layla's face went expressionless. My eyes narrowed in response to the bullshit I'd hoped we were past.

"I don't like messing up."

"First, don't hide your emotions from me. If you're pissed at me then show me. Don't put that mask back on. Secondly, no one likes fucking up, baby. But your reaction to Garrett pointing it out was borderline over the top. You went solid in my arms and you looked afraid. No one in this room is going to judge you. No one's going to think less of you. You don't need to shield yourself from them and certainly not me."

"I wasn't afraid someone was going to judge me," she spat, and I was happy to see her anger boil to the surface. "And I'm sure my reaction was extreme. I have five men relying on me. Five men who have trusted me for ten years. And now they're on the verge of finally coming home and I find out I missed something. I can't miss things, Kevin. I have to bring them home. *All* of them."

Fuck. I hadn't thought about that.

"They're all gonna come home, Layla, promise."

The anger slid out of her features, and she stared up at me with so much trust it stole my breath.

"Thank you."

Without thinking, I lowered my head and pressed my lips against hers.

If there had been any doubt that I was now a true-blue believer in Kismet that kiss would've erased it.

17

MY LIPS WERE STILL TINGLING from Kevin's closed-mouth peck on the lips. I was fairly certain when he'd taken his lips off of mine, he'd somehow pulled my soul out of my body and my heart, too.

It was an impossible notion, but I'd felt it happen. I knew it sounded crazy, and if someone had told me that I'd fall in love at a glance I would've laughed. Not to their face, of course, that would be rude. But later in the privacy of my home, I would've laughed hysterically. As a matter of fact, I felt like tossing out my no-fun rule—oh, who was I kidding, that rule was toast. I'd laughed and smiled more in the last few days than I had in the last few years.

"I'm just saying, Garrett, you have a weak spot." I heard Kira and was pulled back into the room. "His name is Zane Lewis and he watches far too many YouTube videos on how to butcher animals."

The man in question shrugged and stared at the laptop screen.

"What? I'm always up to learning new techniques.

Gotta keep my skills sharp, you never know when I'll have to perform a good old-fashioned disembowelment."

There was something deeply disturbing about that. Mostly because I knew he wasn't joking despite him chuckling.

"And what's with all the searches on condom jokes?" Kira continued.

"Damn, woman! Can't a man have some privacy?"

"I knew you didn't make all those jokes up yourself," Owen huffed. "You're not that witty."

"Owen's been searching for real estate," Kira ratted him out.

"You better not tell Nat or you'll find yourself back in the naughty corner," Owen snarled.

Damn, the man sounded serious. It was time for me to put a stop to this.

No-fun Layla to the rescue.

"Other than snooping on the guys' internet searches did you find anything useful?"

"Useful?" Kira huffed. "We haven't gotten to Kevin's searches yet, Bosslady. We're talking butt plugs and flavored lube. How's that for useful?"

My alarmed eyes shot to Kevin.

Kevin was wearing one of his sexy, movie star smiles.

I glanced around the rest of the room to see them all smiling as well.

"Kevin's ass fetish has been outted." Owen whooped. "Payback is so sweet, even if it wasn't me who instigated it."

Kevin still hadn't said anything to deny he'd been searching for butt plugs on the internet.

"You're such a motherfucker!" Cooper blurted out.

And that was when Kevin lost it—full-blown raucous laughter thundered out of him. So much so his arms wrapped around his middle and he bent at the waist. The rest of the room watched him. Everyone was still smiling. Zane and Garrett joined in and chuckled. But Cooper looked perturbed.

"For six fucking months I've been getting butt plugs in the mail—*weekly*. I hope that shit cost you a whack!"

At Cooper's proclamation, the rest of the guys busted out laughing, too. I didn't laugh, I felt great relief that Kevin hadn't been ordering butt plugs for himself. I was all for "to each their own" but a hard piece of plastic wasn't going near my booty.

"But did you keep them?" Kevin asked.

"You know Coop's got a drawer full of butt plugs." Gabe snickered. "Hope one of your women don't snoop or you'll have some explaining to do."

One of his women? How many women did Cooper have?

"Well, damn, I was hoping Kevin was some sort of Kink God," Kira muttered, sounding completely dejected.

A rush of jealousy hit, hot and unwanted.

"Did you show Bronson the pictures?" I snapped.

"Yep. And we have a winner. 'Liam Martin' is Scumbag Numero Uno, Harrison Washington."

I wanted to sigh and maybe scold Kira for not starting with that important tidbit of information.

"Glad we got that cleared up and confirmed. Harrison's first attempt to flush Theo out was using his brother. Is Bronson still alive?"

"Alive but a little bruised up. They've stopped throwing rocks at him. Lincoln and Scary Max spent a few hours interrogating him. They didn't get anything new. I guess tomorrow starts what Max calls reprogramming. It sounds a little sci-fi, so I'm sitting in on the relearning sessions." She used air quotes and wagged her eyebrows. "Maybe they'll teach me something new."

"I don't think I want you learning how to reprogram a person. You're scary enough behind your keyboard."

"Right! You should explain this to Linc. He's irritating and is going to find his identity on the dark web if he doesn't start being nice to me."

Oh, shit.

"You shouldn't do that," I told her, and at the same time Kevin asked, "Have you met his wife?"

"Jasmin? Oh, yeah, she's a riot. I have a full-on girl crush. She's given me permission. I guess she's been asking him to take her car in to get new tires and he keeps putting it off."

My gaze skidded to Zane's. He was staring at my cyber specialist like she was the most awesome person on the planet—besides his wife, Ivy, of course. He would be no help, so I looked at Garrett. He was frowning. Perfect.

"Can you cut off her internet access from here? She might be serious."

"I'm gonna do more than cut off her access if she doesn't get out of my office," he growled.

Someone was touchy about their things being...well, touched.

"Any-who, the drone's up. Realtime footage is now available for your viewing pleasure."

"What has gotten into you?" I asked.

Kira was naturally funny. I was as close to her as I'd allowed myself to be. But I'd never seen her playful. Was it me who'd staunched her personality all these years? My no-fun rule was self-imposed, but I'd stopped her when she'd cracked jokes.

"I learned something when Two was taken and I should've learned it when my brother was murdered. Life's too fuckin' short, Bosslady. We've spent ten years on this project. So many hours, I've lost track. We've been so mission-focused both of us forgot we were living, breathing humans who should be having a real life instead of working twenty-four-seven. I'm just ready for this to be over. Maybe have a date that's not just me and a bag of popcorn for dinner. I think I'm the only woman in her thirties who's had sex with only two men and not in recent memory. I want our guys home, Harrison nailed to a cross, and to get laid. In that order and hopefully soon."

All the men in the room looked uncomfortable except for Zane.

"My guys are off-limits, Kira. No joke."

Kira's gaze went to Cooper and she mumbled, "Well, that's a damn shame."

"She says that knowing he's got twenty-four butt plugs at his house. Brave or kinky. I'm not sure which."

Kira looked at Gabe and winked. "Maybe a little of both."

"On that note," Garrett grumbled. "You're done. Thanks for the drone, now get out of my office."

"Jeez! Someone's got their undies in a bunch."

"I don't wear undies," Garrett told her.

"Neither do I," Coop noted and winked at Kira.

Oh, boy, those two are going to be trouble.

"How about we stop poking the bear when I need him to go get Theo?" I suggested.

"Right. I'll poke him later. Maybe Cooper can—"

Garrett exited out of the video feed, cutting Kira off midsentence. I thought that wise since there was no telling what was going to come out of her mouth next.

"We're out the door in two hours," Zane announced and left the small dining area.

The rest of the men scattered, leaving me, Garrett, and Kevin the only ones standing around the table.

"You should go take a nap, too," I told Garrett. "I'll keep an eye on the drone and wake you up if I see anything."

Garrett scrubbed his face, looking more tired than he did when we arrived at the house. We'd been traveling over twenty-three hours; he and Zane were the only two who hadn't slept on one of the three planes we'd used to get to Armenia.

I glanced down at my watch. A little after five in the morning East Coast time, meaning Garrett had been up at least twenty-four hours. The mission to rescue Theo was set to happen just after sunset. If Garrett was lucky and he knocked right out he'd get a solid hour of sleep before he had to get ready.

"Appreciate the offer but an hour's not gonna do anything. I'll sleep on the way home."

"Right," I mused. "Once a SEAL always a SEAL. Or I should say once a Special Operator always a Special Operator? Y'all are the same. The Scorpions who worked my base in Afghanistan were the same as the GB guys I worked with in Syria. They could be up for thirty hours prepping for a mission, be out six hours and come back, then pull out their secret stash of hootch and sit around a barrel fire for hours before they racked out."

"I don't remember you out in the field," Garrett said.

Kevin came close and when he did his arm went around my lower back and his hand settled on my hip. I wanted to sigh like a silly schoolgirl at his embrace. I'd gone from nothing and no one to obsessed with Kevin's nearness. I was so used to being by myself, so sure I'd spend the rest of my life alone, I never considered how good it would feel to have someone at my side. But Kevin wasn't just *someone*, he was meant to be *mine*. He was the man who would make me whole. And I wasn't ashamed to admit, I was *that* woman. The kind of woman who needed a man to help her find her way. In my professional life, I was competent and well-respected, very powerful men and women listened to me. They valued my opinions; they were impressed with the intelligence I gathered. It was exhausting. I worked ten-hour days at the Pentagon and gave ten hours to my team. I barely slept, I barely ate, and I absolutely didn't think about my emotional wellbeing. Everyone else came before me. So, yes, I was one of those women who was so stressed, so full of anxiety, that I needed a strong man at my side to help carry some of the burden.

I leaned into Kevin and answered Garrett, "I never worked with your team. Though it was my intel that led the Drifter squad to capturing Casper."

"No shit?" Garrett's head tilted to the side and he smiled as if remembering something fondly. "That was a good op. We'd been sent out three times to grab Awan, the intel was always wrong. We weren't exactly optimists when we were sent out a fourth time. But damn if he wasn't there. He was shocked as fuck when we entered. I'll never forget the look on his face. He was eating dinner. We came in and he put his hands up."

I was proud of that capture. Casper's IEDs had killed a lot of Afghani soldiers and injured American servicemen and civilians. It took me months to track down someone who had good intel.

"All part of the game in the sandbox. Everyone wants CIA money and will tell one truth for every three lies. It takes a long time to weed through the bullshit."

"Bet you're happy you're out."

"I am," I confirmed. "And when my team's home, I'll be out for good."

Kevin's hand on my hip tightened, but he stayed silent.

"Seriously? You're out?"

"Until recently, ten years working two jobs. Burning the candle at both ends has taken too much from me. During the day I have to play a game I don't like. Lies and secrets. Then I'd go home and spend hours scouring through reports my guys send from the field, having to read about the dredges of humanity, follow the intel to more scum of the earth, and devise plans to take them down. One would think it's rewarding to know that they had a hand in taking down some seriously horrible people. But at the end of the day, it takes too much. I can't unsee and unknow what I know; my mind will forever be clogged with the horrors that happen around the world. There is no peace for me, but I have a shot at finding balance and some happiness. Once my team's safe, I'm done."

I hadn't realized Kevin had gone solid next to me until I was done speaking. I turned to look at him and found he was already staring at me.

"You got the recon?" Kevin asked, not taking his eyes off of me.

"Sure do," Garrett returned.

"See you in an hour."

Kevin slid his arm free but tagged my hand and gave it a firm yank. Next thing I knew he was dragging me across the small living room. He didn't slow when we hit the stairs—up we went, Kevin dragging me behind him. The door to the room I'd used to shower was open. Kevin entered, closed the door, and turned the lock, then I found myself with my back against that door, Kevin's palms flat against it on either side of me.

What in the world was happening?

"How quiet can you be?"

He asked his question as his mouth was descending toward mine. All things considered, I was more than a little confused.

"What?"

Kevin stopped his descent, his mouth a hair's breadth away from mine. So close I could feel his breath on my lips, and there was something so intimate about it that I felt my body heating up.

"We're not gonna make it forty-eight hours."

He spoke those words against my lips; I heard *and* felt them. The vibration ricocheted through me from top to bottom; from my scalp all the way down to my toes, my skin prickled with awareness.

"We're not?"

"Thought I could, but I can't. So, how quiet can you be?"

"You thought you could, but you can't?"

Kevin didn't answer, he diverted his lips instead. This would've made me incredibly sad had he not detoured to my throat. Along with that, one of his hands went to my hip, the other gathered my hair in his fist and he used his grip to tilt my head.

"Say yes."

I had no idea what he wanted me to say yes to but my answer was a no-brainer. Which was a good thing because I could barely think straight.

"Yes."

My answer was not met with the response I had expected. Kevin immediately pushed away from me, his gaze slid from my face, down to my chest, then lower to my jeans. His right hand reached around his back and moments later he came back with his wallet. He pulled out a small square packet then promptly tossed his wallet to the floor.

"Clothes off, Layla."

Three growled words that made my already damp panties drenched.

I didn't take my clothes off. I didn't take a single breath as I watched Kevin take his shirt off. And when his bare chest came into view I inhaled sharply at the sight. His body was perfection—washboard abs, chiseled pecs, broad shoulders. Every woman's fantasy.

When his fingers went to the button of his cargo pants, I caught the slight tremor in his hand. There was something about seeing that tremor that made my desire skyrocket. It also spurred me into action. I pushed away from the door, tore my shirt off, and went to work on my jeans. I was in my bra and panties by the time Kevin had toed off his boots and discarded his pants.

And there both of us were, standing in nothing but our underwear. My arms hung at my sides, hands empty. Kevin was the same except he had a condom in his right hand. Neither of us moved, both of us riveted, taking in the sights before us. My eyes roamed, eating up the magnificence before me. Kevin did the same. I wondered if he could feel my eyes on him the same way I could feel his. Each time his gaze skimmed over me I could feel it, the same as if he were using his fingertips.

I hoped he could.

The longer we stared at each other the more I needed to know, so I asked him, "Can you feel it, too?"

His gaze that had been focused on my chest came up and our eyes locked. No, not our eyes, our connection. The one we'd felt days ago when we first saw each other. An enigmatic connection that I was beginning to think was destiny. We were supposed to meet. There was a reason that no man had ever interested me before him. I'd never felt a spark that set off an explosion of emotions. I'd never felt desire this acute. Kevin didn't need to touch me for my body to be ready for him. All he needed to do was look at me.

"Oh, yeah," he whispered.

"You can feel my eyes on you? Because I swear it feels like you're touching me and you're two feet away from me."

That space was eaten up when Kevin moved—not only the two feet that had separated us, but *all* the space. My chest was pressed tight against his, my arms went around his shoulders, and my hands journeyed up and down his back, relishing in his warm, firm skin. The pads of his fingers dug into my sides, I felt the corner of the condom packet scrape my skin, and as odd as it was, I thought that felt erotic. A reminder of what was to come. The promise of pleasure. I melted deeper into Kevin, my hips automatically seeking his hard length I could feel resting on my stomach. I did not need, nor did I want, foreplay.

I wanted Kevin.

"Kev—"

"What is it about you?"

"I don't know."

"I'm standing here with you in my arms, and I still can't believe you're real. I need you to be sure about this, baby. I need to know that when this is over, you're not gonna run from me. This right here, what's happening between us, means something to me."

My heart wanted to swoon at this big, former Navy SEAL sharing his feelings openly. I didn't have to ask to know that was not something he normally did. My head could barely process what he'd admitted. My soul simply sighed.

Destiny. Fate. Magic. I didn't care what had brought us together. But at that moment looking at him, feeling him, breathing him in, everything changed for me. I'd thought it had happened on the plane. I'd been wrong. It might've started then, but it wasn't until that very moment that I knew with absolute clarity I would never run from Kevin.

"You're my forever," I whispered. "My balance."

Kevin's mouth slammed onto mine, his tongue swept my bottom lip, but before I could process how good that felt his hand slipped into my panties and his finger slid through my wetness. His tongue surged in my mouth and at the same time, two fingers breached my opening. Kevin didn't start slow and give me time to get my bearings. His kiss was only slightly better than what was happening between my legs and that was only because the taste of him was so intoxicating I was lightheaded. I did my best to keep up with his plundering. My tongue danced with his until I couldn't anymore because his thumb was rubbing slow torturous circles over my clit.

I moaned in his mouth as the pleasure mounted. And by the time my orgasm broke, I knew I wasn't being quiet when Kevin took a deep kiss even deeper. Plundering turned into devouring as he used our kiss to stifle the sounds of my excitement.

The buildup was fast, but it rolled through me in waves of ecstasy.

Best orgasm ever.

Kevin broke the kiss and my eyes slowly drifted open. Then I was moving, but it wasn't my feet doing the work. Kevin had swept me off my feet—literally and figuratively.

His knee went to the mattress, taking me with him until we were in the middle. I felt my back hit the mattress I immediately wrapped my legs around his hips and his face went to my neck. His tongue swept down to the place where my shoulder met my neck, his teeth grazed the skin there, and a blaze lit inside of me. My nails scraped down his back, my hips lifted off the bed, and I ground against his erection. The friction felt so good I moaned.

"Unwrap your legs."

I did as he asked and unhooked my ankles, letting my legs fall open.

As soon as I did, I was rewarded. Kevin yanked the cup of my bra down and his tongue circled my nipple before he drew it into his mouth. That felt so good I arched, and he pulled my nipple deeper. He let go and moved to the other side. The same thing happened; he pulled my bra out of the way, and the moment my breast was exposed he pulled that nipple into his mouth and fire erupted.

"Holy...I...need—"

I didn't finish, not that I had anything coherent to say. But whatever it was I was going to babble died when Kevin's head came up.

Unbridled hunger heated his gaze.

His jaw was set, his expression severe. He looked like he was holding onto his control by the skin of his teeth. I didn't want him to hold back. I needed all of him and I knew how I was going to get it. I reached between us and bucked my hips. Thankfully, Kevin read me and shifted so I could shimmy out of my panties. I was too far gone to be graceful; I was sure there was nothing sexy about the way I wiggled and kicked my legs. And as soon as my panties were kicked to the side, I attacked.

My hands went for his boxers, my mouth went to his

chest. I kissed and licked every part of him I could reach. I clawed and pulled and yanked until his erection was freed, then I gave up pulling at his boxers and wrapped my hand around his hard length, and began to stroke. He was long and thick and when my thumb grazed the leaking tip I heard it—a rumble that started in his stomach and vibrated up to his chest before he growled out the sexy sound that spurred me on. I found his nipple with my tongue and circled it the same way he had mine. I moved to the other side and sucked.

And that did it.

Kevin went in search of the condom I'd dropped on the bed. I knew he found it when he knocked my hand out of the way. I didn't see him tear open the foil, I didn't watch him roll it down his cock, I was too busy memorizing his beautiful body. I wasn't nearly done with my exploration when his arm went under me and he lifted me off the bed, so I shifted my lips higher and tasted his neck. My legs automatically went around him as he came up on his knees and he slammed into me.

My head tipped back, but before I could scream, Kevin's mouth was on mine and his tongue swept in.

Oh. My. Lord.

I was full, so full I cried out and it was only partly muffled by his mouth. Kevin stilled and I panted.

He waited and I panted some more.

Throughout this, we were not kissing. Our mouths were connected, our lips lingered, but we were simply breathing each other in. It was the single most extraordinary experience of my life. It was a closeness that I couldn't explain. It was sheer harmony and exhilaration mixed together.

Kevin's hand on my ass squeezed and I nodded.

A wordless answer to his silent question.

Totally in sync.

He pitched forward and controlled our fall back to the bed.

A slow slide out, a hard glide in, and I moaned.

He stayed planted deep and pulled his lips from mine.

"I see you can't be quiet."

I would've been concerned if all I had to go on was the gruffness of his tone, but he was smiling down at me. This was altogether a new smile—a sex-fueled, wolfish smile that topped his sexy movie star grin.

"Seems not."

"Right."

Kevin shifted his weight to his elbow and cupped my cheek with his now-free hand.

"Earlier I was thinking about how beautiful you are," he said, and as he did, he pulled out a few inches and slowly rocked back into me. "I thought about how sexy you look in your fancy skirt and blouse, all made up." Another slow glide in and out. "How pretty you looked when we were at The Cape." A hard rock in and out. "How stunning you looked after your shower with your hair wet and no make-up." He hitched my leg up higher and thrust deeper. "But this right here, the way you're looking at me, the blush on your cheeks is hot as fuck, baby." He pulled out all the way to the tip and slammed back in, leaving me gasping. "Gonna need you to find a way to be quiet, Layla. And since I wanna look at your beautiful face when you come for me you need to find a way to be quiet. Can you do that for me?"

I was in serious doubt, but since he thought I was beautiful and I liked that so much I'd do my best even though I was pretty sure I'd fail I still nodded.

Soon I found not only was I going to fail, but I was

going to do it spectacularly and that was because minutes later, with my teeth biting my bottom lip, I was moaning.

"Fuck it."

Everything that had been slow and measured turned into fierce and punishing.

"Wrap me up tighter, baby."

I locked my ankles and dug my heels into his lower back, rocking into thrusts as he powered down. My fingernails dug in, too. I was holding on and while I was, my body came alive. Every part of me was sensitized and with every drive of his cock, I became more aware. Deeply aware, scarily aware. I felt him inside out. I felt him everywhere.

"Harder," I whispered.

Kevin's drives became more powerful but as they did his thumb swept the apple of my cheek sweetly. A whisper-soft touch that was contrasting to how roughly he was taking me.

Soft and rough.

Balance.

I felt him thrusting, I felt my thighs burning from holding him so tight, I felt my pussy flutter, but I was suspended in the beauty of the moment. Floating while Kevin kept me grounded. Out of my body even though I was under his.

I was there, right there, on the edge, but instead of looking down, I was looking up straight into the eyes of the man who'd never let me go.

I could jump and he'd catch me.

I knew it.

I felt it.

So, I let go and fell. I fell, and fell, and fell.

My mouth opened on a silent scream, and I came apart.

This orgasm didn't slowly roll through me. It was sharp and painful and ripped my insides out.

It was glorious.

It was earth-shattering.

It was so good, I was so lost, that I barely came back to myself to witness the last of Kevin's. His eyes were at half-mast, his muscles bunched, his jaw clenched, and he twitched as his release poured into me.

Beautiful.

I waited until his eyes fully opened before I moved. When I unlocked my ankles and let my feet fall to the bed, I groaned when my muscles protested.

"I see the way to keep you quiet is to fuck you so hard you can't breathe."

He wasn't wrong.

And I was too relaxed to prepare a snappy comeback.

So instead, I glared up at him. But even that took too much energy so my glare fizzled out before it could be effective.

"Are you okay, baby?"

"I'm perfect," I whispered.

"That you are." He dropped a kiss to my forehead then said, "I'm gonna go clean up. You've got an hour to sleep. I'll wake you up before we head out."

Suddenly I was thrust back to reality.

"No, I'm fine. I need to get up."

"Layla—"

"No, really, I'm fine. If I nap, I'll just be groggy. I'm your eyes in the sky tonight; I need to be sharp."

Kevin stared down at me a beat then slowly pulled out. The loss of him and his heat sent a chill over my skin. Fortunately, this didn't last long when he rolled off the bed, reached back, and plucked me off the mattress.

"You wanna shower with me?"

"Will showering with you result in an orgasm?"

"You just had two."

"Is it a rule I only get two a day?"

Kevin shook his head and laughed. While he did I stood staring up at him, memorizing every nuance. I was pretty sure I looked like a lovesick puppy while I did it. I was also sure I didn't give a shit.

And boy was I glad I did.

If I had known how long that memory had to last me, I would've stared harder. I wouldn't have let him drag me to the bathroom and into the shower. And as spectacular as my third orgasm of the day was, I still would've watched him smile just a bit longer.

18

I HAD Zane at my side, Layla and Kira in my ear, and a drone overhead, and I still had a bad feeling.

Before we left the house we'd discussed the possibility of Theo being used as bait. But if Harrison didn't know about Patheon and the other guys, which Garrett confirmed there was no evidence suggesting he did, then who was the trap for? Layla? But that didn't make sense either. Harrison had known for months that Theo was alive.

"One, you and Cooper have movement at your three o'clock, hold fast." I heard Layla over the coms.

Garrett and Cooper were on approach from the east side of the property. Gabe was a hundred yards out to the north in a sniper position. Owen was to the south three hundred yards out and on a higher peak. He'd have the best vantage point from his position and was overwatch. Zane and I were coming over the west ridge and I was right—the smell closer to the reservoir was putrid.

"Copy," Garrett returned.

"All's still quiet," Kira added.

She was monitoring local chatter, something she'd done

since Theo was taken. He was seen—or Armen Apcar was seen—dragging a hooded, bound man out of a van and into the larger of the two houses.

No positive confirmation.

No blueprints of the structures.

No weeks of careful planning.

That had to be why the ball in my gut was growing by the second.

"Jesus, that stinks," Zane griped.

Thankfully, the air was cool but the breeze coming from the southwest was blowing the rancid sulfur smell off the reservoir. It was like it was chasing us down the mountain.

"We're almost in the valley," I noted. "At least it'll block the wind."

We had three hundred yards to go before we hit the gorge that would take us to the back of the property. Armen's homestead was surrounded.

Something was wrong.

I tapped my chest, triple-checking I'd remembered to load my vest with plates. I moved my hand across my extra magazine—all four of them loaded and secure. I touched my thigh rig, Sig holstered, my .308 in my hand. I could feel my ankle holster tucked under my cargos and my knife was on my belt.

"Brother, you got a nervous tic?"

"I feel like I'm missing something," I admitted.

"By the sounds I heard, about a gallon of—"

"Don't," I warned.

"Don't what? Tell you that you shook that rickety old house with your bedroom gymnastics? Seriously, though, I'm impressed. It was like a two-point-five earthquake," Zane continued.

"Two-point-five?" Garrett asked. "I was downstairs and

it felt more like five-point-one. I think some of the ceiling crumbled."

"You all know I'm on the line and can hear you, right?" Layla came back on.

"Damn," Kira whined. "Now it's official. I'm the only one not getting any. Though, way to go, Bosslady. Breaking your dry spell with a five-point-one."

"You're fired," Layla hissed.

Fucking hell.

"Doesn't work," Zane told Layla. "I've fired all these fuckers at least twice and they don't leave. I don't know what's wrong with them; I'm a total asshole and you'd think they'd be happy I fired them. But, nope, they stick around."

"You've never fired me," Coop noted.

"That's because you're my favorite. You keep your dick to yourself."

"Opposed to what?" Layla joined in. "Do the rest of your men chase you around the office with theirs?"

"It would really suck if I busted a gut and alerted the bad guys to my location," Gabe grunted. "Maybe we can, you know, grab Theo and bolt before someone catches on we're here. I'd like to be back on a plane in less than an hour."

"Yes. Rule number seven: no fun on an op," I announced.

"Damn, I like you," Layla muttered.

My step faltered and my chest started to burn. Obviously, I knew she liked me. But hearing her say it in a sweet, low tone made it sound like she more than *liked* me. For the life of me, with all the flights we'd taken and the time zone changes, I couldn't remember what day it was. I thought we were moving into our third day knowing each other but time for us didn't seem to matter.

I more than liked her and I was well on my way to falling in love.

Zane slapped me on the back and propelled me forward. After a couple of yards, he whispered so no one else could hear.

"Happy for you."

It was a barely-there waft of a sound, but I heard it.

For all of Zane's sarcasm and gruff talk, the man was a softy.

"Thanks, brother."

"We got eyes on the house," Zane called in our location.

Thirty yards.

And that fucking rock in my gut just wouldn't quit.

"How we looking, Ghost One?" Garrett asked.

I smiled at Garrett using Layla's call sign. It gave me hope when the time came, he'd be ready for Cash, Easton, Smith, and Jonas.

"You're all clear for entry."

"Ready," Owen called.

"Ready," Gabe followed.

"Your call, Z," Cooper invited.

"Hold," Zane ordered.

It was just after sunset, with a first-quarter moon giving us enough light to maneuver but plenty of shadows. On Zane's order, Garrett and Coop would break north and take the small house. Zane and I would take the larger house where we assumed Theo was being held.

Assumed.

Fuck. I hated that word.

No confirmation.

"You good?" Zane tapped his mic off and asked as we approached our final checkpoint before entry.

I followed suit, taking a huge risk having a conversation so close to the target, but I couldn't let this go.

"Gotta feeling we're missing something."

"Brother, there's a lotta shit we're missing. Status FUBAR when dealing with the fucknuts at the agency. There's always an ulterior motive. Something buried under so many layers of shit you'll be digging for years before you find the answer and when you do it'll be so unbelievable you wish you wouldn't have wasted your time."

Damn if he wasn't right.

"This isn't that. This feels sloppy. If Garrett's right, Harrison's been at this a long fuckin' time. And suddenly he decides to show his hand? He personally visits Bronson, knowing he can be identified. He personally meets with Armen, knowing Theo's in Turkey. And if he knew where he was, why not kill him right then? Why send Bronson to fuck with you? Why not nab Bronson and put the word out he had him? If Harrison wanted Theo to break cover that would've been the fastest way. Why put Layla on the Matrix list when he could've taken her out a hundred times over?" *Christ, that thought makes me sick to my stomach.* "And why kidnap Theo? Why not just kill him?"

"Harrison wants the intel and evidence," Zane surmised. "He doesn't know if Layla and Theo are working alone. Killing them doesn't do him any good if he goes down."

"Okay. But then why put Layla on the kill list?"

"This is one of those times when digging for a reason one of those assholes does anything they do is gonna give you a fuckin' migraine. Either Theo's here and we're taking him home, or we take out a bunch of bad guys and go home empty-handed. For your woman's sake, I hope Theo's here.

The alternative is, he's buried somewhere between Turkey and Armenia."

I hoped like fuck Theo wasn't dead. Not only because that would mean a good man lost his life after he'd given the last ten years to a mission that I wasn't so sure was worth it. A one-team crusade to flush out corruption at the CIA. But Theo's death would haunt Layla. She'd put undue blame on herself.

"What if Theo allowed himself to be captured? A Hail Mary to end a long game? He lasted ten years in the field. No backup. Totally alone. And suddenly a low-level criminal gets the drop on him? Doesn't seem right."

"Fuck," Zane snarled. He reached up and tapped his mic before he asked, "Ghost One, do you copy?"

"Copy."

"Before we hit this is there anything you haven't told us?"

"Negative."

I believed that Layla wouldn't allow us to walk into a trap. If she had the slightest inclination Theo's kidnapping was a setup, she would've said so. But I was beginning to wonder if Theo had gone rogue. Got fed up with waiting and wanted to nail Harrison. But the end was near; Layla had said they were wrapping up and ready for the take-down. Impatience? No, Theo was a special operator; he'd have patience in spades.

Fucking hell, I was confusing myself with all the different scenarios I should've been running back at the house before we geared up for the mission. Instead, I'd been buried balls deep inside Layla's sweet body. I couldn't find an ounce of regret for that, but I should've been paying more attention to the mission. Now I was playing Monday morning quarterback, tactical style *while* on the battlefield *before* the mission.

Totally fucked.

"Thirty minutes until you lose sky watch. Then you're waiting three hours for new eyes," Kira warned.

"Team Two, standby," Zane ordered.

"Copy."

Garrett sounded aggravated at the delay. He spent a lot of time behind his computer and in the last few years he'd only gone out into the field a couple of times. He must've forgotten the hurry-up-and-wait. Not that we often discussed the particulars of an operation while we were executing said mission. And by often, I meant never. We were always prepared. Backup plans for backup plans. Multiple infil and exfil points.

We were flying blind.

Fuck it.

"We're good. Let's grab the package and roll."

I flicked my mic back on, adjusted my rifle, and exhaled.

It took more effort than it normally did, but once I found it—the bump of adrenaline, the headspace needed to turn off the noise and focus solely on my mission—I slipped into it naturally. A familiar place where instinct took over.

"On my count." Zane didn't wait for anyone to respond. "Three, two, go."

Zane took point, I was on his heels, and he wasted no time eating up the last ten yards to the back door. We needed to time this right.

Shock and awe.

Zane's favorite way to kick a door in. One of the reasons we were going in at dusk, not in the middle of the night. Bad guys expected bad things to happen in the dead of night. They didn't expect visitors at dinnertime.

Zane jerked his head to the blacked-out window, telling me something I already knew—flying fucking blind. I turned to the side, watching Zane's six as he easily picked the lock. I felt him tap my shoulder, slowly turned back to the door, and bold as brass Zane Lewis clomped into the house. He didn't go easy, he didn't take his time and move silently like I knew he could, he just walked into the motherfucking house like he owned it.

Crazy motherfucker.

I heard movement to my right and peeked around the corner. Two men—*not Theo or Armen*—were getting up from a kitchen table. My gaze swung around the room; I saw half a dozen rifles in the corner leaning against the wall. That was good enough for me to feel my life was in danger. I popped off two rounds and both men went down.

Shots fired meant we'd officially popped the cherry and woken up the cavalry.

"Two down," I called in my kills.

The rest of the kitchen was clear. I moved into the living area. Nice furniture, huge wall-mounted flat-screen TV, artwork on the walls. It would seem Armen did well in the kidnap and ransom business. There was a volley of gunfire from the house next door then three pops closer.

"Three down." Zane came over the coms. "Second floor clear."

"Four down, one woman," Garrett announced. "Moving to the second floor."

"Anyone got eyes on the target or package?" Zane asked.

Cooper and Garrett replied in the negative and I continued to scan the room—no electronics other than the TV, tables littered with trash including ashtrays of cigarette butts, no doors. I made my way back through the kitchen, ignoring the two dead guys, and found a utility room full of junk, but no tangos.

"I got a closed door in a room behind the kitchen," I called in.

I heard two short whistles behind me. What I had not heard were Zane's footsteps. Meaning the crazy bastard could be deadly quiet when he wanted to be.

As soon as I felt his hand on my shoulder I reached for the knob, turned it slowly, and dropped to a knee, the barrel of my .308 up and at the ready as soon as the door creaked open. Zane was right behind me going high.

Empty.

Dirt floor with a four-by-eight sheet of plywood lying in the middle of the room. I got to my feet, took two steps in, and stopped.

"Smell that?" I asked.

"All I smell is dirt."

I sniffed again. Mixed with the clean, earthy smell was tobacco. The kind that would cling to the clothes of a pack-a-day smoker.

"Watch the door," I told Zane and moved farther into the room. No windows, only one way out.

"Status." I heard Layla's sweet voice in my ear and for the first time since I'd entered the house, my heart started to beat faster.

And that was all it took to trigger the rock in my stomach to roll.

I listened to my teammates all call in their updates. No sign of Theo or Armen.

I toed the edge of the board, moving it a few inches.

"So that's it?" I started. "Nine guys. Five here, four in the other house. No Armen, no Theo. No hooded hostage? No computers..." I trailed off when I saw something on the ground that made my heart cease beating. I stepped back and blinked, praying the sliver of an opening was a mirage. An ill-timed flashback to Afghanistan.

When I opened my eyes, it was still there.

"Well, fuck me running with a camel on my back," Zane mumbled.

"Team Two, we have a tunnel if you're done—"

"Stay put, Team Two. Three vehicles approaching from the south. Still on the road but moving slowly," Owen called in.

"Copy," Cooper answered then went on. "We have blood over here and not a little. Bathtub is covered. Bedroom upstairs has a bloody mattress, sheets, towels. But no body. We bagged a few phones, took fingerprints and pictures."

Fucking shit.

"Bag a towel," Layla clipped.

"Layla—"

"I'm good."

She didn't sound good but before I could radio her back Zane gestured to the hole that had been partially uncovered as he moved around the board and slowly pulled the board away. Every inch he uncovered made my chest burn. I hated tunnels, despised them more than anything. The closest I'd come to dying had been in a tunnel in Afghanistan. Nothing good came from going underground.

With the barrel of my rifle pointed down into a dark abyss, I sucked in the musty air knowing my ass was going into that goddamn hole. In the teams we had options—send a K9 in first or toss a few T-bombs in the hole and frag out the bad guys. But we didn't have a dog and we couldn't throw a grenade down there not knowing where Theo was.

Once again, flying fucking blind.

"I'll take point. Cover me."

Zane flipped on the flashlight on the rail of his AR and I was happy to see one of us had our shit together since I hadn't even thought about engaging mine.

I was too busy staring into a dark hole.

Zane didn't wait for my reply before he used the ladder to descend.

Goddamn it.

"Team One's engaging the tunnel," I radioed.

"One vehicle passed the property," Owen updated. "Two have pulled to the side of the road. Team Two, continue to hold. I don't have a lock on the drivers. Ghost One standby, I'll try to get images for you to run."

Good call on Owen's part. No one wanted to take out innocent bystanders who happened to stop someplace dangerous.

"Wait for—"

I really hated to do it but I interrupted Layla. "Z's down. I'm going in."

"Long and empty." Zane's whispered voice sounded in my ear.

As quickly as I could I navigated down the ladder. The air temperature immediately dropped and the smell of mold and decay hit my nostrils.

At least it smells different than Afghanistan.

"Goddamn, I hate tunnels," Zane voiced my exact thought.

"Yep."

"You good?"

"Fuck no. Let's hurry this up so we can get out."

We silently made our way farther into the tunnel that didn't seem to end but was getting narrower, and before long we could no longer walk side by side.

"They got lazy," Z muttered from in front of me.

He wasn't wrong—the tunnel was getting smaller and smaller height-wise as well as width.

Sweat trickled down my back and my skin started to crawl.

This was wrong. All the signs were there. It started as a bad feeling; now that sixth sense that had never failed me was blaring a warning in my head. I reached for the back of Zane's vest to pull him to a stop, but before I could he halted and looked down.

"Fuck, Goddamn!"

I followed his gaze and saw the broken wire. There was no telling what Zane had inadvertently set off. Booby trap? An alarm? An explosive device?

"Two, do you copy?"

All I heard was static and a few broken words that didn't make sense.

"Go!"

I didn't look to see what had Zane spooked; I turn and ran. When I heard Zane's boots pounding dirt behind me I kicked it up a notch and hauled ass.

I heard the boom from above us before I felt it. A beat later debris started falling from the ceiling of the cave.

A second blast echoed in the tunnel. My first thought was this was gonna hurt. I didn't get a second thought before the concussion hit and everything went black.

19

"GET US ANOTHER DRONE!" I half-yelled, half-panted as I ran down the street.

I needed a goddamn car. Why the hell were there no goddamn cars on this street?

"Get back to the house." Lincoln wasn't half yelling in my ear, he was just yelling.

"If you can't get us a drone call Sheep Dog and get a satellite."

"I'm working on it." Kira sounded almost as out of breath as I was, and she was behind a desk in Maryland.

Finally, a fucking car.

"Hang on."

I lowered my phone from my ear, used the butt of my gun, and smashed the window. I waited a beat and when there was no alarm, I reached in and popped the lock. I didn't bother brushing the broken glass off the seat before I slid in and slammed the door.

"Okay, back." I cradled the phone with my shoulder and pulled my knife out of my back pocket.

"Was that glass breaking?" Lincoln asked.

"I might never get to visit Russia after this," Kira announced. "I got into a satellite but I didn't have time to bounce my connection and I got in sloppy. If I wind up in the Black Dolphin it was nice knowing you."

The Black Dolphin was the most notorious prison in Russia, the worst of the worst criminals were housed there. And as much as I wanted to assure my friend she wouldn't get locked up with cannibals and murderers, I was running low on patience.

The last thing I saw before I ran out the door was the second RPG hit the house Kevin and Zane were in. Minutes later when I finally got my hands to stop shaking enough to call Kira for an update, we'd lost the live drone footage. I didn't know what had caused the feed to cut early and I didn't care, all I wanted was eyes on the property.

"Fuck. Goddamn," Lincoln growled.

"What do you see?"

I had the plastic underneath the steering column off and was feeling around for wires, *while* trying not to drop my phone, *while* my heart felt like it was pounding out of my chest, *while* trying to hotwire a car in the dark and do it before the owner came out and found me.

Please God, let Kevin and Zane be alive.

"Get back to the house and wait for extraction. I'm sending a team."

That wasn't going to happen.

"I have to set the phone down."

I heard Linc still yelling when I tossed the phone onto the seat next to me and leaned to the side.

I needed to find the red wires.

"Come on, find the red wires, Layla," I whispered out loud.

My fingers felt too stiff, my legs trembled from running, I was fumbling more than I was making progress.

I closed my eyes and pinched my eyelids together until I saw white spots behind my lids.

Pull your shit together.

Breathe, you need to get to Kevin.

On a long exhale, I opened my eyes and found the wiring harness for the ignition. I inhaled and slowly felt around for the other bundle of wires.

Come on...

There!

I used my knife to slice through the wires then stripped the plastic coating off. I tossed my knife and touched the battery wires with the ignition wire and the sweetest sound ever filled my ears.

Success.

Thank the Lord for old nineteen-nineties Hondas.

I put the car in drive, hit the accelerator, reached over, and grabbed my phone.

"Back. Anything new?"

"What the fuck just happened?"

"Has anyone ever told you, you yell more than your brother?" I asked instead of answering.

"The image is total shit, but we have visuals on One, Cooper, Owen, and Gabe."

"What's the ETA on locals?"

"They might beat you there," Kira told me, and I pushed down on the gas. "I've sent some messages out to assets we have in the area."

I needed to get there before the road was blocked off.

What if I'm too late? What if Kevin and Zane are already dead? No one could survive two direct hits from an RPG.

Please, God.

Please, please, *please, I'm begging you, please let Kevin and Zane be alive. Please don't take him from me.*

"Where are you?" Kira inquired. "I'm not used to not being able to track you."

Shit. I forgot I was on a burner phone.

"I'm passing the hotel by the airport."

"What's the word?" I heard someone ask on Kira and Lincoln's end.

The road I was on narrowed down to two lanes. Rundown houses on one side, beautiful countryside on the other, both flew past in a blur.

Please don't let Kevin die.

"No communication with Zane or Kevin. The team's digging through the rubble," Lincoln answered.

"Gold's geared up and ready to roll."

"Kira?"

"Yeah, Bosslady?"

"Call Ashcroft. I'm calling in my marker."

"Lay—"

"Do it. Turn everything we have over. And call the guys in."

My order was met with silence.

I checked the rearview mirror and didn't see anyone behind me. No first responders, no police, no other cars. The one damn time I wanted the locals to intervene they weren't showing up; how's that for fucked-up luck?

I rounded a bend and saw the haze of smoke.

That sight alone caused my eyes to water.

He has to be alive.

"Layla, we don't even know—"

"Kira!" I snapped. "I love you, girl, but I'm the TL. This is done. Do you understand me, fucking *done*. Tell Ashcroft to turn everything we have over, as is. Then pull my goddamn team from the field and get them on standby and ready to roll out on my orders. One way or another this is over. And if Kevin and Zane are..." I stopped just short of saying the words that couldn't be true. I couldn't accept them to be true. "Just get me my team and if Ashcroft has an issue with it you remind him about Libya, and you tell him this is my payback for that. I expect someone to burn in hell for this and if Ashcroft's gotta use his resources then he damn well better start calling in favors now."

"I'll have the team ready within the hour," she returned softly.

"Thanks, honey." I tried to use the same soft tone she had, but I failed. The words felt like sandpaper as they came out of my throat.

"Brooks already had Gold Team ready to go," Linc argued.

"Great, then we'll have three teams. But I'm not waiting for Gold to get here, so you might be wasting your time. I gotta go, I'm here."

I didn't bother to disconnect when I threw my phone on the passenger seat and I prayed Kira was smart enough to give the guys the heads up I was on the way because I was coming in hot and I really didn't want to be riddled with bullets.

The poor old Honda fishtailed when I made the turn off the paved road on the dirt lane that led down to the homestead. I held my breath and prepared to dive under the dash if one of the men started firing. Fortunately, that didn't happen. Unfortunately, the brakes sucked, and my ungraceful arrival included me smashing into a tree. Okay, so it was more of a minor collision, but the car was toast, and a newer model would've had airbag deployment.

Please let Kevin be alive.

I tried to open the door, and after three attempts, I gave up and climbed out the broken window. I ran toward the smoldering pile of rubble.

Rubble.

Kevin and Zane were under there.

I skidded to a stop and my gaze locked with Garrett's.

Fury was written all over him.

I didn't dare look at anyone else.

I couldn't.

I did the only thing I could do.

I went to work.

Stone by stone. Brick by brick.

I dug.

Please don't let me find him only to lose him.

20

Garrett

Garrett looked down at his phone, feeling heavy fatigue and a fear he hadn't felt in a very long time. The kind of fear that wormed its way into your veins. The kind that ate at your insides until they were raw. The kind that if you let it would bring you to your knees.

He glanced up and looked at the house, or what was left of the house. It had been reduced to a pile of wreckage.

It had been hours and Layla was still pawing at the debris, dedicated to her task of digging Kevin out.

Kira had worked magic. When the cops arrived not one of them asked why a group of Americans were at a known criminal's house. Nor had they asked how the house had exploded. An hour into us digging by hand, a man with a backhoe had shown up and carefully started moving the large sections of concrete.

That man who hadn't introduced himself was still working and Layla was still digging by hand. She was in the way, but no one had the heart to tell her to stop.

The woman was a fucking mess.

Any doubt Garrett had about her loyalty was gone.

Layla was getting down into that tunnel one way or another and she was not going to stop until the last stone was moved. It was what they were going to find when they got in there that made Garrett feel like he'd swallowed battery acid.

The still-ringing phone in his hand was a different kind of problem. One he wasn't ready to face but no longer had the option of putting off.

You never should've put it off, you fucking coward.

"Easton?" Garrett's greeting was met with silence. "You there?"

"Goddamn, brother, it's good to hear your voice."

That scored through Garrett, leaving painful shards of shrapnel in his chest. Kira had warned him Easton was going to call; he'd had hours to prepare yet he wasn't. The guilt Garrett had preserved over the years swelled, the regret still as fresh as the day he quit his team and left without warning.

He couldn't even remember why he'd done it, why he'd tucked tail and ran like a pussy. Finn Winters, that was why. Watching Finn's head be severed from his body was why. He thought he'd fucked up, then watched Finn die because of him and he couldn't sleep, he couldn't eat, he couldn't function. So he ran. And kept running until Zane had found him and told him the truth.

But he'd turned his back on his brothers. And when they kept calling, he threw his phone away and kept running.

"You there?" Easton called out.

"Yeah, sorry." Garrett stopped to clear his throat. "I... um...fuck, Two, I don't know what to say."

"Not Two anymore." He chuckled. "Demoted, man."

Layla had mentioned no one on the team used the call sign One. That was Garrett's.

"How many times did Smith fuck that up? Remember when we first got to the unit, he made us all name tags with our numbers so he wouldn't forget?"

The memory hit hard and fast. Good times in the middle of the desert in a rundown old outpost.

"Ghost has bitched from time to time that he still calls in as Four. He's now Five and Cash is King was bumped to Six."

Speaking of Ghost, Garrett lifted his gaze from his boots to Layla. She was still shifting through the rubble.

"She's fucked-up," he started then rushed to continue. "Not physically, but her and my teammate Kevin have gotten tight. She was TOC for the mission, saw the RPGs hit, hotwired a car, hauled ass here, came in so hot she pulled a Dukes of Hazzard. It's been hours, her hands are a bloody fucking mess, and she's still trying to dig her man and my boss out."

A sudden sadness washed over Garrett, thinking about another woman he knew with the same kind of tenacity. The same blind love. But that was a long time ago and he felt like he'd lived a hundred lives since the day he'd left her. Then she left him a different way. He left and she stayed and found the life he'd always wanted for her. Solid, steady, happy, white picket fence, all the shit Garrett couldn't give her.

"That's Layla. I didn't know what to make of her when all of this started. But there's a reason why I stayed on for ten years and it ain't for the job satisfaction. When that woman sinks her teeth in, you know shit's gonna get done. If she wants to dig her man out, she won't stop until she's done it and that's a guarantee." Easton paused and when Garrett heard his inhale, he braced. "I made her do it. All this is on me. I talked Smith, Jonas, and Cash into it. They wanted her to tell you straightaway. It was me who wanted to tell you. I was pissed and fucking hurt. It was a fucked-up thing to do, I know that now. But at the time, I needed to be the one to tell you, you didn't fuck that mission, you left us for no reason."

More regret. More guilt. Did it ever stop?

"I got no call to be pissed at you. I'm the one that walked away and fucked you over. Fucked the whole team. We got shit to talk about, lots of it, and I'm hoping for that opportunity after I get my brothers outta the ground."

Garrett refused to believe Zane and Kevin were dead. He wouldn't even allow the thought to creep into his brain. They were alive—period, end of story.

"Kira said she called in Auggie for an assist. Good guy, he owns a construction company, he's been an asset for years."

So the backhoe operator's name was Auggie, good to know.

"I got word from a man I work with in Turkey," Easton continued. "He's mostly a piece of shit because he's a criminal and on Harrison's payroll but his intel has always been good. Anyway, word is Harrison's in Sarp. Beautiful seaside village on the border with Georgia. I'm in Istanbul now on my way to you, but I'm thinking I need to reroute to Sarp. I don't know if Ghost told you or not, but Harrison's favorite way to take out an enemy is with a bomb. He likes the impact, the fear it instills in those who think to double-cross him. Two RPGs, that's his style. Even if he wasn't there to personally deploy them, it's his calling card. And I don't like that he's in Turkey. Makes me think he's planning another surprise or he's running. Either way, I need to catch up with him. We didn't work this long for the fucker to slip through our fingers at the final hour."

Garrett processed the news that Harrison was in Turkey, then asked something that had plagued him since he'd started researching Theo.

"Do you think Theo let himself get taken? I read his reports. The guy's been in some tough spots before; seems unlikely a K&R criminal got the drop on him."

"Theo has one fatal flaw."

When Easton didn't continue, Garrett prompted, "And that is?"

"His morality. Even after all this time, the guy cannot see the gray. He would sacrifice himself before he allowed someone who he respects or cares about to get burned. So what I'm saying is, if Armen had something that would hurt one of us—Ghost, Sheep Dog, Zane, you, the Kid Genius— he'd turn himself over without a fight."

Garrett assumed the Kid Genius was Kira, which was a safe assumption seeing as the woman was wicked smart. She'd easily slid into Garrett's job back at HQ. He would've been more impressed if he wasn't so pissed she'd cleaned up his office. But that was an argument for another day.

A day when Kevin and Zane weren't buried alive.

"That makes more sense. You head to Sarp. What's happening with the others? Where are they?"

"Has Ghost not filled you in?"

"Brother, I told you she's fucked-up. Maybe I didn't properly express the level of fucked-up she is. She's been at it for nearly five hours. Her hands are dripping blood, if one of us gets near her she yells at us to get back. Her arms are trembling so badly I don't know how she's still throwing pieces of concrete. She hasn't stopped to drink. She hasn't spoken to any of us other than to tell us to shut up and get back to fucking work. So, to answer your question she hasn't filled us in on shit."

"She pulled the plug. Had Kira call Sheep Dog to turn in the evidence we had on Harrison and he's meeting with the president now. Now, don't get me wrong, we were wrapping up, but there were still a few loose ends we needed to tie up. But that's done now. Mission complete. You've got Jonas, Smith, and Cash en route to you. She also called in some favor Sheep Dog owed her. I don't know what that means, but the Kid Genius sounded worried, though I don't know if she knows what the favor is either. But there is one thing I do know; if something happens to your teammates, she'll set the world on fire, and she won't care if it takes her another ten years before it blazes. And that's what I'm assuming she's set in motion—if the worst case happens she'll have a plan at the ready."

Christ.

Garrett liked that for Kevin. He liked what it said about Layla. But even more, his respect grew exponentially for the crazy woman.

"Fuck, she scares me a little," Garrett joked in an attempt to loosen the knot in his chest.

"She should, brother. The woman is scary fierce. She had to be to gain the loyalty and respect of four old salty sailors with gigantic chips on their shoulders. She went all-out for Two, for Zane, for you, for her country. She gave up her life to see this through. Now her mission has shifted to your brothers. And you better believe she'll have your back on this."

Garrett saw Owen approaching so he wrapped up his call.

"Gotta get back to it. Keep me updated."

"Will do, brother. Be safe and I'll be seeing you soon."

Easton disconnected and Garrett turned his focus to Owen.

"Find anything?"

"Man, someone's gotta tranq her," Owen growled. "I cannot watch that shit anymore. She's trembling so bad she's wobbling. Kevin would be pissed as all fuck his woman was bleeding and ready to fall out. She won't give up and when she finally does pass the fuck out she's gonna be mad at herself that she did. Someone's gotta put her down and I vote that someone's you."

Owen wasn't wrong. When Layla finally did pass out from exertion, she'd consider that a weakness. It was better she woke up pissed at Garrett than think she failed.

"Find me a syringe and I'll fill you in on my call with Easton."

"Brave fucker," Owen mumbled. "You know she's gonna beat your ass when she wakes up."

"Wouldn't be the first time I've taken one for the team."

Except the time I abandoned my post and my brothers.

21

LINCOLN

Lincoln Parker stood in Zane's office and not for the first time thought he was damn proud of the man his brother had become. And that pride had nothing to do with the battalion of commandos he employed, nothing to do with the business he'd made successful, and everything to do with the family he'd built.

Zane was a man other men wanted to know. He was the type of man who inspired loyalty and that in part was why they were in this fuckup.

Theo Jackson.

A former CIA officer who had barely known Zane yet had respected him enough to make moves to protect Zane's reputation and possibly his freedom. It was debatable if Theo had made the right call, but that was for another day.

Linc had other things to do and as he stood looking out the window at the Naval Academy Chapel dome just like he'd seen his brother do a thousand times he now understood why his big brother chose this spot to contemplate his day. The view was spectacular, even in the middle of the afternoon. But it was more than the beauty of the campus or the Severn River. It was what the academy represented—the hope, the future, the young leaders who would graduate full of promise, the warriors waiting for their turn.

One day, they'll take our place and take up the fight.

And Zane was determined to leave them with something better.

"Hey, you wanted to see me?" Ivy asked as she walked into her husband's office. "What's going on down there, did they find Theo? And please tell me y'all are done with that poor idiot. I can't take another day listening to him cry."

Bronson had been a belligerent fuck, until Kira and Leo had spent some time explaining who his brother really was. After that, he'd smartened up and started to apologize for everything he'd done. Then he'd started crying when Kira told him his brother was now missing for real.

The guy was a blubbering idiot but no longer a concern.

Lincoln had more important things to worry about.

Linc turned and when he did, Ivy flinched and took a step back.

"Ivy—"

"Just..." Her hand came up, palm extended, and her eyes slowly drifted closed. "Give me a second."

The bile that had been churning in his gut the last eight hours since he'd seen the house his brother was in explode threatened to slither up his throat and choke him.

"How bad?" Ivy whispered.

"Let's sit—"

"How bad, Linc?"

Lincoln had forgotten how tough his sister-in-law was. In his own despair and anger, he'd forgotten his warrior brother had married a woman who was equally as strong as he was.

"We don't know yet, he hasn't been located."

Ivy's eyes popped open, her lip trembled, but she stood strong.

"Just tell me fast, Linc. All at once."

Linc's gaze dropped to Ivy's stomach and the stinging in his chest burned his heart.

"He told you I'm pregnant?"

Ivy was five months pregnant, and they hadn't told anyone. As soon as she was safely into her second trimester Bronson was still pulling his shit, so Zane wanted to wait to share the news with the team. But Zane had told Linc the moment they'd found out and had sworn him to secrecy. For a group of observant men, no one had noticed Ivy's wardrobe change over the last few months, but with everything going on it wasn't that surprising.

"He told me," Linc confirmed.

"He won't give up," Ivy stated. "He'll come home to me. To us."

"Damn right he will," Lincoln agreed and crossed the room.

When he got close, Ivy buried her face in his chest and he wrapped his arms around his brother's wife.

It was then, standing in his big brother's office, holding his brother's wife and unborn child, that Lincoln Parker remembered the fragility of life.

One life snug in his or her mother's womb.

The other... unknown.

22

I FELT MY SHOULDER DISLOCATE, I tasted blood, and I smelled fear.

Not mine, Armen Apcar's.

The cocky fucker's attitude changed when my hood came off.

Before he saw my face he'd had fun taunting Zane and me with all the ways he was going to torture us before he killed us. His threats were unoriginal and would've been amusing if they hadn't been joined with snide comments about how he'd captured the great Zane Lewis.

Those had stung like a motherfucker.

I admit, waking up hogtied and hooded bruised a man's ego in general, but a dipshit like Armen being able to pull it off was a whole new level of *what the fuck*. And the what-the-fucks continued from there.

"I'll take you to your friend if you tell me your name."

My friend? Did he mean Zane, or had he captured all of us?

Zane and I had been easy targets down in that goddamn tunnel. Too goddamn easy. I knew not to go down there. I fucking *knew*, felt it in my gut before we hit the house something had been wrong. I knew better than to ignore my instincts; bad shit happened when that voice says stop yet you still proceed. Bad shit like waking up on a plane with your wrists tied to your ankles and a sack over your head. The kind where you don't know where you are or how long you've been unconscious. The kind where you don't know where the rest of your team is.

And now, the kind where you worry about where your woman is and if she's safe. That last one was new for me. That was the thought that sent my blood pressure through the roof. We'd left Layla unprotected. We'd left her back at the house to watch our backs with no one watching hers.

Jesus.

If Armen—or worse, Harrison—got her, there'd be hell to pay.

"Fuck." I spat a mouthful of blood onto the concrete. "You."

Armen and his team had fucked up huge. So huge, this asshole was going to find himself dead soon.

They should've left me hooded and tied up.

Armen's stupidity or arrogance or both meant after I was tossed into this room, knocked out with what felt like a hammer to the back of my head, I'd woken up with only my hands zip-tied behind my back. If they'd done the same with Zane, whoever was guarding him was dead. This was by and far the stupidest mistake Armen had made in his life.

"What's your fucking name?" Armen shouted and landed a right hook to my ribs.

Come on, asshole, give me something good before I kill you.

"Why do you want to know my name?"

"I like to know the names of the men I kill."

Lying sack of shit.

"No one's gonna pay ransom for me if that's what you're after. I'm no one special."

"Someone already paid for you." Armen smiled.

Bullshit! Armen was worried, getting more desperate by the second. He saw my face, knew he'd nabbed the wrong guy, and now he needed to know who I was.

"How do you not know my name if someone paid you to kidnap me?"

"Kill you," he corrected and scowled.

Maybe Armen's frown coupled with his glare was supposed to be scary. Maybe he thought I was like one of the rich travelers he carjacked and kidnapped. I bet this scene would be frightening for someone who hadn't been captured and tortured by actual terrorists. Maybe he was used to shouting in people's faces and having them cower. It was obvious this guy had no idea what the fuck he was doing. I was on my feet, freely walking around a room, with only my arms zip-tied behind my back.

The only reason I hadn't killed him yet was because I wanted to know who he thought I was. He certainly didn't know my name, and something had changed when he saw my face.

"Tell me who you're supposed to kill, and I'll tell you if you have the right guy."

Two more swift punches to my middle. The guy had decent speed but there was no power. I could stand there all day and take his baby fists, but he couldn't. I wasn't sure if he was breathing heavily because he was scared or out of shape. Either way, not even five minutes into this bullshit interrogation he was winded.

"You think this is a joke?" Armen leaned closer and shouted. "This isn't a fucking joke!"

The pounding in my head intensified, reminding me my head was still jacked from multiple concussions. My ears were still ringing from the grenade that exploded so fucking close it was like God had whispered *not today* and by some miracle, we didn't die.

I needed this to be over more than I needed answers. Once the adrenaline waned, nausea would set in, and if I was unlucky so would blurry vision.

"I think *you're* a motherfucking joke!"

Armen reared back like he'd never encountered a victim that yelled back, which he probably hadn't. "Such a fucking joke you grabbed the wrong guy. So fucking stupid you thought you'd bring your fists to the fight instead of a gun."

"I can—"

Armen didn't finish. The sole of my boot connected with his gut, he stumbled back, and the dumbfuck leaned forward to catch his breath. It was as if he was begging for my knee to break his nose. Without thought, I obliged. I heard the crack, not just his nose but I'd bet his zygomatic bone shattered, too. A howl of pain was accompanied by his hands going to his face, leaving the rest of his body unprotected. I swept his legs out from under him. He rolled to his side to ball up. And that was it.

The door flew open and men rushed in.

I didn't wait for them to come to me; if I was getting my ass kicked I was taking down as many as I could.

I charged the first man, planting a kick to the outside of his knee. It buckled and as he fell, he twisted to grab the man behind him. They both started to go down when the third man shoved them out of his way and the big motherfucker started swinging. His first shot grazed my chest, but he landed the second one. Thankfully, his swing had lost some momentum seeing as the laces of my boots were now embedded in his balls. I would've felt bad for the asshole that his testicles were now lodged in his bladder if hadn't been trying to kill me.

Unfortunately, my luck had run out when the last two men jumped on me at the same time. The elbow to my fucked-up shoulder sent excruciating pain down my right shoulder and arm, all the way down to the tips of my fingers. I hadn't recovered when the second guy used my torso like a punching bag.

"Enough!"

Thank fuck!

I sucked in a pain-filled breath and immediately regretted it. Shallow breaths were all I could handle without groaning in agony. And I'd be goddamned before I made a noise that resembled pain. I gritted my teeth and looked at the newcomer.

Perfectly styled salt-and-pepper hair, nice suit, nice shoes. He looked about sixty, maybe a little younger.

Harrison Washington.

"You had one job, you stupid fuck. Just one. Bring me Zane Lewis and Garrett Davis. And you fuck up and bring me Kevin Monroe."

Well, at least Harrison knew who I was.

Bad news was he'd wanted Garrett. Good news was he didn't have Garrett, or he wouldn't've been so pissed.

"I thought—"

"That's the problem," Harrison cut Armen off. "You thought. I don't pay you to think. I pay you to execute my plans."

"You said they'd come in the middle of the night."

"Someone kill this whiny fuck!" Harrison exploded.

A moment later a gunshot rang out. I wanted to fall to my knees and praise Jesus the weapon was suppressed; one more loud noise, and I was afraid my eardrums would have permanent damage.

Harrison turned his attention to me. And the way he smiled sent a shiver down my spine. Harrison Washington wasn't stupid. He wasn't an amateur like Armen. Whatever Harrison had planned for me was going to hurt like a motherfucker.

"Chain him up."

I moved. Unfortunately, four men moved with me.

For every kick I landed, they landed four more. My body absorbed one punishing blow after the next.

I was fighting a losing battle. And as the haze and darkness started to pull me under I was still fighting. When the pain morphed into nothingness I was still standing. That was, until my vision went black.

23

MY FIST CONNECTED WITH A STRONG, hard jaw and I winced as some of the cuts on my palm opened back up.

"That's your second and last shot," Garrett growled and rubbed his chin.

"You tranq'd me, you asshole!"

"Yeah, woman, I did, and I let you get yours back, *twice*. You hit me again and I'm tranqing you *again*."

Was he fucking serious?!

"I've been asleep for seven hours!" I shouted.

"Good, now you're all rested up."

My gaze went around the room full of men. Men who didn't include Kevin and Zane but now included Easton, Smith, Jonas, and Cash. When I had awoken, I was *informed* I was now in Turkey. My team had arrived while I was still knocked out and I was *informed* it was Easton who'd gotten the lead that Harrison was in Sarp. Further, I was *informed* that Easton had scouted the house of one of Harrison's known associates, who was also an asset of ours, and found Armen and his guys already there. I was again informed that the tunnel had been undamaged and empty. When Owen and Gabe had followed it to the end, they found Zane's watch. I didn't understand the meaning, but Garrett explained that meant Zane had been alive to take it off and drop it for the team to find.

That gave me hope.

But I was more than a little angry I'd been treated like luggage and carted onto a plane, offloaded when we'd arrived, and carried into a safe house and put to bed.

I'd slept while the guys had all worked.

I'd snoozed seven hours away while Kevin was... being tortured, beaten, hurt?

Please still be alive.

"I'm all rested up?" I whispered. "Seriously, Garrett, that's what you have to say to me?"

Garrett stepped closer and I took a step back, too afraid that if he was in punching distance I'd swing again. I wasn't stupid enough to think he'd let me hit him again and smart enough to know he'd let me land the first two.

I felt hands curl around my biceps from behind me. I knew it was Jonas who had stopped my retreat when I heard his deep gravelly voice murmur, "Calm down, Ghost."

I didn't calm down, but I wanted to turn around and hug him. My gaze went to the rest of my team and now I was pissed for a new reason. Ten years ago, we'd spent seven days holed up in Ashcroft's house going over intel and the plan. Then I handed each of them a packet with multiple identities and cash and said goodbye. They were strangers to me then. But over the years I'd gotten to know them. What had started as exchanges of information turned into more. I was their handler but as the years slipped by I'd started to care for them. I hadn't seen them in person with my own eyes in ten very long years and I'd been asleep when they arrived.

I'd missed welcoming them home.

Well, not home. We were in Turkey, not the U.S., but still.

"Now what I have to say to you is gonna piss you off more than you already are, but here goes—you were in the way. You weren't gonna stop digging until you hit that tunnel and I needed the backhoe, not your hands. Which brings me to your hands; they're fucked, Layla. You were bleeding, you were shaking, you were at it for hours, exhausted and ready to fall out. Now, something you need to know about Kevin; he would lose his fucking mind if he saw what we all saw. More than that, if one of us didn't step up and take care of you he'd lose his shit in a way that would end in bloodshed. And rightfully so. You're his, which means you're ours. And we take care of our own, including tranqing them when they are causing themselves harm. So, now you're rested up and ready to roll. I assume even with your hands fucked you can still carry a rifle."

I ignored all the stuff Garrett said about Kevin losing his mind. I couldn't think about how good it felt to belong to Kevin, and through him, the rest of the guys. If I did, I'd start thinking about how scared I was to lose it. How I'd only dipped my foot in the water, but I was already drowning. I couldn't find him only to have him for a couple days then have it all be gone.

So instead, I focused on the last part and latched onto my bitchy attitude because that was better than all the guys knowing I was scared out of my head.

"Oh, so I get a gun, now?"

Unfortunately, my attitude didn't faze Garrett.

"I get it," he whispered. "I get being scared, thinking

you're gonna lose something important, *someone* you care about. I get the anger that builds. I never was any good at taking advice, so regrettably this didn't sink in when it should've, but maybe it will for you—use your anger intelligently, Layla. Use it to strengthen your resolve. You're angry Kevin's not here. We all are. We have a mission, focus your anger and come with us to get your man. And Zane, though I'm warning you, Zane likes a mess—so it's a crapshoot what we'll find. If he's gotten loose on his own, you could see intestines. He wasn't joking when he told Kira he likes to keep his skills sharp."

I really hoped that was Garrett's way of cutting the tension with a joke.

"He's not kidding," Owen said, dashing my hopes. "Brace, honey, it could be bad."

I wasn't sure how much more bad I could take.

And there was still no sign of Theo.

My fingers curled into fists, my nails dug into my scraped-up palms. The pain reminded me of the hours I'd spent moving rocks. Hours that Kevin and Zane had spent with Armen.

And I suddenly got it.

Everything faded away except for you and the danger you were in, and I felt fear. Bone-deep fear of losing you. Of losing something special before I had the chance to really have it.

I had not felt the exhaustion, I hadn't felt the rocks as they cut into my palms, I hadn't felt anything except bone-deep fear of losing Kevin. I wouldn't have stopped digging. I would've kept going, slowing down the process because I'd been single-minded in my terror.

Garrett was right, I needed to focus my anger and fear, or I'd be a liability. I'd get in the way and slow them down.

I wouldn't risk losing my something special.

"I'm sorry," I told Garrett. "Not for punching you but for being a bitch."

"Right."

"And thank you for sorting me out."

"Anytime."

Apparently, the guys had all been waiting on me, not so patiently it would seem.

"Here." I'd barely looked in Gabe's direction when he tossed me a vest.

"You're loaded and ready to go." Cooper pointed to the table and my eyes followed. "We found Kevin's .308 in the tunnel. You good with iron sights?"

My throat started to burn.

"Yes."

I pulled the vest on over my black sweatshirt and adjusted the webbing on the sides. It was loose but would have to do. I reached down to the table and started loading the full magazines into the front pockets.

When I was done, Owen walked over and nudged my shoulder. "My lucky knife. Do us a favor and don't get yourself killed."

"Copy that." I took the knife and shoved it in my pocket. He turned to walk away but before he got far, I reached out and grabbed his forearm. "Thanks."

"He's tough. You know that, right?"

I wasn't sure where Owen was going with this, but I wasn't sure I could handle much more.

"I know."

"No, Layla, he's tough—hardheaded, straightforward, bossy, stubborn. He needed someone who he could go toe-to-toe with him. He needed someone just as tough and stubborn as him. He wouldn't mean to do it, but he'd walk all over a sweet, docile woman. He needed an equal, someone to keep him in check." Owen paused and dipped his chin. "I'm pleased as fuck he finally found it. And not just because I now get to pay him back for busting my balls about Natasha. Though when we get him back, I'll give you a hundred bucks if the first thing you whisper into his ear is *meat*."

Um...what?

"I'm hoping there's a story behind that and you're not a closet weirdo."

Owen's smile told me I was right, there was a story, and as much as I really, *really* wanted to hear it—no, I wanted to hear all the stories. I wanted backyard barbeques, and dinner parties, and other times besides. I wanted to listen to Kevin and his friends laugh and tell a hundred stories. But right then I wanted to get on the road and bring back Kevin and Zane.

"Aren't we all closet weirdos?"

"No, Owen, having a peculiar fascination with meat is a whole nother level of strange."

"I'll pitch in a hundred if you tell him meat," Gabe added from the other room.

"Shit, I'll talk Zane into expensing your honeymoon if the first thing to say to Kevin is meat." Garrett laughed.

My honeymoon.

God, I wanted a honeymoon so bad.

And that was just bizarre. Not because I just met Kevin, because a week ago I'd convinced myself I was going to grow old and die alone, and now I couldn't imagine my life alone if something happened to Kevin. I might walk the earth, but my soul would leave with Kevin.

Please, God, let them be okay.

"I have no idea what the hell y'all are talking about. I mean, I'm a meat-eater but..."

I didn't get the rest of my sentence out before four grown men dissolved into a bunch of cackling, little boys.

Whatever. At least they were all strapping on gear while they laughed themselves stupid.

I nabbed Kevin's Springfield off the coffee table and paused. The weight of the weapon settled my rioting thoughts. I wished like hell Kevin was still in possession of his rifle, or better yet it had been used to dispatch the assholes in the tunnel who had taken him and Zane. But if the .308 wasn't in her rightful owner's hands, I was happy she was in mine. There would be a certain justice in that. There was only one thing I wanted more than putting a round between Armen's eyes and that was Kevin coming home safe and whole. Okay, two things—I wanted Zane and all his snark and sarcasm to come home safe, too.

I made my way across the room to Easton, Smith, and Cash. I looked around but didn't see Jonas.

"He stepped out to make a call," Easton told me as I approached.

"Kira?"

"Yeah. She was freaking out the last time we checked in," Cash told me.

"Freaking out?"

Kira didn't freak out; she was levelheaded and calm, always.

"Sweetheart, she got word you were knocked out and she freaked the fuck out and threatened her cyber-geek shit that she swears will be more painful than an airport rectal exam. I'm not sure she understands that TSA doesn't actually crawl up your ass, it's a figure of speech, but she was carrying on, so Jonas went to call her to update her on your status." Smith smiled.

I felt tears wet my lashes. Everything hitting me all at once. I'd been so lost for so many years I hadn't recognized or considered that Kira cared about me enough to freak the fuck out, as Easton had put it.

"Sorry." I waved a hand in front of my face.

"A lot going on. How're you holdin' up?" Easton inquired.

"I was gonna ask you the same."

Easton's gaze went over my shoulder and I knew he was staring at Garrett.

"Shit time for a reunion. Not how any of us wanted it to go, but we're all good. Right now we gotta common goal, we're focusing on that. Everything else we'll deal with later."

"And the team? I mean Coop, Owen, and Gabe. They were cool with you guys?"

Easton's face gentled and he gave me a sad smile.

"Their concern was you. Now it's Kevin, Zane, and you. They welcomed our help. We spent some time going over the op and that's as far as we got."

"Easton, listen—"

"Later, Layla. We're rolling out of here any minute. Best case is, Theo's locked up with Zane and Kevin. If he's not, me and the team go hunting. But for you, it's over. You're on a plane home with your man."

"And if I don't want that?" I snapped.

"You do, sweetheart. You want it so badly you called the mission," Cash reminded me.

Guilt clawed at my stomach. I'd kept the team out for years longer than we'd thought.

"Get that look off your face," Easton started and

grabbed my hand. "Something I don't think you ever understood, we were all-in to follow you anywhere you wanted to take us for as long as you wanted us there. But Garrett was right; it's time someone stepped up and took care of you. You're our TL, we should've been paying closer attention to you. We fucked up and put the mission before you. And by the way, don't be mad at Garrett, it was me who told him you wouldn't stop digging your man out. We know you, we know your loyalty, we know you'll stick by us for as long as it takes. So we've decided to quit. Ashcroft turned over our intel. Last I heard, Graham was havin' a kitten and Ashcroft was answering some uncomfortable questions, but federal warrants were being written. As soon as we have Theo back this is over for all of us."

Garrett was right, it's time someone stepped up and took care of you. So maybe I sucked at taking care of myself. But I bet I'd be better at it with Kevin by my side, and I was going to make damn sure I was good at taking care of him.

"It's good you quit, because so do I."

Four men chuckled but it was Smith who said, "I'm proud of you. You're keeping your cool."

I no longer needed to guard my emotions or choose my words carefully to conceal the truth. I could be open and as honest as I wanted to be.

"I'm dying inside. My heart feels like it's been ripped from my chest. If it wouldn't make me sound insane, I'd swear I can feel his pain. I'm too scared to think. I'm more afraid than I've ever been in my life. I'm so mad the anger is filling my chest and I can barely breathe. I'm trying so hard not to scream because I'm so fucking furious, I'm scared I won't be able to stop if I start. I'm terrified of what we're gonna find that I'm almost paralyzed. And if everyone doesn't hurry the fuck up and start loading out, I'm gonna flip my shit."

"Load out!" Easton shouted then looked down at me and smiled. "Let's go get your man so I can give him a once-over."

Jonas came back into the room. His gaze moved through it until it stopped on Garrett.

"Kira's got eyes on the property and confirmed the cameras are offline. Harrison showed up ten minutes ago."

"That's good news, so why the look?" Garrett inquired.

"She said two guys got what appeared to be a body wrapped in plastic or a black blanket out of the trunk."

"Theo," I whispered, and I felt my heart shrivel.

"Last thing," Jonas clipped. "Our asset's still in the house and confirmed Monroe and Lewis are in the basement. Prepare—they've been worked over but alive. Our guy's a douche but he did us a solid getting us intel and disabling the security system, so try not to kill him unless you have to. He's wearing a green tie and he'll be hiding in a closet."

Worked over but alive.

Worked over but alive.

A body wrapped in plastic.

I was going to fucking kill Harrison.

―――

"YOU DO NOT LEAVE MY SIDE."

I fought the urge to roll my eyes. That now made four times Easton had repeated himself in the last five minutes since all nine of us had packed into the van Gabe was driving.

"You're not going to have to worry about me staying by

your side because we're gonna die before we get there," I complained.

"Just be grateful Myles isn't driving," Owen muttered.

I gritted my teeth and looked from the sheer drop out my window down to my lap.

"She's a control freak and wouldn't even let the GBers in Gan drive her around," Cash rightly noted.

"How do you know that?"

"Woman, you don't think people didn't talk about the hot, stubborn CIA chick with control issues?"

"By *people,* I assume you mean *men,* and you never told me you'd heard stories about me."

"There was nothing to tell. You're hot, stubborn, and have control issues. I figured you knew all that already and didn't need circle time to discuss it."

"If I wasn't concentrating so hard visualizing myself on a beach somewhere relaxing, instead of having a near-death experience I'd flip you off."

"There's a nice beach right *down* there about four hundred meters." Smith leaned over me to point out my window to the Black Sea.

I kept my head bowed and closed my eyes. I pushed the fear and anger aside and allowed my thoughts to run. First I pictured Kevin's smile, the first one he gave me when he told me it was possible he was going to turn me in for breaking my oath. A quick, barely-there smile that had hooked me. The smile he gave me in the car on the way to the Cape that stole my breath. His movie star smile that was so sexy it made me tingle all over. His hungry like a wolf smile that held the promise of good things to come. I remembered Kevin making love to me. The way he felt, the way he looked at me, the way he touched me. All of it so beautiful my heart ached for more moments. There was so much more to say, more to learn, more days to have. Just *more*. I wanted all of it, I wanted to know everything, I wanted to tell him that when I told him I liked him what I really meant was I was falling in love. It was crazy, it was scary, it was insanely wonderful and beautiful. And it was the honest-to-God truth.

Life was too short, it was fragile, it could change in an instant. But for however many more days I had, I wanted to spend them next to Kevin.

Please, God, don't take him from me.

———

IT WAS LATE AFTERNOON; we had no cover of darkness.

We had one shot to use the element of surprise.

Owen parked the van down the street less than a quarter-mile away.

The plan was to hit hard and fast.

My team was going in the front, Garrett's team entering from the back. Cash and Owen would clear the first floor. Gabe and Smith, the second level. Easton, Garrett, Jonas, and myself, the basement. Cooper would go where he was needed. Kira had eyes in the sky, but we had no overwatch. No fallback plan. We weren't leaving without Kevin, Zane, and Theo.

"Clear to make entry," Kira said over the radio.

The doors to the van opened, and an eerie calm settled over me. I couldn't fail, I couldn't let Kevin down.

I *wouldn't* let him down.

Failure wasn't an option.

I slid out of the van. The rest of the guys followed, closing their doors gently. Then we were moving down the quiet street in a beautiful hilltop neighborhood above an equally beautiful seaside village. To the north, the stark white knobbly observation tower at the Georgia border crossing jutted into the sky. To the west, the Black Sea went all the way to the horizon. But the real beauty was the greenery—rolling hills, mountain peaks, with red roofs the only other color in an ocean of green.

The house came into view. Garrett, Owen, Gabe, and Cooper found an opening in the dense trees and disappeared. The rest of us were out in the open. A five-person army marching down the street ready for battle, not giving a single fuck we were going to turn a lovely, peaceful community into a war zone. We'd contain the battle of course, but this sleepy community was about to get rocked.

"Three, we're in place." Garrett's voice sounded in my ear.

Steady. Calm. Determined.

"Copy, One. Ready on your call."

"Six?" Garrett called for Cash.

"*Cash is King*," Six muttered.

I glanced over at Easton, then to Jonas, Smith, and finally Cash. All four men had identical grins. It was as if something in each of them had mended. Or maybe I was delusional and saw what I wanted to see. Believed what I needed to believe so my heart could mend, too.

Garrett counted us down to entry.

Three...inhale.

Two...exhale.

One...balance.

Cash opened the door, and everything slowed down as much as it sped up. I followed Easton through the door. He immediately went right. I followed, ignoring the elegance of the room. Kevin's rifle was up, the buttstock snug against my shoulder, safety off, ready to fire.

I heard gunshots, men shouting. The sounds melded together in the background. I was single-minded in my mission to get to the basement. We made it to the stairs without having to fire a single shot. Our luck drastically changed when four men came running up the stairs firing wildly—rifles at their hips, gangster style.

We returned fire. No jumping for cover, no diving behind furniture. We advanced like a death squad, not missing a step, not slowing. Four shots, four men down.

No one spoke.

There was no chatter over the coms.

There was no jackassing around like I'd heard during the last operation.

I skirted the bodies, careful not to step in the pooling blood, and followed Easton as he made his way down the stairs.

"Let me take point," Garrett said from behind me and stutter-stepped past me down the stairs.

I felt Jonas's hand on my shoulder. He leaned closer to whisper, "Don't worry, I got your back."

I wasn't worried. I was anxious to get down into the basement and through the door at the bottom. Thankfully, it was ajar. All Garrett would need to do was nudge it open.

Garrett jerked his chin. Easton obviously read the silent communication and nodded.

And in a dangerous-as-all-fuck move that would've made Kevin tackle me to the ground, we ran down the rest of the stairs and busted through the door.

Then I had to suck in a breath. The only way to describe the sight in front of me was carnage.

Absolute chaos with a dash of disturbing.

My gaze stopped on Zane Lewis, covered in blood. Head to toe. Face, hands, body. I had no idea if it was his or if it belonged to one of the dead men who littered the floor. All I knew was there was no amount of warning a girl could get to prepare for the massacre Zane Lewis had somehow pulled off.

And at Zane's feet was Eddy Stallone.

Holy fuck.

Zane lifted his hand holding a knife still dripping with blood and pointed it to a closed door. The man looked utterly spent. Exhausted and deranged. Psychotic and relieved.

Easton turned, not waiting for me or anyone else, and reached for the handle. As soon as he opened the door I heard a shot and Easton's big body jerked back. No blood, his plates took the round. Thank God. Then I learned a new meaning of chaos. The men jumped into action. The sound of gunfire was deafening—even with earpro, my ears rang. The sound echoed, reverberating through me. Fury built and what was left of my sanity snapped when I followed Garrett into the small room.

Harrison Washington, down. Two other men on the blood-soaked floor, dead.

But that wasn't what had my world tilting.

Kevin's limp, beaten body, chained with his arms over his head, was all I could see.

It filled my vision.

A nightmare's nightmare.

My soul wept.

"Someone get him down!" I might've screamed, I might've whispered, I might've simply imagined I'd said the words.

But suddenly Garrett and Jonas were there, and Kevin

was no longer hanging. I swung my rifle over my shoulder, felt it catch on the sling, and dropped to my knees by Kevin's side. The steel head of Owen's knife dug into my hip. I reached into my pocket to shift it to the side, and in my peripheral I caught movement. Harrison's hand was coming up and with it the muzzle of his gun. My hand came out of my pocket, I flicked the blade open, and jumped.

"Gun!"

I didn't know which came first, my warning, me sinking the blade into Harrison's throat, or him pulling the trigger at point-blank range.

All the oxygen whooshed from my lungs—all of it. I couldn't pull in a breath. The impact of the bullet jerked my body back, my shoulders hunched forward, my spine arched, my vision blurred, and I still couldn't breathe.

"Jesus fucking hell!" someone yelled over the ringing in my head.

I felt hands on me, lifting me, moving me, then a violent shake.

"Fucking breathe!" Garrett shouted in my face.

I wheezed in a shallow breath.

"Oh…" I tried again to suck in more air. "Kay."

Garrett set me down and I turned my head to look at Kevin. Eyes swollen shut, blood coming out of his ears, caked in his beard—fresh and dried.

"Get her vest off."

There was more pulling and jostling.

I kept my eyes glued to Kevin.

My hand slid across the small space separating me and Kevin until I found his limp hand and curled my fingers around it.

Hands roamed over my stomach and chest.

I stared at Kevin.

"Jesus fuck! Aren't they a pair?"

That was Zane.

I felt it. It was faint, but I felt Kevin's hand twitch in mine.

I sucked in a lungful of air ignoring the smell of blood, chaos, and carnage, and smiled.

24

"HOW DO you feel about me moving in with you?"

Layla's toes curled as I dug my thumb into the arch of her foot. Her cute electric blue toenails caught my attention and I smiled at the memory of her sitting on her bathroom vanity with her foot mostly in the sink basin, her toes on the edge as she painted them.

"Is there something wrong with your house?"

There was absolutely nothing wrong with my house, but hers was bigger and she had way more shit than I did. I could round up the guys and they could move me in one trip. We'd need to hire a moving crew and a Wayfair semi to move Layla.

"Nope," I answered. "But you have a bigger backyard and your landscaping's nicer than mine, and your couch is way more comfortable."

"And I have a three-car garage, one more bedroom than you, my house is closer to the office, and the better takeout places are near my house," she deduced. "Plus you're thinking about how heavy my bedroom furniture is and how many men you'd have to hire to move it."

A lot had changed in the last four months. But not one of the changes had to do with her reasoning and observation skills.

Some of the changes were big, some were inconsequential, but all of them meant I had Layla.

All of her.

She was still the competent, strong woman she was when I met her. She still wore her sexy, designer skirts to work, but at the end of the workday they now ended up on the floor next to whichever bed we were sleeping in. Tonight, it would be her bed seeing as last week we'd stayed at my place all week. The going back and forth between houses was getting old. It was time for us to settle.

And as the weeks turned into months, her intelligence still impressed me. The only difference was I got to witness her brilliance every day at the office. She'd quit her job at the Pentagon the day we'd gotten home from Turkey and accepted Zane's offer to come work at Z Corps. Layla then took it upon herself to hire Kira. This of course led to a twenty-minute tirade from Zane bemoaning about how he'd lost control of his company where at the end of his bitching he fired Layla. She'd simply rolled her eyes and told him she'd start after everything with Patheon was wrapped up.

Then there was Layla's tenacity and determination—that wasn't a change, it'd always been there—it was just that I got to witness it firsthand. The first two months we were home were painful, made more so by my injuries. Layla had run herself ragged back and forth from D.C. almost daily for briefings and depositions. She'd spend hours on the road, hours in meetings, then she'd come home and play nurse. The guys and their wives and girlfriends had all offered to pitch in and help, but Layla wouldn't hear of it. If she had to be gone all day, she allowed someone to come sit with me, but the moment she got home she'd take over. During one of the afternoons Garrett had been on babysitting duty, he told me about how Layla had tried to dig me out of that tunnel with her bare hands. My chest had burned with fury thinking about Layla with bloodied hands, dripping with sweat, exhausted.

"It was as beautiful as it was painful, brother, watching her try to dig you out." After Garrett had delivered that news, the burning in my chest lost its ferocity but the heat remained. But when he went on to tell me about the day Zane and I had been rescued and finally told me what everyone had been keeping a secret—that Layla had taken a round to the chest, the plate she'd been wearing the only thing between her and death—the anger came back tenfold.

It had been too much. It wasn't my proudest moment but the frustration of my injuries keeping me bedridden while Layla and everyone else ran themselves sick to take care of me made me lose my shit. Layla had witnessed my meltdown. She'd stood in my bedroom while I threw a man-sized temper tantrum that included shouting, throwing my phone across the room, and punching the mattress. Thankfully, none of my venom was directed *at* her, but she'd watched. And when I was done, she crawled into my bed and very carefully wrapped herself around me and cried—which I learned that day she hadn't done yet. Not when she watched the house explode, not when she was digging me out, not when she woke up in Turkey, not when she found me hanging from a chain half-dead, and not when she was shot in the fucking chest. My broken ribs screamed in protest when I held her to me as tightly as I could. That meltdown and those tears started the healing process. We clung to each other, each of us lost in our own thoughts, but doing it together.

But the biggest change was that something had broken free inside of Layla. She no longer hid a single emotion. If she felt it, she expressed it. She smiled all the time, she laughed, she was open, and when something pissed her off, she had no issue throwing attitude—though that wasn't new.

"Correct. Your furniture weighs a ton. But my bed's a king so it comes with me."

I smiled and she narrowed her eyes.

"So, let me see if I have this right; you want to move in with me, but you haven't even taken me out on a proper date yet."

She was correct about that, too.

My hand left her foot and glided over her ankle and up her leg, stopping at a scar mid-shin. A tiny scar from when she was eight and had fallen off her bike. The road rash was so bad she'd had to go to the hospital to have the pebbles and debris picked out. A story she'd told me one of the many times we'd lain in bed and shared.

In the four months we'd been together, the majority of that time was spent with me recovering from my injuries. At first, I'd been irritated about this, but I quickly found the upside to being bedbound—Layla being in that bed with me. Unfortunately, my body had been beaten to hell, which meant all physical activity had been maddeningly out of the question. But it also meant we'd had the time we hadn't before Turkey to get to know each other. And that was when I'd learned just how much Layla had changed—no more hesitation before she answered a question and often-times, she'd lie next to me and offer stories about growing up in Oregon. She touched on her mother here and there but mostly kept to lighter topics. Some of those topics led to some seriously heated debates. I mean, I couldn't let her comment about Dr. Seuss being the best children's books author of all time go without argument. *Hello*, Shel Silverstein. She didn't agree that *Silence of the Lambs* was the best movie ever made and I sure as hell didn't agree with her that *Naked and Afraid* was quality TV.

Something else happened in the beginning that I'd protested vigorously. It had led to a fight—not an argument, a bona fide fight—her bathing me. My male ego couldn't fucking take it. Layla seeing me weak and broken had played havoc on my self-esteem. She was red-hot pissed when I'd flatly refused to allow her to give me a sponge bath after she saw me struggling to stand at the bathroom sink. My arm was in a cast, my shoulder and ribs were broken. Everything fucking hurt and standing was excruciating. But I was determined to power through it.

Until Layla broke down. When she pulled herself together, she blasted me.

"Tell me how you'd feel if I refused you. If I made you watch me grit my teeth and sway. How would you feel if you knew I was hurting but too goddamned stubborn to let you help? You know what you're telling me by not letting me help you? That you don't trust me to take care of you. And I promised myself that when I got you back, I'd do better about taking care of me and I made that promise to myself so I'd be good at taking care of *you*."

Her words had gutted me. Each of them felt like a blade slicing my already bruised flesh.

There would be no way in fuck I'd stand by and watch her in pain. So she'd made her point. And from then on she'd bathed me until I could get in the shower. When I could do that, she'd come in with me. That was a form of torture—her soft, wet, soapy hands roaming my body and me only having one hand and one good arm to repay the favor.

But something that came from that was an intimacy I'd never known. A down-to-your-soul closeness that only comes from vulnerability. There were no walls, no barriers, no room to hide when you had to rely on another person for everything. And Layla came through in every way.

"Earth to Kevin," she called and pulled me back to the present.

I took in her bare legs, my eyes stopping at the juncture between her thighs. The crotch of her red lace panties was barely visible under the hem of my tee that had ridden up when she'd lounged back and put her feet in my lap for her nightly foot rub. I continued my perusal up to her chest. Another thing I learned about Layla was as soon as she changed after work her bra came off. For two long months, all I had of her were sponge baths and cuddling. Cuddling that included her tits pressed against my side, her bare thigh resting on mine, and a rock-hard dick that didn't get the message that the rest of my body was too fucked-up to perform.

When I could stand long enough to shower without passing out, we added hand jobs and I got her off with my fingers. But it would take another month before my face was healed enough to kiss her. I then added going down on her and she'd return the favor and suck me off. But the seal on sex had officially broken three weeks ago when the doc gave my ribs and shoulder the all-clear and I seriously appreciated the easy access to her body, and I knew she felt the same.

My gaze made it to her beautiful face, her pretty eyes already full of desire.

"I was saving our first date for the proposal."

She blinked and tilted her head.

"What proposal?"

"The one where I ask you to marry me."

I watched with avid fascination as her eyes slowly drifted closed and a hint of a smile pulled at the corners of her lips.

"You're gonna ask me to marry you?" she whispered.

"Yep. On our first date," I confirmed.

Layla's lips finished that upward curve into a full-blown smile.

Goddamn, the woman was crazy beautiful, but when she smiled that beauty went next level. It never failed to ignite a chain reaction of emotions that started with a soft blow of affection but always concluded with the need to fuck her.

She kept her eyes closed and continued whispering when she said, "Okay."

My hand traveled back down her calf. I lifted it and at the same time, I leaned forward and kissed her ankle. Then I waited for the shiver.

"You know how much I love it when you tremble when my lips are on you?"

"It feels good."

"You know what else feels good?"

"Your mouth between my legs?"

I let out a sharp bark of laughter and bared my teeth, giving her a little bite. She shivered again, and again when I trailed my mouth up her leg until I reached her knee.

"Baby, I ate you not even an hour ago."

"Is there a rule that says I only get your mouth once a day? Because I'm pretty certain you've had mine more than once in twenty-four hours."

She wasn't wrong. Back when I was recovering, I learned that not only was Layla excellent with her mouth, but she liked doing it. She liked it better when she was on her knees, with her ass and pussy within my reach and I could finger-fuck her while she sucked me off. My woman liked to get off and she liked getting me off. And since we now had privacy, she was vocal about both.

My hands went under her shirt. I hooked her panties and roughly yanked them down her legs and tossed them to the side. While I was lifting one of her legs to the back of the couch I told her, "New rule; when you get home and change, panties come off with your bra."

"Any changes to the rule book need to be submitted in writing," she sassed.

I pushed her other leg off my lap. Her foot settled on the floor next to the couch and my palms went to her inner thighs, spreading her wide. Her pretty pink pussy came into view and my dick twitched at the sight.

"Writing, huh?" I asked as my hand slid higher.

"Yes," she moaned.

My thumbs teased her wet folds, gathering her excitement as they went.

"Kevin."

Breathy, desire-filled, but I wanted her mindless.

I dipped a finger inside and Layla's head tipped back into the armrest.

"Pull your shirt up, baby. I wanna see all of you."

Slowly she pulled the hem of the t-shirt up. It was debatable who was more of a tease. I could draw out her pleasure and make her wait for her orgasm, but Layla liked to torture me until I lost control. The results were explosive.

Without me having to ask, Layla cupped her tits, squeezed them together, and strummed her nipples.

I pulled my finger out and added a second.

"I'm gonna eat you but you come around my dick."

"Okay."

"You gonna be able to hold out?"

"No."

I smiled as I lowered my face between her thighs and replaced my fingers with my tongue.

Layla's hands immediately went to the back of my head and her hips tipped up.

"Hands back on your tits, Layla."

She groaned her displeasure, but her hands disappeared. As a reward, I tongue-fucked her until she was squirming and I had to slide my hands under her and grip her ass to keep her still.

"I can't hold out."

She never could and she lied and said she would.

My lips moved up to her clit and that was all it took. I sucked the bundle of nerves deep and her body locked, followed by her sweet groan of pleasure.

I surged over her, slammed my mouth on hers. Her tongue came out and she licked my lower lip.

"Mmm," she hummed.

"Reach down and pull me out."

Her hands worked the front of my shorts while one of mine slid into her hair. The other moved down to toy with a pebbled nipple. I rolled it and pulled while Layla stroked my length from root to tip in firm, hard tugs.

Ah-fucking-mazing.

"Put me in, baby."

She didn't put me in. I felt the tip glide through her wet up to her clit. She rolled her hips and used my shaft to split her pussy lips open and the head to bump her clit as she essentially masturbated using my dick.

"That feel good?" I asked and gave her nipple a firm pinch.

"Yes."

"You like getting yourself off with my dick?"

"Yes," she hissed and slid her pussy over my length. *Tease.*

I dropped my lips back to hers, our tongues met, the kiss deepened, and I let her play until she was panting in my mouth. The friction felt damn good, but it wasn't enough. I shifted my hips and the next time she rolled her hips back, I drove inside.

At the feel of her sleek, warm, tight pussy swallowing my dick and her nails going to my back and digging in, I went at her hard. With each downward drive, she lifted her hips, reaching for what she wanted. I heard the hitch in her breath, felt the quiver around my dick, and when she broke our kiss, I looked down and watched it happen. The effect was no less moving than the first or the second or the tenth time I'd witnessed it. Each time it happened I watched if I could. Layla's look of surprise right before she flew apart. The hunger in those gorgeous eyes, the way they locked with mine unfocused, lost in pleasure. But the best part was the love I saw shining back at me.

Layla would say I brought her balance.

She didn't balance my life; she made me feel extremes.

Extreme emotions. Extreme pleasure. Extreme happiness.

Over-the-top love.

"Honey," she panted.

"Let go."

"*Kevin.*"

"Give it to me, Layla."

Her back arched and her head tipped back.

She was close. I was closer.

"Love you, Layla."

With one last stroke, I planted deep, ground down, and

together we went. The feel of her pussy contracting felt so fucking good I shoved my face in her throat and groaned my orgasm against her skin.

When we were both breathing normally again, I touched my tongue to her throat and waited.

She gave me a shiver and whispered, "Love you, honey."

Christ, I loved hearing her tell me she loved me.

25

I WAS at my desk when Theo hobbled in. Four months after his capture and he was still using crutches. If Kevin and Zane had been messed up, Theo had been all but dead. It was so close; I didn't think he'd make it.

But he did.

It would seem Theo had nine lives.

Thank God.

"When'd you get back?" I asked.

"Yesterday."

After Theo spent a week in a Turkish hospital, we brought him back to the States. His mom had come down from Canada and it was both heartbreaking and mending to watch the hospital room reunion. A miracle had happened; her son was back from the dead, only to be on death's door. A month later, Theo was released and went to Canada with his family—and yes, they'd taken Bronson with them.

"Did you get your new papers?"

Aaron Cardon would officially stay dead, and in his place, Theo Jackson was officially born.

"Yes. Thank you."

I pushed back from my desk, stood, and took in my old teammate. Other than the crutches he looked good. It would take some more time before he was fighting fit, and I knew his body would bear the scars of his torture. Not to mention, it would take a while before he'd emotionally heal.

"Everything all right?"

"I need to apologize."

I felt my spine snap straight and my stomach did a somersault.

"No, you don't."

"Yeah, I do. I fucked up and we both know it. I thought I could play with Armen. I let him take me, and in doing so I fucked the mission and nearly got Kevin and Zane killed. It was a bullshit, hotshot maneuver. We were nearing the end, I knew it, and what I did was stupid. Whatever intel I thought I could get on Harrison through Armen wasn't worth the chance I took."

I thought about what Theo said and realized how much alike we'd been—taking unnecessary risks, thinking we were fighting a war by ourselves, forgetting we had a team to back us up.

"I think we both got impatient. Neither of us thought it would take so long and when we saw the light at the end of the tunnel..." *Ugh. I hated that word.* "We were in a rush to get there. But it's over. Well and truly done. Harrison's dead. Eddy's dead. Ashcroft helped the current IG clean house and the agency's swept the stain under the rug and they're moving on. Whatever happens there now, it's not our concern."

"Edward Fucking Stallone. I didn't see that coming. The guy was a spineless weasel. I had no idea Harrison trusted him enough to bring him on board. It stings a little none of us caught on. He flew under the radar for four years."

Theo was wrong. It didn't sting that Eddy outplayed us —it felt like a hot poker to the ego. After Leif Robinson died and Harrison decided it was time for him to step up and take control instead of hanging back letting other people play frontman, he'd turned Eddy and we'd had no clue. I never would've given Eddy a single thought if he hadn't been the one inside my apartment that night.

In the course of our ten-year investigation, we'd fucked up twice. Both big, but the first oversight that Harrison Washington was the kingpin was the bigger of the two. We'd always known a top dog was pulling the strings, we'd looked, we'd ruled people out, but we never suspected it was Harrison. Garrett had found that connection. A good reminder that fresh eyes and teamwork's a hell of a lot better than exhausting yourself as a one-person squad.

I was done talking about the past. It was time to move us to the future.

"Did you think about Zane's offer?" I asked.

"Yeah. I'm here to talk to him but I wanted to see you first."

My heart swelled.

I'd missed Theo while he'd been gone. Hell, I missed all the guys. I was still getting used to hearing from them via text instead of encrypted emails. But what didn't take getting used to was getting to know them better. Our once strictly professional relationship that had very little person-ality injected into the emails we exchanged had morphed into true friendships.

The guys had also admitted that they'd broken some rules. It was forbidden for any of the men to meet during the operation, yet they'd met up whenever they could.

Sometimes two of them would get together, sometimes all of them. In all honesty, I wasn't completely surprised former SEALs and SAC operators would do whatever the hell they wanted to do, rules be damned. I also learned that when Easton had contacted Garrett he was in the U.S. and wanted to meet with Garrett to tell him the truth. That didn't surprise me as did Garrett not holding any grudges.

Once we brought Theo back to the States and he was on the mend, the guys had scattered. They'd spent ten years on a mission. Last I heard, and I heard from all of them daily, they were enjoying living again. "Breathing clean" as Easton called it.

"Well, I'm glad you stopped by so I can warn you, Zane's in a mood."

"What kind of mood?"

Poor Theo, he had no clue about the many moods of Zane Lewis and how they could swing from moment to moment.

"The kind he gets in when he's arguing with his pregnant wife, and she rightly refuses to listen to his overprotective nonsense."

"You must be talking about the boss," Kevin said.

I looked to the side and my heart rate slowed as I watched my man walk into my office. When he got close and hooked me around my waist and dropped a kiss on my forehead, my heart rate accelerated to a fast thud in my chest.

Slow. Fast.

Balance.

"Hey, man, good to see you," Kevin greeted.

Theo studiously took us in until he saw whatever he was searching for. Then he smiled.

"Good to see you up and around."

Kevin chuckled and motioned to Theo's crutches. "How much longer on those?"

"Few weeks at most. Now that I'm back in Maryland and everything's wrapped up I can give more time to PT."

"Speaking of wrapping up, Zane needs us in the conference room." Kevin looked back at me and added, "You, too, baby."

"Fabulous," I muttered under my breath.

I wasn't exaggerating when I said Zane was in a mood. Ivy had spun him up good and tight today when she explained she was working until the day their daughter popped out.

"I need to grab something before we go."

I slid out from Kevin's embrace and went to my desk. I pulled out something I was saving for such an occasion.

"What's that?"

I held up the adult coloring book and a pack of colored pencils.

"Baby, it says 'Fuckity. Fuck. Fuck. Fuck.' on the cover."

"Yep. A *Sweary As Fuck* coloring book. I'm hoping him coloring in all the curse words will stop him from saying them out loud. I have the first page picked out for him."

I flipped through the coloring book and found the page I had dogeared.

"Gerbil Fucker," I announced and turned the book around.

Kevin's laughter started as a chuckle but soon he was roaring with it.

Theo was laughing, too, but still managed to say, "Totally missed out working with you all these years. Not gonna miss out again."

I got what Theo meant. We'd worked together but from afar. We were teammates but not close ones. Theo telling me he wasn't going to miss out again meant he was taking Zane's offer.

And since I was no longer the closed-off, no-fun Layla, I whooped and smiled.

"I'm so happy to hear that."

"Glad to hear that, sweetheart. Let's go talk to Zane and see if we can make you happier." Theo paused and his eyes went to Kevin. "Though I'm thinking there's nothing I can do to top the kind of happy you already are."

Theo was right.

Nothing could top the kind of happy Kevin made me.

But when I walked into the conference room and found Jonas, Smith, Cash, and Easton I was pretty damn happy to see all of them. And what made it even better was Garrett standing in the middle of their huddle, smiling.

Good Lord, I was going to cry. So I covered it up with a snappy comment.

"What's this? A party I wasn't invited to?"

All heads turned my way but it was Easton who broke away and bravely pulled me from Kevin and hugged me.

"Missed you, Ghost."

"Missed you, too, Three."

Easton rocked me back and forth until we heard Kevin growl.

"I was gonna pass you off to the others so they could get their fix but now I'm not so sure that's a good idea."

"It's not," Kevin said.

Even though he couldn't see me, I rolled my eyes.

"Ah, yes, the gift that keeps giving," Owen said from somewhere in the room. "Kevin just keeps stepping in it."

I didn't understand what that meant until Cooper pulled me out of Easton's arms and swung his around me.

"Haven't had my Layla fix yet." Cooper winked at me and this time when I rolled my eyes Kevin saw.

"You think it's funny," Kevin grunted.

"Kinda, honey. You know they're fucking with you and yet you keep growling like a bear when one of them hugs me. They don't actually like me as much as they like pissing you off."

"Oh, we like you, Layla." Coop continued to poke the now very angry bear.

I pushed away from Coop and tucked myself under Kevin's arm.

"You know it's gonna be fun when you get a woman," Kevin told Cooper.

"Coop's getting a woman?" Kira asked as she entered the room with Zane behind her. "Like a real live woman or the blow-up kind?"

Cooper's gaze went to my friend and he gave her a megawatt smile that would melt the panties off a woman—real or otherwise.

Kira, as it turned out, was even more of a smartass than I'd thought.

"Dayum." Kira waved her hand in front of her face. "Is it too late to sign up to see that smile in the morning?"

"Not sure he sticks around until morning," Gabe mumbled.

"Even better," Kira returned.

Four pissed-off men turned their angry eyes her way.

"Standdown, killers, I'm joking."

"You damn well better be." Cash spoke for the group.

"I got signed contracts!" Zane boomed and pointed to Kira, which surprised me. "No dipping your wick in the company ink."

There were chuckles and muttered curses. Some apologizing for Zane, some praying for his tongue to fall out, but mostly the guys just groaned. Kira, however, wasn't deterred.

"Seeing as I don't have a wick, that means I'm the ink in that metaphor. But even if that wasn't the case, the employment contract I signed said I wouldn't play naked Twister with clients nor would I clean the cobwebs for the womb room with anyone who cost you money. Nowhere did it say I couldn't do a no-pants dance with an employee."

Zane smiled at Kira until his dimples popped out.

"I knew I liked you."

"You like her because her sex euphemisms are as bad as yours," Myles pointed out.

"Yep," Zane confirmed and looked around the room until his gaze landed on me. "What's that?"

"Something that is no longer needed since you seem in a better mood."

Zane lifted his hand and motioned me closer, and I knew from experience the man wouldn't give up until he got what he wanted. But I didn't move closer. I set the book on the table and pushed it across the smooth, polished surface. Zane reached out and snatched it off the table and I sent the colored pencils sailing the same way. He didn't bother picking those up, he was too busy thumbing through the book.

"Knob jockey. Cock goblin. Turd burglar. Shit wizard." He read the pages out loud and continued flipping. "Loose butthole."

He closed the book and slammed it on the table. His head tipped back and his laughter thundered in the room. Kevin gave me a squeeze and I glanced up at him.

He was smiling down at me with his sexy movie star

smile. I felt my panties flood, my nipples tingled, and I shivered.

Kevin's smile went electric right before he dropped his mouth to my ear. "As soon as this meeting's over I'm pulling that sexy skirt up and bending you over your desk."

It wouldn't be the first time.

One of the many job perks.

"Everyone take a seat before Kevin drags Layla back to the love den...I mean, her office," Zane snarked.

Kevin didn't deny that was exactly what he'd planned to do, and I knew better than to give Zane ammo, so I quietly shuffled to the table. Kevin pulled out a chair for me and once we were all seated, Zane remained standing.

"First, for the sake of national security Theo, Cash, Jonas, Easton, and Smith are coming to work for us."

I sucked in a breath so big it was a wonder I left any oxygen in the room. I glanced to my right. All of the Blue Team sat at the table along with Garrett.

All smiling.

Welcoming.

Then I looked to my left and all the guys were staring at me.

"What do you say, TL?" Easton started.

TL?

Team leader, me?

My gaze went to Zane and I lifted my brow in question.

"It was all or none," he started. "Garrett's spread thin as it is with Red, Gold, and Blue so Kira's been a big help. The two of them can geek out together and run intel, but even with Kira, I can't lose Garrett in cyber. So that leaves you to keep these five in line."

"Hell yes!"

No hesitation.

I wanted my team if it meant having them like this. Open, clean, living.

"I feel like the band's back together." Jonas patted Cash on the shoulder. "No more wandering around aimless."

"You weren't aimless, brother. You forget I've been with you the last two months. Your aim was true."

"You're right." Jonas smirked.

I didn't want to know what that smirk meant but I was fairly certain I knew.

"Good news, baby," Kevin whispered.

"Great news."

His hand in mine tightened. He knew how worried I'd been about my team and I'd been nervous about how they'd assimilate back into regular living.

Now I wouldn't worry.

They'd be with us at Z Corps.

"Last order of business then I'm going up to my wife's office and executing a kidnapping. And if one of you fuckers thinks to come to her aid you're fired."

"You mean to your aid when she knocks out that tooth you just fixed?"

Zane smiled, showing off his new front tooth.

"I was thinking of staying hillbilly but as Kira pointed out missing a tooth lessened the effect of the dimples."

I tried damn hard not to think about the carnage of that horrible day. It could be said, Zane Lewis really didn't like being held hostage. Further, he didn't like being tortured. I still didn't know—and I never wanted to know—how he'd managed to kill all those men with his bare hands and a knife. Though I did hear him say he lost his front tooth ripping a man's throat out with his teeth. I am praying that wasn't the truth. But it was Zane Lewis, so it might be.

I shook my head to dislodge the image of Zane standing

in the basement with blood all over his face, Hannibal Lecter style, and refocused on the room.

"That was a good call," Owen confirmed.

"So, last order of business. Graham released the final report on Harrison Washington."

I sat up straighter and so did the rest of the guys. We'd found a safety deposit box in his name and had been waiting for the search warrant to be executed. To say that the President of the United States was ticked off when he learned the truth about Patheon and what we'd been doing wasn't an understatement—it was a gross distortion of reality. The POTUS was off the hook, pissed. I'm talking DEFCON 1, full nuclear meltdown, threats of me and my team in rendition for the rest of our lives. Zane had called former President Anderson and the two of them had a talk with the current president, and whatever was said in the meeting had changed Graham's mind. But we weren't allowed anywhere near the federal investigation beyond testifying when needed.

"Louis Patterson was Harrison's first frontman," Zane started.

Damn. I really hated that someone whom I'd liked was really a dirty, lying sonofabitch.

"Did he really die of a heart attack or was he murdered?" I asked.

"Heart attack. Leif took over, Harrison stayed in the background." Zane paused and his eyes turned pensive. "Leif's dead, so some of this is speculation, but from what the Inspector General concluded, Leif used me to threaten Theo because he was pissed at me. Well, me and Theo. I didn't remember the op until I read the IG report. A pipeline was being tapped in South Sudan. I fed Theo the intel and the CIA was able to share that information with JSOC and a Delta team was deployed to take out the warlord. Finn was on that team."

Zane stopped again and looked over at Kira. When she acknowledged his soft look, which I was shocked he was able to pull off, he continued. "That pipeline was making Leif a lot of money and through Leif, Harrison was getting his cut. It would be a safe bet both of them were pretty fucking unhappy Theo and I fucked up their money flow. So what it comes down to is, Leif had a hard-on for me. It was a win-win for Leif. Theo would either heed the threat and stop demanding an investigation or he wouldn't, and Leif could take me down, then take Theo out. And that's that. Layla took out Harrison with Owen's lucky knife. I snapped Eddy's neck. Leif's been rotting in hell for years, and a station chief, an analyst, and a targeting officer are all now guests of the agency in a foreign prison, hopefully getting jungle rot between their ass cheeks. It's over. And when I say that, I mean it is *over*. Those are the only answers we're gonna get. Any of you think to dig, the deal I made to keep you out of the pokey will be voided and the best I'll be able to do for you is...well, nothing. You'll be fucked and I'll look like an asshole. And just so we're clear, I get seriously fuckin' cranky when I look like an ass. Any questions?"

"Yeah," Smith called. "When do we start?"

Zane shot Smith a bright white smile showing off his new fake tooth.

"Ask your boss." Zane pointed to me. "I got a wife to kidnap and handcuff. And a..." He paused and opened the book. "Shit sipper to color."

With that, Zane Lewis left the room chuckling to himself.

"You got ten minutes to brief your team, baby," Kevin whispered in my ear.

Hmm.

Talk to my team or go to my office with my man?

No brainer.

I stood and tugged Kevin's hand.

"Garrett will show you around," I announced.

Kevin's body shook but he wisely didn't vocalize his laughter as he stood.

"Damn, brother, command performance," Gabe snickered.

We were at the door when I looked over my shoulder.

Garrett and Easton were sharing a smile.

That made my heart happy.

But when Kevin scooped me up into his arms while the rest of the guys hooted and hollered, that was pure happiness. The kind that seeped into your bones. I didn't give one shit that the guys knew what Kevin and I were going to do. There was no embarrassment, no awkwardness.

I was no longer alone. I had Kevin, and with him came a band of brothers who were fiercely loyal and protective. They were also immature and liked to bust each other's chops, and now that included mine.

"You know they're gonna give you shit for carrying me down the hall."

"Don't care."

Neither did I.

"Have I ever told you how sexy I think it is when you go all knuckle-dragger caveman?"

"You haven't, but it's good you think it's sexy because you're about to learn what happens when you play along with their antics."

"Antics?" I laughed.

"Glad you think it's amusing, baby." He brushed his lips over my cheek and used the toe of his boot to open my office door. Then he used his heel to kick it closed. "Let's see if you're still laughing when I'm done."

Kevin set me on my feet, yanked my skirt up, turned me around, and pushed his erection into my ass.

"Bend over, Layla."

With one of his hands trailing up my thigh, the other in the middle of my back pushing me forward, he growled, "Now."

I bent forward and he followed me down and curled his big body over mine.

"You've got a sweet ass," he murmured close to my ear.

His breath fanned over my neck, causing a full-body tremble.

"Fuck, I love the feel of you." He cupped my pussy and circled my clit over my panties. "You gonna be quiet?"

"Not likely," I told him the truth.

"Try."

"Okay."

"Love you," he whispered.

I felt his hand working open his cargos, then I felt him push my panties to the side.

My eyes drifted closed, and my soul sighed.

"I know you do."

"Good."

In one single hard thrust, we were connected.

"Love you, too," I wheezed.

"I know."

In the end, I was quiet, but only because Kevin kissed me through my orgasm and I returned the favor and swallowed his groans.

"Hurry up, you two!" Gabe shouted from the hall.

"Owen ordered lunch. Charcuterie boards have been delivered."

"What the hell is a charcuterie board?" Kevin shouted back.

"A fancy meat platter."

I'd heard the story. I'd heard dozens and dozens of stories about Kevin and his team. And since I'd heard all the stories and met all the women, I was sure it was actually sweet Natasha who'd ordered lunch, which made the meat and cheese platter ten times funnier.

"Come on, honey, let's go eat some meat." I laughed.

"Yeah, Kev, come eat some meat!" Gabe yelled.

"Tacos, goddamit. I like tacos!"

Yeah, my man loved tacos.

Lucky me.

26

COOPER CAIN

"So let me get this straight." Kira's pale green eyes danced with humor as she glanced between Gabe and me. "You want me to sit in a chair in the middle of the dance floor, and you want Cooper to put *that* on me."

"Yes."

"I think you forgot the part where Evette tosses—"

"Okay," Kira chirped.

"Great."

Gabe's slap on my shoulder before he went in search of his new wife to tell her the good news that he'd found two suckers to embarrass, was a warning. I might've no longer been the "new guy" seeing as the teams now had five new guys to haze, but I was still the newest member of my team, and being that, I was still subjected to their foolishness.

Unfortunately for them, I didn't embarrass easily. Unfortunately for me, Kira Winters struck me as a woman who was up for anything. And the wicked smile she was aiming my way told me I was in for a world of hurt. The kind of hurt that was going to start in my balls but eventually, the pain would travel to my chest when she ripped my heart out and stomped on it.

Kira was the kind of woman a man fell for. It wasn't her extreme beauty, it wasn't her shiny blonde hair, it wasn't her eyes that resembled pastel jade ice crystals, it wasn't her body that had mine aching every time I saw her. It was all of it, what those eyes said when she looked at me. It was her fun, flirty, outgoing, up-for-anything personality. It was how gracefully she moved. The promise of all that was her. She'd be down to lounge around in sweats all day in front of the TV. She'd be happy going skydiving. She'd let me fuck her breathless on the hood of my GTO. She'd let me tie her up and smack her ass, or she'd ride me slow and sweet.

Anything.

Absolutely anything.

And I knew this because she'd camped out on my couch all day watching old sitcoms with me more than a few times over the last five months, and she did it looking sexy as all fuck. She ate popcorn by the handfuls, and she drank whiskey on the rocks, she wore ratty sweats paired with tight tank tops that showed off her flat stomach. She laughed like she didn't give a single fuck what anyone thought about her. She grabbed life by the balls and did whatever the hell she wanted to when the spirit moved her to do it. Including calling me at midnight to tell me she'd made reservations for the next day for us to go skydiving. And when she jumped out of the plane, she yelled with wild abandon all the way back to the ground. But when the mood hit her, she could be quiet and thoughtful.

The woman drove me to the brink of insanity.

"You're looking a little scared, my friend."

Scared was the last thing I was. On the verge of taking her home and putting us both out of our misery was more like it. Ending the five months of foreplay that she'd instigated and that I'd been doing my best to ignore.

"How'd you get here?"

A slow sexy smile pulled at her lips. It was no less effective at making my cock jump in my slacks than the wickedness of her previous grin.

"Kevin and Layla."

"After this, I'm taking you home."

A perfectly manicured eyebrow arched, and yeah, that, too, made my cock twitch.

"You are?" she asked under the pretense she was pondering my statement.

"I am," I confirmed.

"And will you be walking me to my front door like a gentleman, so I can ask you in for a drink?"

Brink. Of. Insanity.

I heard the music change then the MC called our names over the opening electric guitar riff of an old, familiar Guns N' Roses song.

"Shall we?" Kira laughed and offered me her elbow to escort her to the dance floor.

Fuck that.

I stepped closer, tagged her around the waist, and dropped my mouth to her ear.

"There's not gonna be one thing gentlemanly about tonight, baby."

"Thank God. I was starting to get worried you were a prude."

I dragged Kira out onto the dance floor, deposited her in the chair that had been set out for this purpose, and dropped to my knees in front of her. Without a word, I pulled the ugly-as-fuck hot pink satin garter belt out of my pocket, then lifted her right foot.

In the background, "Welcome to the Jungle" barely drowned out all the hoots and hollers of our teammates. I was sure I was supposed to put on a show, go slow and drag out the spectacle of a wedding tradition I had no interest in participating in. But when my fingertips glided up Kira's silky-smooth skin, all thoughts except one vanished. I shoved the garter over her knee and my hands dipped beneath her skirt.

Now that my hands were no longer in view of the guests, it was time to educate Miss Winters.

My right hand continued to maneuver the garter into place while my left went higher, and I watched those sexy eyes get hazy when my fingers brushed over her wet panties.

Kira looked down at me and tilted her head in a taunt that made my cock jerk. She was calling me out, knowing I wouldn't go any further with everyone watching.

The woman was crazy.

I yanked my hands free, helped her stand, and paused just long enough to take in her triumphant smile.

I could look at that smile every day for the rest of my life, and it wouldn't be enough. I'd still want more of it.

"You think you won," I noted.

"I did."

"Game's not over, sweetheart."

———

FIVE MINUTES LATER—PARKING *lot behind Gabe and Evette's wedding reception.*

"This still feels like winning," Kira panted.

My fingers dug into her hips, the material of her skirt bunched under my hands, my seat pushed back as far as it would go, not giving her much room to move. But she didn't need space, not when the feel of her slick, tight pussy was enough to send me over the edge. The swivel of her hips only intensified the pleasure.

I slipped one of my hands down between us and my thumb instantly found my target. I gave her a few slow circles.

"That feel like winning, baby?"

"Yes," she moaned.

Fuck yeah, it did.

"Harder, Kira."

I let go of her dress, slid my hand around to her ass, and groaned when she slammed down on my cock, hard.

"So good. I'm close, honey."

Her back arched, her drives became uncoordinated, and I felt her pussy clench.

And there I sat, Kira riding my cock with wild abandon just like I knew she would, fucking me hard and fast until she was breathless. The feel of her so goddamn good I saw stars. She fucked me through her orgasm, she fucked me through mine, she threw her head back and moaned her pleasure like she didn't give a fuck who heard. The woman was out of this world. Best sex of my life, bar none. I never had better, and I knew with my cock planted deep in her sleek, wet pussy I never would. No one would ever compare to Kira Winters. Not in any way.

She'd be the woman who ruined me.

She'd take what I could give then demand more.

She'd take and steal until she had all of me.

The fuck of it was, I knew how it would end. I knew

she'd spent ten years working in the dark, and she was ready to live her life again. She was ready to drink it in and drown in as many experiences as she could. She'd use me until she was full, then she'd move on.

And I was going to let her.

Grab your copy of Cooper Here

ALSO BY RILEY EDWARDS

Thaddeus

Kyle

Maximus

Declan

Blue Team - Susan Stoker Universe

Owen

Gabe

Myles

Kevin

Cooper

The 707 Freedom Series

Free

Freeing Jasper

Finally Free

Freedom

The Next Generation (707 spinoff)

Saving Meadow

Chasing Honor

Finding Mercy

Claiming Tuesday

Adoring Delaney

Keeping Quinn

Taking Liberty

Triple Canopy

Damaged

Flawed

Imperfect

Tarnished

Tainted

Conquered

The Collective

Unbroken

Trust

Standalone

Romancing Rayne

Falling for the Delta Co-written with Susan Stoker

BE A REBEL

Riley Edwards is a USA Today and WSJ bestselling author, wife, and military mom. Riley was born and raised in Los Angeles but now resides on the east coast with her fantastic husband and children.

Riley writes heart-stopping romance with sexy alpha heroes and even stronger heroines. Riley's favorite genres to write are romantic suspense and military romance.

Don't forget to sign up for Riley's newsletter and never miss another release, sale, or exclusive bonus material.

Rebels Newsletter

Facebook Fan Group

www.rileyedwardsromance.com

facebook.com/Novelist.Riley.Edwards
instagram.com/rileyedwardsromance
bookbub.com/authors/riley-edwards
amazon.com/author/rileyedwards

ACKNOWLEDGMENTS

To all of you – the readers: Thank you for picking up this book and giving me a few hours of your time. Whether this is the first book of mine you've read or you've been with me from the beginning, thank you for your support. It is because of you I have the coolest job in the world.

Made in United States
North Haven, CT
27 February 2022

16566762R00166